ASYLUM

K.A. Tucker

Papoti Books

Library and Archives Canada Cataloguing in Publication

Tucker, K. A. (Kathleen A.), 1978-

Asylum / K.A. Tucker.

Issued also in electronic formats.

ISBN 978-0-9869155-4-3

I. Title.

PS8639.U325A79 2012 jC813'.6 C2011-907864-3

Editing by Marg Gilks

Front Cover Design by Extended Imagery

Printed in the U.S.A

v1

Published by Papoti Books

www.katuckerbooks.com

To Lia and Sadie, my very own Curly Lock girls.

To Paul, for surviving another book.

To my beta readers, Mindy and Jaime — you two are why people write books.

To Gina, for giving me the gift of time.

To Marg Gilks, my editor, for waving her magic wand again.

1. SAFE

"Forgive me," I whispered, knowing my words would never reach her ears. She was already gone. Safe—safe from this deadly atrium; safe from Mortimer and Viggo; safe from me.

Now for damage control.

I scanned the crowd of a hundred-odd depraved vampires, their wild eyes and expressions varying from bewilderment to crazed blood lust after the briefest scent of a human, until I spotted four familiar faces. The four who needed to survive. Relief flickered through me. *Thank God for those pictures.*

I closed my eyes, searching for one last thread of energy, just enough to cast another spell. *There*—a miniscule, glowing purple helix coil, much like a DNA strand, floating beside my heart. I grasped it with my mental hand, and yanked. It immediately took flight, shooting up to my fingertips. Armed with magic, I raised my hand toward the pyre burning brightly atop Veronique's tomb. A thought brought embers soaring toward my fingertips as if magnetized.

Then I struck.

Sparks shot from my hand and erupted into flaming circles around Evangeline's friends, forming a formidable barrier of protection—large enough not to ignite them but tight enough to keep them from leaping out and making a run for it.

"Sofie?" Mortimer hollered, his voice tinged with uncertainty.

I turned to see shock masking his face. He stood next to Viggo, both of them frozen like ice sculptures, struggling to grasp the events of the past ten seconds. I knew that confusion would quickly give way to understanding, followed by retaliation.

I'll deal with them later. For my sister's sake, they needed to survive; for my sake, in a subdued fashion. Another flick of my hand produced three flaming circles—one around each of them and the last around me. *There. That should hold them until I'm finished.*

Now, elimination.

From the corner of my eye, I caught the telltale silvery white hair and hideous face of a mutant. I shuddered; their very existence was truly repulsive, but worse—I knew the Merth-laced building couldn't confine them. The last thing we needed were those monsters running loose in New York City.

Flames shot from my fingertips to ignite the hideous creature, consuming his body as if it were made from highly flammable fabric. His one shrill scream echoed through the atrium, sending a chill down my spine. I didn't let it distract my focus, though. Spotting two more mutants, I quickly dispatched them as well.

Heads started to turn, the screams attracting the attention of the other vampires. Soon enough, they'd figure out the fate I had in store for them. Then I'd have mass hysteria and vampires hiding in every nook and cranny of Viggo's palace. I didn't have time to hunt them all down individually for dispatch.

I hurled sparks of fire freely from my fingertips toward any vampire in sight. Within seconds, dozens of flaming bodies crumpled to thrash on the ground, scorching the leaves and petals of the atrium's plants and engulfing any vampires caught in their proximity. But I knew there were more vampires out there, blocked from my view within Viggo's urban jungle.

There was only one thing left to do. I had to torch the entire atrium—

and hope I could control the fire well enough to prevent the entire building from going up in flames. Inhaling deeply, reconciled to the plan, I raised both hands—

Only to be distracted by a body lying on the ground, bound by Merth—a vampire with jet-black hair and lemon eyes.

Rachel.

Jaw clenched, I pictured myself slowly tearing the flesh off her body as she screamed, only to allow it to grow back so I could do it again . . .

But there was no time for that. Sighing my disappointment, I raised a finger toward her, preparing to rid everyone of the viper once and for all.

"Caden, no!"

The scream stilled the spark about to fly from my hand. My eyes swung to the four flame-encircled figures in time to see Caden, his expression lost, vacant, step toward the flames. I gasped. He was going to kill himself!

With the last bit of magic I had left after Evangeline's complicated transportation spell, I instantly extinguished every flame in the atrium before he could succeed. Caden stared back at me, resentment marring his stunning face—but unharmed. *That's okay. You can hate me. You're safe.*

A powerful hand grabbed me by the neck and hoisted me into the air. "Where is she?" Viggo growled, rage blazing in his eyes.

Despite everything, I laughed. I continued to laugh as I sailed through the air and slammed into a brick wall sixty feet away, my bones splintering on impact. Pain ripped through my body as I tumbled to the ground and lay in a heap, my face twisted in agony, awaiting the second attack that would surely begin before my bones had a chance to heal.

I was right.

Mortimer wrapped a hand around a fistful of my hair and yanked my head back. He crouched in front of me, his chocolate-brown eyes smoldering with rage. "I knew we were fools to trust you," he growled through gritted teeth. "What else do you have up your sleeve, witch?"

"I had no choice," I managed to whisper, pain making me wince with each word.

"Lies!" Mortimer boomed. With a fierce shove, he propelled me facedown onto the cobblestones. I felt my forehead split open and my delicate nose explode. A metallic taste filled my mouth as blood poured in.

Normally I used my sorceress powers to numb the pain of my physical scuffles with Viggo and Mortimer. But until my magic had time to rejuvenate, I would have to endure for the next few minutes. With great difficulty, I turned my head to rest my cheek on the stone. I lay unmoving on my stomach, focusing all of my attention on the destruction around the atrium and on the spectators, only half hiding, intrigued by this violent exchange. I just needed five seconds, and my face would regenerate. Within ten seconds, I'd be as good as new. *Relax, Sofie. You can handle ten seconds . . .*

I gasped as a blunt object tore through the middle of my back, through my ribcage, to exit through my stomach and thud against the cobblestones beneath me. Viggo's signature move. *Bastard!*

It made healing hard. I had to get it out. Gritting my teeth, I flexed my arms and pushed my broken body up until I rested on my knees. I grasped the jagged end of the steel pipe with shaking hands, took a deep breath—*One . . . two*—and jerked it forward. My scream filled the silent atrium as the steel slid through my flesh. *Again . . .* I had no choice. I had to get it out now. Clenching my teeth, I prepared for another tug.

A swift kick between my shoulder blades sent me sprawling on my stomach again, shoving the pipe back into my stomach. Another lightning bolt of agony raced through my battered body. Something against my back—presumably a foot—pinned me down.

"I'm sure Sofie can explain everything," a musical but authoritative female voice called out above me, adding, "once you stop torturing her."

From my position, I could see Evangeline's two female friends—Fiona and Amelie—standing forty feet away. It clearly wasn't either of them speaking. Evangeline had no other friends. The hairs on the back of my neck spiked. *How does this vampire know my name?* "Who—" I began, then gasped as someone ripped the pipe out of my body and tossed it clattering onto the stones beside me. The weight lifted off my back. Again I lay waiting until my regenerative abilities—a magnificent vampirism—kicked in, praying that Viggo and Mortimer would allow me time to heal. This time, they did.

Once mended, I flew to my feet to assess the scene before me: the players, the situation, the threat. The atrium was no longer the scene of bedlam it had been only minutes ago. It was now a scene of silent chaos. Charred heaps—the remains of unlucky vampires—littered the ground. Scorched foliage and billowing smoke filled the once-picturesque atrium. I scanned the crowd, quickly counting the remaining Ratheus vampires. Forty. They were scattered, appearing ready to dive behind benches and statues at the first sign of a magical assault. Forty blood-crazed vampires, their eyes dancing wildly as they searched the atrium for humans. If only I had a few sparks of magic, I could level the rest of them. I could—

"Right, Sofie?" the unknown vampiress said, interrupting my plotting.

I turned toward the voice to find Viggo and Mortimer squared off opposite a diminutive, Asian-looking woman with porcelain skin and juicy red lips.

"Right . . . Sofie?" the woman repeated, regarding me with black, almond-shaped eyes. "I'm sure there's a good reason why Evangeline vanished into thin air and you just charred seventy of your own kind?"

Gritting my teeth, I forced a small smile. *You are not my kind.* "Right," I answered as levelly as I could, determined to match her confidence. The problem was, I couldn't. I couldn't even answer her by name. *Who is she?* I needed information—quick. Reaching inside once again, I scoured my body for a magical helix. Just one. Normally I had thousands of tiny purple coils floating around my body, ready to be plucked for various spells. I just needed one to send out a probe, to dissect this vampire's very core, to grasp her true intentions, to know everything there was to know about her. But I was empty. I had drained my magical tank and until it began to regenerate I would need to rely on my wits. *Damn it!*

Viggo's smooth croon broke the silence. "Of course there is! Excuse my rudeness. My desperation got the better of me." He flashed one of his brilliant smiles. "So sorry, Sofie. That was barbaric of me."

I sneered in response, his charming façade kindling a desire to punch him in his perfect nose. It was the same façade he had used to lure Evangeline in, to gain her trust. Worse, I had to stand by and watch him spin his repulsive web, powerless to stop him for fear of how he would punish her for my interference. I had learned that horrible lesson five years ago. The last time I overtly crossed him, he murdered Evangeline's mother, leaving her orphaned.

But he couldn't hurt her now. She was buried deep within the untouched mountains of Siberia, surrounded by miles of remote wilderness, warm and comfortable in the haven I had spent ten years building. I no longer needed to give Viggo satisfaction by playing along. "You'll never see Evangeline again!" I sang out, mustering my most obnoxious grin, feeling suddenly giddy.

Viggo's jaw clenched. Finally, a ripple in that handsome, iron-cast mask. "Is that so?" He took a rigid step toward me but a pale, delicate hand flew to his chest, stopping him. It didn't actually touch him; it hovered, palm out, inches in front of his charcoal wool suit. Intrigued, I watched Viggo's cobalt-blue eyes study the little hand for a long moment before sliding up to meet the owner—this undaunted, mysterious female leader who knew my name.

He doesn't know what to think of her either. I knew how Viggo's psychopathic mind worked. I had spent a hundred and twenty years with him breathing down my neck. He wondered how old she was. More precisely, he wondered if she could be stronger than him—the oldest vampire on Earth—given that she'd had no human nourishment for seven hundred years. I caught the curious sparkle in his eyes. He was wondering if he should test her. If he failed, he would prove inferior in front of an atrium full of witnesses. Any edge would be lost.

Do it, Viggo, I silently prayed. Not because I wanted to see him fall—

though I so desperately did—but because I needed to see what this vampiress was made of.

"Where is Evangeline?" Mortimer's deep Parisian voice cut through the tension like a sharp blade. It took the tall, dark-haired vampire only half a dozen strides to tower ominously over me. "What is this new game you're playing with us? Have we not suffered enough?" Mortimer didn't bother with an act, which was a refreshing change, despite his naturally unpleasant demeanor. He hadn't always been surly. It had slowly crept in over the years as he waited for my sister's release from the magical tomb where I had put her. Between the long wait and the anxiety that she would choose Viggo over him, the being my sister had fallen in love with had vanished. Deep down, I pitied him. What a terrible unknown to endure.

But for now, my resentment with these two outweighed any compassion I might dig up from my deepest recesses. I was, for once, enjoying the upper hand, as spiteful as that was. I felt another wicked smile stretch my lips. I dared to reach up to adjust the lapel of Mortimer's black wool suit jacket. "Somewhere you will never find her. You can—"

"To protect her or harm her?" the little vampiress interjected, suddenly appearing beside Mortimer. Something strange flickered in her eyes. Fury, possibly, though I didn't see why.

I felt my lips purse tightly, and my minty green eyes narrowed to slits. Try as I might, I couldn't school my emotions from my face. *Who the hell is she to question my intentions for Evangeline?* "To protect her, of course," I delivered in a crisp tone.

"From us?" She indicated the group of hungry Ratheus vampires with a wave of her hand.

I speared her with the flattest look I could muster. "Yes. You." My eyes flitted over to Caden, who stood huddled within a small circle with his friends some distance away, whispering quietly while watching the event unfold. My eyes shifted to Viggo and Mortimer. "And them."

"We would never hurt Evangeline," Viggo began.

"Drop the act," I snapped. "No one's buying it."

"You must be Viggo," the vampiress murmured, smiling knowingly at him.

Another intense wave of panic rolled through me. *She knows too much.*

Viggo responded with a broad, toothy grin and an overly-dramatic bow. "And who might you be, my beautiful creature?" I noticed his fingertips drum lightly against his thigh, the only indication of his tension—one he usually acknowledged and ceased within seconds. This time, though, those long, manicured fingers kept drumming.

The vampiress's upper lip twitched slightly but otherwise her face remained serene, unreadable. "Mage."

Evangeline never mentioned a Mage . . . Who was she?

"Well, Mage. Welcome to our fabulous planet." Viggo thrust his arms out dramatically. "Full of living, bleeding humans! We're so happy you've finally made it."

At the mention of blood, a chorus of growls and deep inhalations rose from the crowd of depraved vampires. My attention darted to Evangeline's friends again to see their eyes morph in anticipation.

"Settle down, everyone!" Mage's stern voice rang out above the noise. "Don't behave like wild animals." As if her words had a tranquilizing effect, the noise in the atrium quieted to a low murmur.

"Now tell me, dear Mage, because I am in awe of your power . . . Are you the first?" Viggo asked. The first . . . he meant the first vampire.

Mage ignored him, turning to direct her next question to me in a sharp, direct tone. "Why do you believe Viggo wishes harm to Evangeline?" She was focused. She wanted information. But why did she care?

"Yes, Sofie," Viggo interjected, his brow creasing as if he were confused and hurt. "Why, exactly? We made a deal. Once our sweet Evangeline brought back a vampire, she'd be free to go with her extorted money and her little friends. Remember?" he asked innocently. "So why exactly don't you want to finish the spell? Don't you want to release your sister?" He gestured at Mortimer. "Are you punishing us for something? Or," his eyes narrowed, "perhaps you want *more* money for yourself?"

I sighed, absorbing the onslaught of accusations. There was no point in continuing the eighteen-year-old lie anymore. They wouldn't find Evangeline. But I had to lay the truth out carefully. "The spell isn't over." I held my hand up in surrender as the words left my mouth, focusing now on Evangeline's friends, hoping to explain before they exploded, before they decided I should die for deceiving Evangeline. To my surprise, my confession brought no reaction. Nothing, aside from a flicker of mild surprise in Amelie's emerald eyes. From Caden and the cute couple standing behind him, nothing. Their expressions were stony, indifferent. *Strange.*

I did get a reaction from Viggo and Mortimer, though. "What?" they screeched in unison, Mortimer's voice two octaves above his normally deep, ominous level.

I adjusted my stance as I explained, expecting one of them to fly at me. "The pendant can't come off Evangeline yet and I need the pendant to release Veronique."

"And when can it come off?" Mortimer whispered, hovering over me, his glare icy enough to freeze a normal person stiff.

"When I figure out how to get it off Evangeline without killing her," I answered, matching his coolness.

"You're choosing that girl over your own flesh and blood?" Each word left Viggo's mouth with slow, sharp precision.

The accusation pierced my heart as surely as if he had stabbed me. "No, that's not true," I began, but I faltered, the guilt of my betrayal a weight on my shoulders. I loved my sister. I ached to see her. But Evangeline . . . She may as well be my own flesh and blood, for what she had come to mean to me. I had watched her grow from a tiny, soft baby into a beautiful, gentle woman. I would carve a path of destruction through anyone who wished her harm. I would protect her until my very last second of existence.

"How long have you known?" Mortimer hissed.

Always. The moment the Fates answered my Causal Enchantment, I knew each and every step that needed to take place. But I didn't answer Mortimer. Instead I locked eyes with Viggo, relishing the moment as recognition passed across those callous, two-thousand-year-old eyes. Recognition that he had been played a fool. I didn't need to answer. I just smiled.

Viggo's eyes narrowed to slits. His lips pursed into a tight smile that evolved into a grimace as he stared intently at me. I knew he was visually tearing out my throat, weighing the value of the desire, deciding if it was worth keeping me here. And he could easily dispose of me if he wanted to; without my magic, I was no match for the ancient demon's strength. In the end, he only sighed. "Well played, witch." His lips parted into a wicked smile. "Now it's my turn."

He flew toward Caden with superhuman speed. A gasp caught in my throat, his intentions immediately clear to me.

Caden met him face-on, as if expecting the threat. Of equal height, they stood chest to chest, regarding each other as predators would before a battle. "What will happen, do you think, when Evangeline finds out her precious Caden is dead?" Viggo purred, shifting his weight, preparing to pounce.

No, you mustn't harm him. He is Evangeline's life. It will kill her. I haphazardly pushed Mortimer out of my way as I edged forward, terrified that my sudden movement would serve as a catalyst.

Caden's head tilted back, his Adam's apple protruding sharply as he broke out in boisterous laughter.

It stayed Viggo's hands. He cocked his head to the left and said curiously, "Is that amusing? Your death, after all of this, is amusing?"

Mortimer suddenly appeared next to Viggo—as an ally, or as someone with a vested interest, I wasn't sure. Either way, the two of them against Caden would be disastrous. I needed to stop this from happening. My heels scraped over the cobblestones as I shifted closer, the thirty feet between us feeling like a thousand.

"Yeah, actually, it is," Caden answered levelly, those beautiful, piercing jade eyes sizing up both Viggo and Mortimer, undaunted. They were physically the same size, though Caden appeared ten years younger in human years. "We used the human to get here and now you're threatening me because of it? I didn't do anything you wouldn't do."

My feet froze. His words . . . *the human*. So impersonal. So cold. So . . . treacherous. Wariness crept into me.

"It worked! And now we're here!" Amelie suddenly squeaked, cutting into their exchange with an excited lilt in her voice. She skipped forward and placed her hand on Mortimer's chest, not intimidated by his ominous, towering presence. "You must be Mortimer, right? So tall and handsome! I'm Amelie. I think we could be good friends, don't you?" She flashed a brilliantly adorable smile—so adorable that it completely disarmed Mortimer. He faltered, blinking several times, and eventually allowed a subdued grin.

The smile didn't work on Viggo. "So you're saying you don't care for Evangeline?" he asked lightly, though I knew his mood was anything but light.

"I'm saying we did what we needed to do to get here," Caden answered, shrugging. Something in his tone . . . he sounded . . . bored? Detached? It sparked a wave of rage within me.

Viggo's left eyebrow arched. "I don't know if I believe you."

"I don't give a rat's ass what you believe," Caden answered with a sneer, his chest puffing out aggressively, "except for one thing. Believe this: if any of you so much as look at us the wrong way—" those mesmerizing, blue-green eyes shifted to me "—any of you . . . you will die."

Viggo's responding chuckle would have sent a chill through any sane person's soul. "I'm not so sure you should be throwing threats around, given your youthfulness and lack of human blood."

Another smug grin stretched across Caden's face. "Youthfulness?"

"Why, yes! Seven hundred, is it? Give or take? A baby, next to some of us."

"You assume what we told the human was true." All four of them chuckled now, the young, blonde Bishop in the back throwing his arm lazily over Fiona's shoulders. "How much of what you know about me do you think is real?" Caden continued.

This can't be happening. I was so sure of his feelings. How could anyone not fall in love with her? Panic twisted my stomach. My worst nightmare was coming true. Could they really have lied to Evangeline about everything? Yes! Of course! Why wouldn't they? Or . . . they could be lying to Viggo, distancing themselves from his target. Either was possible. But now they were toying with my trust.

Ruse or not, Caden's ploy was working. Viggo's lips compressed as he realized he could very well be picking a battle with a vampire twice his age, with three more flanking him.

Anxiety tore at my insides. I needed to know the truth. Had he lied to Evangeline? Used her to get here? If they had . . .

I'd tear them all to pieces.

I stepped forward, keeping my target in sight as my mental eye scoured my insides for a spark. I only needed one little helix to read Caden's soul. Just one tiny little bud, even . . . .

Mage stepped in front of me, blocking my path. "Move," I growled.

"You cannot blame them for deceiving Evangeline to get what they wanted. After all, you did the same," Mage reminded me.

"What I did was nothing like that!" *Go away! You're distracting me!* I sidestepped around her. Just one spark—one—and I'd burn them to the ground. *There!* I found one floating beneath my left lung. I plucked at it, pulling it up and forward, releasing it from my fingertip. The tiny, glowing purple bud, visible only to me, sailed toward Caden.

A sharp spasm shot through my back as something dug into my collarbone. I lost my grasp on the helix. Flinching, I watched it drift up and away, now worthless. "I wouldn't do that, if I were you," Mage's voice hummed in my ear. I turned to see her hand on me, and one eyebrow raised. How did she know what I was doing? Vampires couldn't see magic . . . "You mustn't blame Evangeline. Many were tricked. Even other powerful vampires." She gestured with her chin toward Rachel, lying under a charred tree.

That's right! I had forgotten. Was the whole Rachel-Caden thing a charade as well? Desperate for answers, I spun on my heels, breaking free of Mage's grasp, and flew to the raven-haired demon. Bending down, I tore the Merth bindings from her wrists and legs, wincing at the sting.

She was on her feet in a second, her hate-filled yellow eyes locked on Mage. I watched a secret look pass between them.

"No harm intended, Rachel," Mage offered mildly.

"No. Just trying to leave me in that hell hole," Rachel responded coolly, her pinched nose and pouty red lips rendering her face beautiful yet unpleasant.

"Well, you're here and you're free. Bygones, right?" Mage matched her coolness, unruffled by whatever had transpired between them.

"Right." Rachel displayed a toothy grin. She turned to Caden, fury flashing over her face, her hands flexing as if about to rake his eyes out.

"So was all that an act, too?" I asked Caden, leaning in to scrutinize his every twitch, his every shift, for some clue.

"No. That was an added bonus," Caden answered, adding with thick sarcasm, "thanks so much for letting her loose."

Rachel's eyes narrowed further. The hatred was genuine, I decided. But all this just couldn't be . . . Was it all an act? It would certainly be smart of Caden, distancing himself from ties to Evangeline, making himself less of a target for Viggo and Rachel. Again I reached inside for a bud, desperate to read Caden, to end this question once and for all. Regrettably, I couldn't find even one.

"I don't believe you," Viggo finally stated, crossing his arms over his chest.

Caden only shrugged, an infuriating gesture, based on the fleeting twist of Viggo's mouth. If they kept this up, act or no act, Viggo wouldn't restrain himself. I had long-since dissolved his patience.

"Well, while you're not believing, where are the humans? I'm parched," Bishop piped up with an obnoxious grin.

"You'll have to ask Sofie if she can find you—" Viggo began, but voices from inside the building interrupted him.

"Are all the servants on vacation?" a female exclaimed angrily.

Right on cue.

Heads whipped around as Camila Forero stormed through the red doors into the atrium, followed closely by her husband, Carmelo—Viggo and Mortimer's Colombian "beard" family, and the only two humans left in the building. Their children had left with Evangeline for no other reason than that the sweet, optimistic girl had begged me to save them. These two, I'd intentionally left behind.

Camila stopped dead. Her dark brown eyes grew wide as they flitted over the smoldering corpses and landed on the crowd of strangers regarding her with intense interest.

One . . . two . . . . there. Forty sets of nostrils flared. The scent of human blood coursing through delicate human veins had reached the Ratheus vampires. It was all they needed. Eyes began morphing into the hideous red globes of ravenous vampires, the only time one of our kind could be considered grotesque.

Camila's jaw dropped. Her terror flooded my mind like a potent memory. Another vampirism. I knew the others would sense it as well. It would only feed their lust. Camila's feet began sliding backward as she edged stiffly toward the building. Her four inch snakeskin heels scraped against the concrete steps. She stumbled into her husband before pushing past him to run, Carmelo on her heels. I sighed. *Bad move, running.*

"The garage!" I heard Camila whisper to her husband as surely as if she stood next to me.

So they thought they could hide? Despite myself, I chuckled. *Silly humans. There's no hiding . . .*

The swarm took off, Caden and Amelie in the lead, tearing into the building after the humans, in a race to see who would taste human blood first. Sympathy for Evangeline swallowed my anger, the likelihood that her friends had deceived her growing with each minute.

"Wonderful!" Viggo muttered sarcastically, throwing his hands up in the air. "Who's going to clean up the blood?"

I rolled my eyes. "You think there's going to be a drop of blood left?"

Camila's shrill scream silenced any retort.

"How long before they discover they're trapped?" Mortimer asked, the legs of a bistro chair scratching against the cobblestones as he dragged it away from a charred body. He repositioned it on the other side of Veronique's statue. "And how angry do you think this Mage will be?"

"Yes, she may prove thorny," Viggo mused absently as he inspected the leaves of a wild rose bush—an ancient and rare variety that Veronique loved, now a crisp mess.

I wondered the same thing. I began tinkering with the Merth the second Evangeline left for Ratheus for the last time, testing out different magical weaves and chants, combining basic witch binding spells with my own concoctions, adding my own unique signature to make the spell unbreakable by anyone but me. It had taken days to figure out and thousands of helix threads but, in the end, no vampire was getting within twenty feet of an exterior wall without facing paralyzing pain. Given we now had forty vampires within these walls instead of four, I couldn't be more thankful that the spell was in place. It was the only thing I was thankful for.

We didn't have long to wonder how Mage would react. "What have you done to this building?" her crisp voice called out. I turned to see the delicate vampiress gliding toward me, her movements smooth and controlled. She dabbed a blood-stained cloth against her mouth. More dark red stains covered her shirt—a gray button-down meant for Fiona. A mutant accompanied her on her right, the only surviving mutant. To her left, at a distance but clearly intent on hearing the conversation, Rachel slinked.

A flood of Ratheus vampires trailed the three of them through the doors into the atrium, their angry crimson eyes settling on me. I counted twenty-eight now. The rest were no doubt lying on the cold tile within the Merth's border, waiting for someone to drag them to safety. But twenty-eight could still prove difficult to control, that fact driven home as I caught whispers of "witch" and "torture." I glanced from Mage back to them, and to Viggo and Mortimer. *I'm surrounded by angry, desperate vampires.* This couldn't end well. "What do you mean?" I asked, my voice intentionally airy.

Mage paused for a moment to regard me, a knowing smirk touching her lips, her eyes narrowing slightly. She turned to a tall, willowy blonde standing near the security door beside the iron garage gate. "Tanith? Please demonstrate." The blonde vampire hesitated. "Go and open that door," Mage pressed gently, her voice a soothing song.

Tanith stalked toward the metal door. She reached out slowly, her face pinched, her long fingers approaching the metal handle as if anticipating pain. Like a cobra, her hand shot forward the last few inches to graze the handle and pull back.

Her eyes lit up in pleasant surprise; what she had expected hadn't happened. She glanced over at Mage as her hand clamped over the door handle. She gave it a yank. It did little more than creak. I had expected as much, given it was triple-reinforced with titanium deadbolts and a system of iron rods tunneling ten feet into the brick surrounding it. Even Viggo with all his strength couldn't open that door without exerting significant strength.

With a sigh, Mage floated over to the door. She reached out to grasp the handle with her dainty hand as Tanith had before her. She pulled. A hair-raising metal screech echoed through the atrium as Mage ripped the security door out of its frame as if it were nothing more than a sheet of paper, sending concrete and brick flying in every direction. I had never seen a display of strength like that before. It was all I could do to keep my mouth from hanging open. In my peripheral vision, I spied Viggo's jaw drop for a split second before he schooled his expression and clamped his mouth shut. Mage was no longer his competition. She had just proven herself to be vastly superior.

Now, with a gaping hole in the wall, the Ratheus vampires—Caden and friends falling in at the rear—bolted. They poured through the opening into the tunnel, heading toward the exterior door, the final barrier between them and the streets of Manhattan . . . and the blood they'd been craving for seven hundred years.

I wasn't worried about them escaping. Instead I stood frozen, watching as Mage tossed the heap of metal aside and calmly approached me. *I have no magic and I'm facing off against the vampire queen that I've single-handedly trapped in this building.* I wondered how long I would survive. The mutant lingered beside her, his eyes shifting furtively to the gaping hole, no doubt wondering if he could pass.

Shrieks of pain echoed from the tunnel.

Mage crossed her arms over her chest. "That's what I'm referring to."

"Oh, *that.*" I was going for aloof but it came out sounding like a petulant child. "Well . . . " I paused, evaluating my options. What should I tell her? They already knew I was a sorceress. Should I play dumb? Could I pretend I was as much a victim of some witch's trap as she was, that I couldn't get out either? Or could I blame Evangeline's spell, say that this was a consequence? Various webs began spinning at warp speed in my mind. It was all I did lately—lie. Lie to Viggo and Mortimer to protect Evangeline; lie to Evangeline to protect her. Heck, I even lied to myself to ease my guilt over the choices I'd made.

I regarded Mage's shrewd, hawkish eyes and some instinct cautioned me against lying this time. *The truth it is.* A rarity. "We can't have blood-crazed vampires tearing through the streets of our city, especially ones who've already had a hand in the extinction of one world's humans. So, I've laced the building with Merth. None of you will get out until I release the spell." *Go ahead and kill me, Mage. You'll never taste warm human blood again.*

Mage leveled a hard stare at me, the corners of her almond eyes crinkling as she thought. "You're telling me the truth." It was a statement. "I appreciate that. I know it doesn't come naturally for our kind. Thank you." She turned her back on me to walk toward the tunnel. "Everyone, listen!" Mage shouted. She waved them all out of the tunnel to form a circle around her in the atrium. Only fourteen returned, throwing daggered glares in my direction. The rest were caught within the Merth. "I'm sorry, but every one of us will need to stay here for now . . . Jonah, stop!" Her hand flew out toward the mutant Jonah as he slowly edged toward the tunnel exit. He glanced over his shoulder at Mage, his face twisting into something more repulsive, if that were possible. But his feet still moved forward. He could get past the Merth. He could be free.

He can't escape. With desperation on my side, a flame suddenly erupted at my fingertip. *Oh, thank God. My magic is back.* "Stop," I commanded, my hand rising, my finger pointed, ready to burn the mutant to the ground.

Mage suddenly appeared in front of me, her powerful hand clamping over mine, thwarting my plans. Her hand remained on mine as she turned to regard him. "Jonah," she said, her voice calm.

"Just for a bit . . . promise," he murmured, continuing forward.

Viggo and Mortimer appeared before the gaping hole in the wall, their tall, lean frames creating a formidable barrier. Luckily we agreed on one thing—we couldn't have a mutant loose.

"Seriously?" Jonah chuckled arrogantly.

"Now would not be a good time to make your exit." Mortimer's French accent made him sound calm and diplomatic but I could see the mixture of rage and panic in his eyes. Viggo, on the other hand, swayed side to side, hands at the ready, sneering. He was eager to pounce, his distaste for mutants evident.

Jonah rolled his hideous white eyes. "I disagree! I've waited seven hundred years. Now is the perfect time. You two aren't strong enough to match me so I suggest you let me pass before I rip you to shreds."

Great. Another volatile situation. How many more of these would we endure under this roof? How long before one of us died? My attention slid to Evangeline's friends, who now stood in a far corner under a sizeable fig tree, their shirts speckled with blood. Clearly they'd been at the head of the line for the Foreros.

"No, but with my help they are," a prissy voice called out, drawing my eyes back to the hole. Rachel stood next to Viggo, offering Jonah a wicked grin. "Thanks for tying me up, freak." Whatever had transpired on Ratheus, Jonah had made an enemy of her. "If I can't go out there, neither can anyone else." She offered Viggo an over-exaggerated grin and a wink. *She's choosing a side.* "Besides, you can't go out there. You're hideous!" she sneered at the mutant.

Jonah smirked, unperturbed. "So what?"

"So what?" Mortimer shouted, never one to control his anger. "So you'll only attract the attention of a bunch of fanatics watching us every minute of every day, waiting for a reason to uncover us!"

"You're being watched?" Mage glanced at my fingertip and, seeing the flame extinguished, released her grip.

I nodded once.

"Humans?"

A second nod. Not just any humans—the People's Sentinel, a group of zealous humans whose sole mission was to kill vampires. They had been nothing but a thorn in our side for centuries.

"Have they made an alliance with the witches yet?" Mage asked.

Yet? "No . . . " I began, processing her words and her tone. A few had helped the elusive Ursula—a scorned witch from my past—attack Evangeline in Central Park the day she hoodwinked Leo and the dogs. Max was kind enough to bring one of the victims' hands home to show me the awkward crucifix on the thumb: the Sentinel's trademark. I wouldn't call it an alliance, though. The Sentinel hated witches as much as they did vampires.

"And so it begins," Mage murmured.

Unease stirred in my stomach. She knew something. She expected something. I opened my mouth to demand she share her knowledge, but she had already turned her back to me, her attention on Jonah.

"I need you to remain within these walls until we decide how to eliminate this threat," she told him. "We must avoid a repeat of Ratheus. Understand?"

A repeat of Ratheus. She was afraid of a world war ending human life here. She and I shared one thing in common, at least.

"Understand?" Mage repeated more loudly when Jonah's gaunt face twisted in displeasure. After a pause, the mutant nodded, scowling.

It was as if she had power over them, as if she could control them. There was something so elusive about her, so . . . I seized a magic bud and quietly chanted a few lines of a probing spell as I let my magic drift toward her. The glowing tendrils curled around her skull, preparing to enter and download information buried deep within her core. I would know everything there was to know about our dear Mage in fifteen seconds . . .

Black hair fanned outward as she whirled around to face me, anger flashing in her eyes. "Don't you dare," she hissed.

My magical fingers recoiled.

"Don't ever do that again, or you and I will have a problem," she warned quietly.

I pursed my lips tightly, torn between feeling like the child caught with her hand in a cookie jar and pure fascination. How did she know what I was doing?

Satisfied that I would not continue my magical assault, Mage looked to Viggo and Mortimer. "We know everything. We know about your venom issue. We know about Sofie's sister in that tomb over there." She pointed to the statue behind Mortimer. Viggo's eyes bulged with panic, that the secrets he guarded so closely were thrown out into the open. "It's in everyone's best interest that we consider a truce. No more killing—anyone. No more of Sofie's magic." She looked at me to confirm that I heard her. "In return, Jonah stays inside and this group will behave as appreciative guests, accepting your asylum."

Viggo and Mortimer exchanged the briefest look. "Though I am trustworthy," Viggo began, earning an eye roll from me, "how do we know we can we trust this group?"

Mage offered Viggo a honey-sweet smile but when she spoke, her words were laced with deadly warning. "No one defies me. No one."

"No one?" I mimicked, eyeing Rachel, whose vengeful snake eyes hadn't left Caden and his friends.

Understanding my concern, Mage turned to Rachel. "No retaliation, right, Rachel?"

After a pause, a sneering Rachel nodded reluctantly.

"And," Viggo added, his index finger swinging back and forth between Caden and me, "we have a truce as long as they stay away from each other." *Of course.* He was afraid I'd form allegiances.

Caden chuckled in response. "No worries there. I want less to do with that witch than with psycho." He gestured toward Rachel.

"You had better not be lying to me," Viggo warned in a low tone, his blue eyes icy. Caden snorted.

If this is an act, you had better ease off. Though Viggo played the easygoing vampire, getting caught lying to him had disastrous consequences.

"Fine. We're in agreement," Mage said, assuming she had my agreement. "So now what?"

Viggo clapped his hands together, his typical false charm in full swing again. "How about a beverage?"

CR

"Stand back!" Viggo sang out as Mortimer pushed a refrigerated cart along the cobblestone path, its metal frame rattling noisily over the uneven ground. They had insisted on bringing a batch of blood up from the cellar, afraid that exposing the Ratheus vamps to all that blood at once would send them into a crazed tailspin.

K.A.TUCKER

Now, though, asking a group of vampires who had waited seven hundred years for a drop of blood to stand back was too much. All forty vampires—I had rescued the ones from within the Merth-affected perimeter in an effort to gain favor—flocked toward the cart like starving, red-eyed peasants begging for the king's rations. Arms outstretched, they groped eagerly at the metal box.

"You'll all get some!" Viggo chirped as he tossed bags of blood out, adding for my benefit, "It would be faster if we had servants, of course."

The vamps tore through the thick medical plastic with their teeth, desperate to get to the contents. Blood spilled over their hands and splashed onto the ground. Evangeline's friends pushed forward to fill their fists with bags, then scurried to a far corner to feed quietly, whatever promises they'd made about refusing human blood clearly nonexistent. I felt another sharp pang of despair, my hope that they might be deceiving Viggo and Mortimer all but gone.

That much spilled blood proved difficult even for me; I felt the spidery web of veins creep into my eyes and knew I needed to get away. Turning from the crowd, I fled to the only place that offered some semblance of comfort in this asylum of blood-crazed vampires.

2. EXILED

"Am I stupid?"

Leo jerked in his chair as if startled from sleep. My voice had likely done just that. He was past exhaustion, the heavy circles under his eyes so dark they could be mistaken for bruising. But the stubborn old man refused to go to bed. Instead, he slouched in the checkered-print wing chair beside the wood stove in my room, his hand resting lazily on Remington's head. I think he was waiting for me to drift off.

That was the problem. I couldn't drift off. Caden's bloodthirsty red eyes met me every time I tried. Murderous eyes. And no matter how hard I concentrated, no matter how long I stared at the four by six photo of him that I held in my hand, I couldn't call his beautiful jade eyes from my memory.

It had been a little after midnight when Leo escorted me to my second floor bedroom—a simple but cozy cedar-paneled nook with slanted ceilings and two tiny windows overlooking the mountains. A pair of pink flannel pajamas waited for me on a double bed. Just as Sofie had instructed, Leo informed me.

Now, two hours later, I lay under the plush white down duvet with my personal guard dog, Max, stretched out beside me, gazing out at a night sky speckled with brilliant stars, thinking about Caden and the others. Wondering if their previous morals and convictions still held. Wondering if Caden was mad at me for believing everything would be fine. Wondering if I was an idiot for believing in the first place.

"What's that?" Leo murmured, his thick Irish accent as staggering now as it had been the first time I heard it only hours ago, when I learned he wasn't merely a proper British butler, but Sofie's warlock spy, planted in Viggo's household fifteen years ago to keep tabs on his employer.

"Am I stupid? For believing them?"

He chuckled softly. "No, my dear Evangeline. You are far from stupid. Naïve, absolutely. But it's born out of an enormous heart and an enduring need to believe the best of people. Not stupidity."

"But why? After everything that's happened, I still lap up what people give me like a dog!"

Hey, now, Max grumbled.

I patted his massive paw in apology. "You're no ordinary dog, Max." That was an understatement. Max and his brothers were werebeasts, created by Mortimer before Sofie's magic fried all vampire venom in her struggle to do the impossible—turn from witch to vampire. Besides their giant muscular bodies, they had the regenerative abilities and super senses of a human vampire, as well as telepathic links with their maker. Except Max. He was special. When Max switched his allegiance to me after the attack in Central Park, I began hearing him inside my head. It was only one way, unfortunately, but he understood every word that came out of my mouth.

Leo shifted in his chair to face me. "Honestly, I don't know what keeps your spirits so high. With all that has happened to you, we expected one jaded young woman. And yet you keep surprising us with this unworldly resilience." He smiled gently. "That's a good thing, by the way."

"I guess so," I murmured after a moment.

"It is!" he insisted. "It's what makes you so damn lovable."

I leaned into Max's shoulder, hiding the blush I felt creeping into my cheeks at the compliment, such attention unfamiliar to me. I'd spent the last five years utterly invisible. Of course now I knew that was all Sofie's doing, her compelling everyone to keep their distance for fear of Viggo murdering those close to me.

Leo turned back toward the stove, chuckling to himself. "And don't forget, you weren't the only one tricked. I'll bet Viggo and Mortimer are feeling quite foolish right about now."

I propped myself up on my elbows. "Why'd you do it?"

The light from the fire burning in the wood stove coupled with a candle on the side table provided enough light to observe the old man's profile, brows puckered as he frowned, deep in thought. "I was in Sofie's debt."

Shock widened my eyes. "She forced you?"

Leo's head whipped back toward me. "Oh no!" he said, his voice suddenly passionate. "Not in the least. I *wanted* to help her." With a sigh, he bent forward to ease another log into the fire. "Sofie gave me back my wife."

A small gasp escaped my sagging jaw.

"Oh, don't be so shocked! Did you think I was born in a three-piece suit?" he exclaimed, straightening the red and orange argyle sweater vest he had donned, a contrast from the formal clothing he'd worn in Manhattan as Viggo's butler.

Leo . . . in another life? Married? It was reasonable, yet I couldn't picture it. Swallowing my shock, I asked, "How did Sofie . . . give you back your wife?"

He smiled. "One winter, my wife—Maeve—started having difficulty breathing. To this day, I don't know what caused it. A weak heart, perhaps. Being what I am, I tried healing her, but I couldn't. I tried every spell in the book. I begged every sorcerer I knew, who tried every spell in their repertoire. Nothing. No one could fix her. Not with normal magic, anyway." He leaned back in his chair. "A friend of mine suggested I ask the Fates."

The Fates. I remembered Sofie mentioning these Fates. "Isn't that what Sofie did for my spell?"

Leo's head bobbed up and down, his brow furrowing. "Dangerous and powerful stuff, that type of magic. It can be deadly. Few sorcerers will even attempt a Causal Enchantment. Most don't have enough magic in them to call on them, even if they're brave enough. I don't, that's for certain." A wrinkled index finger rose to wag in the air. "But there was one, it seemed, a powerful and fearless French sorceress who had turned herself eighty years earlier using a Causal Enchantment for the love of a vampire, only to accidentally kill him. I had heard about her; she was a fable by that point, really. No one knew if she still lived. Most thought she had met her demise by fire, or something equally poetic. If she did exist, she had dropped off the grid completely.

"I was desperate. I had to find her, had to see what she could do that no one else could. And so I searched. I researched every French sorcery guild tree; I picked the brains of every elderly witch still alive. And I finally found a name: Sofie Girard."

"Girard," I repeated softly. Of course Sofie had a last name!

He nodded. "Once I had her name, I used a type of spell called a 'broadcast spell' to seek her out. I'll explain that another time." He waved away my perplexed look. "Maeve was so weak by this point, her breathing ragged. I didn't expect her to last another week." Leo paused and swallowed heavily.

"The morning after I sent the broadcast out, I walked into our little kitchen in Dublin to find this stunning red-haired woman perched on the counter." He chuckled. "At first I thought she was going to strike me dead for seeking her out—those pale green eyes seemed to dissect me." Leo leaned forward until he perched on the edge of his chair, suddenly animated as he relived the memory. "But she pushed past me without a word and walked over to the couch where my wife lay, wheezing terribly and barely conscious by now. Sofie leaned forward, close to my wife's face. I didn't know what to expect. I was afraid she would do what I couldn't—end my wife's suffering. Or worse, turn her! Of course, I didn't know about the venom problem, that her venom couldn't turn a human." A wistful smile touched Leo's lips.

"But she did no such thing. For two days straight, Sofie sat beside Maeve, holding her hand. I could feel her magic in the house. Such awesome, unparalleled strength that woman has. She is a true rarity in the sorcery world. I sat in the chair next to them, watching. I didn't utter a single word. For two days straight, I sat there, until I finally passed out from exhaustion." Leo leaned back into his chair. "When I awoke, Maeve was sitting next to me with rosy cheeks and vibrant eyes. Sofie was gone."

My heart swelled with relief. "So Maeve's okay? Where is she now?"

Leo smiled sadly. "She's been gone twenty years now, Evangeline. That's the downside of marrying an older woman." He chuckled. "Maeve was nineteen years my senior. When I was a spry fifty-five-year-older, she was in her mid-seventies. Old age took her. But thanks to Sofie, I had thirty wonderful years with her."

"So then what happened?" I felt my eye brow quirk with doubt. "How'd you end up as Viggo's British butler?"

"Well . . . " Leo slowly eased out of his chair. He walked over to gaze out a window, his arms crossed over his chest. "When Maeve died, I was lost. Figured I'd just let myself waste away until I could join her. And then one day about fifteen years ago, Sofie contacted me using a communication spell. It seems the sly woman had kept tabs on me and knew I was widowed." He laughed, shaking his head. "She asked about my British acting skills and my ability to mask my powers. Intrigued and willing to repay her in any way I could, I followed her instructions. I moved to England under an assumed name and fraudulent credentials. I published an advertisement for a job in New York City, and I learned a disguising spell to hide my Irish accent, to create the illusion of a perfect gentleman's man. It didn't take long for Viggo to find me. His last butler met an untimely death." Leo grimaced. "Or timely, for Sofie's sake."

I shuddered, hoping Sofie had nothing to do with it but not feeling overly confident.

"I entered their home just after Viggo killed your mother."

That stabbed at my heart. Since learning the truth of my mother's death—that Viggo had murdered her—I could not think about my mother without seeing the haunting image Max had shown me of Viggo leaning over her broken body. It was etched in my mind, just as Caden's bloody eyes now were. A giant wet nose nuzzled against my ear. Max, comforting me. I gave his head an affectionate scratch.

Leo continued. "At first I knew nothing about you, about the spell, or the venom issue. But slowly, as Sofie learned to trust me, as I began feeding her bits of information and described strange happenings that I heard of with my ear to the ground, she confided in me." He gave me a gentle smile that pulled at the wrinkled skin around his mouth. "By the time you stepped out of Viggo's private jet, I knew you quite well." Returning his gaze to the window, he paused, his mind drifting. "Maeve and I were never able to have children. She was in her forties when we married. We tried, but it never took." Just as quickly, he drifted back into our conversation. "Planting me in there was brilliant on Sofie's part. Unfortunately I knew nothing about Ursula. Viggo kept that one close to his unbeating heart."

"I don't know how Sofie keeps up with all these schemes of hers," I muttered, feeling a twinge of envy over her brilliance. "I mean . . . this place!" I wished I had a hundredth of her cunning. She had designed an escape route for every escape route of every situation, even the most wild and unplanned.

Leo's arms unfolded to punctuate his words with movement. "Oh, you don't know the half of it! The cost and complexity of building this place up here? Creating a fully self-sufficient cabin on undiscovered land? It has taken ten years and countless helicopter crews. She compelled every single builder, supplier, bookkeeper—anyone at all— so as not to risk a trail here for Viggo or Mortimer to follow. There is nothing that woman hasn't thought of regarding your safety, I can promise you that." His declaration allowed me a large sigh of relief; I had a maternal vampiress watching over me.

But then those pulsating red eyes pushed into my memory and my chest tightened. "Leo, will my friends ever be normal again?"

Leo approached slowly and stopped next to my bed. "They were never normal, Evangeline. They're vampires." He paused. "I could help you forget them, if you wanted. But my magic isn't like a vampire's compulsion. I wouldn't be able to isolate specifics. I'd likely wipe out the past month completely. You might not even remember them."

"No!" I exclaimed, more a shout in the dead silence of the night. *Not remember them?* Forget the angelic ring of Amelie's giggles? Forget the shivers that ran through my body every time Caden gazed in my direction? Forget that all-consuming warmth of love? Never. I modulated my voice. "No, that's okay. I don't want to forget what's happened."

Leo smiled. "That's good, because I might accidentally lobotomize you." He placed his hand on my forehead and said somberly, "You need your rest, Evangeline."

I groaned. "I'm trying, but I can't. Every time I close my eyes, I see . . ." My words became garbled as a feeling of calm and peace washed over me; my eyelids became too heavy to keep open.

"Go to sleep now, my dear girl," Leo murmured distantly, following that with a low chant. He was casting a spell, I realized. I didn't care;

the sound of his voice welcomed, soothed. I felt the lightest peck on my forehead just before I drifted off, meadows and children's laughter replacing the image of Caden's burning eyes.

Ș

A gray and white marble hallway stretched ahead of me, illuminated by wall sconces that flickered repeatedly, as if touched by a power surge. It looked like the hallway outside my room in Viggo and Mortimer's home, only different. Was it wider? Longer? I stepped forward and teetered, then looked down at heeled shoes, three inches high, peeking from beneath the silky folds of a jade green evening gown. It was the same outfit I'd worn on the night of my eighteenth birthday. Instinct pulled my head to look over my shoulder for Max, but he was nowhere in sight. I was completely alone—an oddity within these walls, where there always seemed to be eyes on me.

And then it hit me: *I'm dreaming.* All suddenly became clear. This had already happened. I had already lived this.

What should I do? The atrium. Maybe I'll find Sofie there. I walked slowly toward the stairs at the end of the hall, reveling in the feel of my gown, the odd sense of relaxation whirling around me. I hadn't felt this peaceful since my birthday.

Suddenly the stairs disappeared and the hallway stretched out ahead for miles with no end in sight. A surge of anxiety replaced the warm, tranquil feeling; I was late for something, I was sure of it, but I had no idea what. I picked up my pace, rushing down the hall, hoping that the stairs would reappear. But the hall kept stretching farther and farther ahead of me. Finally I kicked off my shoes, hiked up my dress, and ran. My breathing became labored, the need to get to those stairs—to my destination—crushing.

As suddenly as the top of the staircase had vanished, it

rematerialized. I skidded to a halt before I tumbled down the steep flight. I was no longer alone. They were there, climbing up the steps, broad smiles on their faces, Amelie's blonde curls bobbing, Fiona and Bishop hand in hand. Just as I remembered them. They were dressed as finely as I, the girls in matching dresses but different colors—Amelie in crimson and Fiona in violet to compliment her sparkling purple-tinged eyes. Bishop stepped forward in a dashing silver suit.

I grinned. They grinned back as they glided up the stairs toward me, parting before they reached me to stand on either side. And then my breath caught as I glimpsed a mass of chestnut brown hair. Caden ascended the stairs behind them, wearing a custom-tailored black suit like those Viggo and Mortimer wore. He lifted his head and his beautiful jade eyes bored into me, sucking the air out of my lungs. My shoulders slouched with relief. I was where I needed to be. I had made it.

Caden stepped onto the landing and held out his hand. I moved forward and took it, then poured myself into his arms, into his embrace. "It worked," he whispered in my ear, the words tickling my skin, sending shivers through to my fingertips.

I reveled in the feel of his chest against my cheek for a long moment, inhaling the intoxicating scent I had come to realize was Caden. Finally I pulled back far enough to gaze into his eyes as I curled my arms around his neck. They were just as I had remembered, so vibrantly bluish-green, so unhuman.

"I told you it would. You just needed to believe in yourself." He smiled, lifting a hand to hold my chin before leaning forward to press his mouth over mine in a soft kiss. When he broke away, he whispered, "And now we can be together forever."

"Forever?" Forever, with Caden. An impossibility before, but now it couldn't happen soon enough. "When?"

His smile turned my legs to water. "Why not now?"

Something started to burn against my chest. Caden's brow furrowed with confusion as he gazed down. I followed his eyes to the black heart pendant around my neck—the catalyst for my curse—alive with fiery red and orange swirls that danced as they had on Ratheus, when they worked to protect me. When they'd stopped me from being transformed. My stomach tightened with the sickly realization that I couldn't have what I wanted. That I couldn't be with him. Not yet, anyway. How would I explain it to him? Would he wait for me? A renewed sense of panic washed over me. Hesitantly, I looked up . . .

Into the pulsating, blood-red eyes of a thirsty vampire. The same eyes that I had met in the atrium, moments after arriving back with Caden. The same eyes that had poisoned all of my memories. I stumbled backward, gasping for air, terror ripping through me as I tried to distance myself.

"Join us," Amelie's playful voice whispered in my ear. Spinning around, I saw the others closing in on me from all sides, their eyes full of that same hunger. For me. My blood.

"I can't yet!" I shrieked. They would kill me before Sofie reversed this curse! I had to get away, to save myself. I stumbled into a run, barely able to stay on my feet.

"Join us," they whispered, trailing me. "Join us now or die."

I screamed . . .

And bolted upright in bed, the sound of my scream ringing in my ears as it bounced off the wood-paneled walls of my tiny room. I was back in the cabin I'd been exiled to until Caden could control his thirst for blood. Pulling the duvet up around my chin, I focused on my breathing to slow my heart; it was thumping so furiously in my chest, I thought it might explode.

Bad dream? A concerned voice asked. I turned wide eyes on Max, now standing next to my bed. This was all too familiar.

My hands flew to the werebeast's neck, seizing fistfuls of shiny black fur. "Please tell me it was just a nightmare, Max. It wasn't real, right? Please!" I begged, my breathing still ragged, my throat burning as I sucked in icy air.

It was just a bad dream, he reassured me somberly. *I've been by your side all night.*

I exhaled noisily, flopping back into my pillows. "Oh, thank God."

His deep chuckle filled my head. *You'll never have a regular bad dream again without thinking it's real, will you?*

Reaching up, I fumbled with the black heart pendant. "Not while this blasted thing is around my neck." The gift from Sofie was my death sentence if Viggo or Mortimer got hold of me. I lay quietly, replaying the nightmare in my head. As horrific as it was, it had allowed me a glimpse into the recesses of my mind, into my memories of Caden. Memories of what I loved. I needed to hold that in a death grip. If it meant reliving the aftermath, I would do it over and over again, night after night, I realized. But how many times would I wake up to the same inevitable end? How long would I need to torture myself with that fear before I could put it past me?

Staring up at the ceiling, I noticed the cloud billowing above me as my hot breath condensed in the room's frigid air. I shuddered, pulling the heavy duvet up around my neck to ward off the cold. "Why couldn't Sofie send us somewhere tropical?" I grumbled.

Max's deep laughter rumbled inside my head again as he climbed up onto my bed. The bed creaked as if threatening to collapse under his weight, but he didn't seem bothered as he flopped down to take up three-quarters of the mattress and share his body heat.

"So glad I amuse you," I said, pushing myself up to sit cocooned within my covers and scan the tiny room, now bathed in wan morning light. A cedar wardrobe sat in one corner and a matching chest of drawers in another, next to the wing chair that Leo had occupied earlier. A simple room, sparsely furnished. *Except for the artwork,* I thought, focusing on an oil painting hanging on the wall opposite me. A little blonde girl sat on a swing with two young women, one blonde, the other a redhead, standing to either side behind her, as if both were pushing her. The minty green eyes caught my attention immediately. *Sofie*. Swinging my eyes to the other woman, I recognized the face of my mother. There was no doubt. "Sofie painted that?" I asked Max, my eyes locked on the portrait.

Yup. And that one.

His muzzle swung to the wall directly behind me and I followed it to another oil portrait of two women, standing side by side. I recognized the one on the left as me as I was now, an adult. It could be a mirror image, Sofie's depiction was so accurate. The woman on the right was my mother. Seeing us side by side, I now saw my uncanny resemblance to her. It was shocking, how similar we looked, though I had never realized it before. "How many more of these paintings are there, Max?" I asked in awe, my focus sliding back and forth between the two faces.

He chuckled. *Think of it as a parent putting up framed pictures of her child.*

I guessed the answer was "a lot." A shiver ran down my spine, the idea that I had unwittingly modeled as a vampire sorceress's muse for the past eighteen years unsettling.

Her favorite place to watch over you was at the park.

A second shiver ran down my spine. *Watch over me*. That was Sofie. And Max. Both of them had shadowed me my entire life without my knowledge, watching a child as any parent with severe obsessive tendencies would. "Will she always be there?" I asked aloud.

Until you're out of danger. And even then, the ties will be tight until . . . the end.

"The end," I repeated softly, catching the certainty in Max's voice. It wasn't a question of if, but of when. I turned to regard Max's golden eyes, too perceptive for any canine. There was sadness in them. "When is 'the end' for me, Max?"

Silence filled the room as Max shut his eyes. *I will protect you from vampires and witches with every fiber of my body. But I can't protect you from the curse of humans. The curse of expiration.*

"You mean just plain getting old?" I said, smiling softly.

Max grunted in assent.

Join me or die. Their whispers suddenly swirled inside my head. I had forgotten until now. I swallowed, then heard myself say aloud, "Not if I become one of them." A bizarre form of hope blossomed inside me. Why shouldn't it? Why would I stay human? There was nothing left to cling to in my human life. I could be one of them and be safe, be with Caden and the others forever. If I joined them, Sofie and Max wouldn't need to watch over me. I would become the predator. I wouldn't need to be protected from anyone, including Caden.

I hadn't given it a thought since the first time I'd questioned Sofie about it, weeks earlier. At the time it was hopeless, because the pendant's magic wouldn't allow my conversion. But maybe now . . .

As long as that black heart hangs around your neck, your soul is still entwined with Veronique's, Max confirmed.

"Of course." I touched the pendant again, running my thumb over its smooth surface. Somehow I had known that would be the answer. My dream had all but told me. This, the pendant that Sofie couldn't figure out how to remove, the noose around my neck, ruling my actions, confining me, cursing me, was a prize to everyone else, something desirable, something to kill for. The urge to yank the stupid thing off suddenly overwhelmed me. I needed it off if I wanted any hope for a life—human or vampire.

Max must have read the despair in my face because he quickly added, *If anyone can figure out how to get it off, Sofie can.* He finished with a reassuring bump against my shoulder. It didn't help.

The bed creaked in loud relief as Max slid off. *You should eat.* He strode over to the door and used his mouth to pull the lever handle down. The door swung open.

I glanced at the clock on the nightstand. Nine-thirty. I hadn't eaten in . . . forever, it seemed. Beside the clock lay my stack of four by six photos of my friends that Sofie had developed for me—the only thing I had to hold onto, now that my memories were infiltrated with demon-red eyes. I gingerly collected the pictures and slid out of bed, shuddering again as the cool air enveloped my body. I quickly wrapped myself in the plush white velour robe that hung on the bedpost at the bottom of the bed, and slid my feet into the matching slippers.

Max led me out into the hallway and past six closed bedroom doors on the way to the stairs. Not a cough or a whisper came from any of them. It was eerily silent for a cabin containing this many people. We stepped from the dimly lit staircase into the great room, now warmed by sunshine streaming in from various vast windows and a skylight tucked between the thick wood beams supporting a cathedral ceiling.

This way, Max called, heading past the rustic dining table toward the back of the room, where I could hear pots and pans clanking together. I rounded the corner and stepped into the delicious, earthy aroma of a rich soup stock.

"Good morning!" Leo sat at a small table with a cup of coffee in one hand and a wildlife magazine in the other. Relaxing in the wooden chair with his legs crossed, wearing a red and black plaid shirt, he looked completely at ease. A night's sleep had faded the dark circles under his eyes. "Coffee?" he offered, sliding a full mug my way before I could answer.

I smiled and nodded, letting my eyes rove the kitchen. All the luxuries of Viggo and Mortimer's urban kitchen were there—the cappuccino maker, the industrial gas stove and grill, a large refrigerator—but the string of garlic cloves hanging from a nail in the wall and the butcher block counter cluttered with bottles and jars of various spices and oils gave it a rustic air.

Magda and two other staffers hovered over various pots on the stove, the source of that delicious smell, no doubt. I found it remarkable that these women, magically wrenched from their accustomed environment yesterday and exiled into these mountains, continued with their daily duties as if nothing out of the ordinary had happened. I wondered if they had any clue what was going on. Either way, they didn't seem bothered. "We have twelve hungry mouths to feed up here," Leo exclaimed as if reading my mind. "Go on, take a seat." He pushed a chair out with one foot. "Did you sleep well?"

"For the most part. Thanks for . . . whatever you did."

He winked at me, then returned his attention to his magazine. I glanced at the giant brown grizzly on the cover. The image stirred memories of Big Brown and a wave of sadness washed over me. Big Brown had been Bishop's ferocious pet, created to serve as my protector. The evil Council leader, Mage, had killed him when she entrapped Caden. "I guess we don't get regular mail deliveries here?" I said, noting the issue's publication date—1992. *Not exactly current.*

Leo chuckled. "No. I suppose we don't." He sipped his coffee, eyeing me over the rim of his mug.

I studied the cover some more, noting the subhead *Locate the world's remaining grizzly population.* "So," I asked, "are there any grizzlies in these mountains?"

Leo's eyebrows arched. "Hoping for a clue as to where we are?"

"No . . ." *Yes.*

"Hmm. You know there's a map in here, indicating where the world's grizzlies exist. They're in only a few locations around the world. So if I told you there were grizzlies here, you could quickly deduce where we are, right?"

Don't try to outsmart him. He's a wily old man, Max warned from his spot behind me.

"Yes, I've noticed," I grumbled, pouring a heaping teaspoon of sugar into my coffee.

Leo exploded in laughter, his eyes shifting between Max and me. He must have caught the gist of our secret conversation. After a moment I couldn't help giggling as well, caught in Leo's infectious spirit. He put the magazine down. "How do eggs and bacon sound?"

I nodded eagerly. "Yummy."

As if waiting for the signal, Magda abandoned the wooden ladle in her pot and grabbed a frying pan from the hanging rack. In seconds, she had two eggs sizzling.

Hands hugging my coffee mug, I rose from my chair and wandered over to a giant window that displayed a mountain view both breathtaking and daunting. The valleys and sea of trees below us told me we were at a high altitude, yet distant mountains towered over us. Spying a frosted thermometer to one side of the window I leaned in, and found the mercury buried at the minus sixty degree Fahrenheit mark. I shivered reflexively.

"Sit!" Magda instructed in her brusque accent. A plate thumped down on the table behind me. "Your food is ready."

"Thank you." I smiled at her as I headed back to the table.

Her head bobbed once, the only indication that she'd heard me. She moved immediately to another task, tossing a cutting board's worth of chopped potatoes into a pot of simmering water.

I devoured breakfast, using my toast to sop up the yolk from my eggs and accepting a second helping of bacon. I noticed Leo watching from the corner of his eye while pretending to read his magazine, an amused but relieved smirk on his face.

"Good! I'm glad I don't have to worry about you being too miserable to eat," he commented as I set my fork down, finished.

I smiled, gathered my dishes, and carried them to the sink. Magda's helper, a middle-aged, mousy woman named Martha, politely shooed me away, whisking the dishes out of my hand before I had a chance to wash them.

"They are working for you now, per Sofie's instructions," Leo explained.

"Oh." I smiled at Magda, whose eyes flicked to me before refocusing on her pot. I felt my cheeks burn, and wondered what they thought of me. I didn't need servants, but I knew refusing was out of the question, so I didn't bother. I turned to Leo. "Okay, what now?" What did a person do to kill time when they were exiled in the wilderness?

"Relax! Enjoy life," Leo murmured, waving his hand dismissively toward the great room. "There're plenty of books to read."

Taking the hint, I left the kitchen's delicious aroma, my giant werebeast in tow, as usual. "Don't you need to eat?" I asked over my shoulder.

I'm ready to gnaw someone's arm off but I'll go later, when the others get back. We go in shifts so someone's always around here, he explained.

"Why? It's not like anyone's going to find us."

Stranger things have happened.

"I guess." Like talking telepathically to a werebeast who'd decided to switch masters. Or being cursed and sent to another world. Or falling madly in love with a vampire who then tried to kill me. My life was all about the strange.

I rounded the corner to find a dark-haired guy standing and staring out a window, a small hardcover book in his hand. Julian. He half turned at the sound of my footsteps.

Speaking of gnawing on arms, Max muttered.

"Good morning," I said cheerily, ignoring my hungry werebeast's subtle threat. Suddenly conscious of my fuzzy pink pajamas, I pulled the ties of my robe tighter.

There was no need. Julian turned back to gaze out the window without a word, leaving me to stare at the back of his raven-haired head. Not surprising. The young Colombian had yet to show a side that challenged Sofie's derogatory opinion of him. He and his sister, Valentina, were part of Viggo and Mortimer's beard family—a cover for their existence and their lavish home on Fifth Avenue. I had practically begged that they be protected from Viggo's deadly grip, the only reason Sofie hadn't left them in that death trap.

I wouldn't waste my energy on that one, Max said.

I sighed and walked over to scan titles on the bookshelf beside the fireplace, obedient to Leo's instruction to relax. I noticed that one shelf housed every single one of my favorite novels, and a small metal sign posted on the shelf identified them as *Evangeline's Picks.* I smiled. The other shelves were full of unfamiliar titles, surely chosen by Sofie for that very reason.

I grabbed a book with a plum cover and took a step back, only to bump into Max, who had edged up behind me. "Max!" I whispered in exasperation, turning to see the dog eyeing Julian. I followed his gaze to find Julian's attention on us. On me. Our eyes locked. It was the first time I had ever looked at him dead on. Sofie was right—he was really good-looking in that tall, dark, and Latin way. For a second I thought he would speak. But then his brow knitted into a scowl and he turned back to gaze out at the snow, leaving me staring awkwardly at his back for the second time. *Being in exile with him is going to be long and painful.* At least Valentina was here. I had only met her the one time, but she seemed nice enough.

My eyes wandered around the room, looking for something else to fix my attention on. They quickly zoned in on three oil paintings on the opposite wall. Yesterday, distracted with my abrupt arrival and the following revelations, I hadn't noticed the paintings. Now I had time to study them.

Each one depicted a little blonde girl in a different scenario. Me. Me jumping through puddles; me playing with my dolls; me petting a speckled gray Pomeranian. Glancing around the room, I found two more that were very clearly of me. "You weren't kidding, Max," I murmured under my breath, waves of shock rippling through my body. I glanced at Max and saw something close to a grin on his muzzle.

Didn't anyone tell you that vampires can be a tad obsessive?

Sofie was . . . obsessed with me? With a heavy sigh, I headed to a lounge chair beside the stone hearth and pulled my legs up to sit cross-legged. "Relax and enjoy life," I whispered to myself again, as if repeating Leo's words enough would somehow make this feel like a vacation. Maybe I'd get to enjoy all two hundred-odd books, given that I'd be "relaxing and enjoying life" in this asylum for years, I thought bitterly as I cracked the cover. The faint new book scent that wafted from its pages soothed me, at least.

After restarting the first page a dozen times, I realized I wouldn't be putting a dent in my personal reading challenge any time soon. My attention kept drifting to New York . . . How far away was I from Caden? Was it day or night there? What was happening? Had Caden's feelings for me changed?

"What the—" Julian's low mutter distracted me from my musings. I quietly shut my book and looked his way. He hadn't moved from his spot and he was intent on something outside. A moment later the side door opened and Valentina stepped through, her normally olive-colored cheeks glowing a vibrant red and her big brown eyes glassy-looking from the frigid temperatures. She wore nothing to protect her from the elements but mitts, a light sweater, and a pair of boots, the undone laces dragging as she walked.

"Are you insane?" Julian exploded, storming toward his little sister. "What were you doing out there? You could have frozen to death!"

"I went for a quick walk. It's pleasant out," Valentina answered excitedly in that high-pitched, childish voice of hers. I felt my eyes widen with shock at the same time that Julian's did. How anyone without a balaclava and a fur-lined body suit could ever call minus sixty degrees "pleasant" was beyond my understanding.

"I have to agree, Valentina," Leo said sternly in his Irish brogue as he entered the room. "Only an idiot goes out in these temperatures without good reason. Don't leave this cabin again without being properly dressed, and only with someone's knowledge."

Valentina turned to regard Leo, her bright eyes narrowing ever so slightly with displeasure before they relaxed. "Okay," she agreed, smiling sweetly. If Leo's severe reprimand ruffled her, I couldn't tell.

"Why would you . . . " Julian's voice drifted off and he shook his head at his foolish sister one last time before turning to Leo, his expression wary. He opened his mouth to speak, but hesitated. "Do you know what happened to our parents?" he finally asked, his tone more respectful than yesterday's. Leo's blunt threat must have forced him to check his cockiness.

The wrinkles in Leo's heavily creased forehead deepened. He nodded. "That's why I came in here." He paused. "Unfortunately, your parents didn't survive. There were just too many . . . of them to control."

"Too many?" Julian repeated, confusion in his eyes.

He hadn't seen the horde of Ratheus vampires appear, I realized. He had been inside. The guy *really* had no idea what had happened.

"They died quickly, if that's any consolation. I'm sorry." Contrasted with his callousness the day before, Leo's soft tone indicated authenticity. I noticed he wouldn't use the term "vampires," though everyone in the room knew exactly what they were.

I hazarded a glance at Julian to see hollow shock in the eyes that stared back at Leo. Instantly, I pitied him. I knew what he was feeling. It had consumed me only five years ago, the night I received news of my mother's death. He was now an orphan. At least he still had his sister . . .

Julian's brown eyes slowly slid first to the dogs, then to me. The muscles in his jaw tightened. "How are you involved in this?" he asked, barely above a whisper.

Max was instantly between us, his lips curling back to expose razor-sharp teeth. He snarled a warning.

"Calm down, Max," I said sharply.

There was no need. Max's ferocity—normally enough to make anyone wary—went unnoticed. Julian continued to stare at me with haunted eyes. When he spoke again, it was more to himself than anyone else. "They will all die. Every last one of them." With that he stormed off, his words a swift kick to my stomach.

Movement beside me drew my eye. Valentina peeled off her sweater and tossed it haphazardly over a chair as she walked over to the couch nearest to me. She seemed surprisingly . . . fine.

I hesitated. "Are you okay?" I asked as gently as possible, moving to sit beside her. I hadn't spoken to her since the day I helped her up from the cobblestones after her fainting spell.

Confusion flashed in her bright doe eyes while she worked to comprehend my meaning. "Oh! You mean because of my parents? Yeah, I'm fine. I figured they were dead."

A small sound escaped me and my jaw dropped. Had I heard her wrong? She must have realized how callous she sounded, because she quickly added, "I was so sad last night that I cried myself to sleep. It's out of my system now." Her tone held zero sincerity. How could anyone be over their parents' deaths in a night? *Shock! That's how!* I finally realized. That was the only explanation.

I glanced over at Leo; he wore a perplexed frown. Good; it wasn't just me who found the entire exchange strange. Shaking his head, he walked back toward the kitchen, muttering under his breath. I thought I caught the word "fool," but I couldn't be sure.

She's not right in the head, Max mumbled. *And she smells . . . off.*

I shot a disapproving look at the giant dog. Of course she wasn't right in the head. She'd just found out both her parents were murdered by vampires!

With a heavy groan, Max dropped to the ground in front of the fireplace and closed his eyes. I knew he was still listening intently.

"What're you reading?" Valentina asked, eyeing the book I still clutched. Before I could answer, she spied the deck of photos sitting on the coffee table. A picture of Caden sat on top. "Oh. He's hot!" She reached over to grab the photo. The sleeve of her black shirt slid up, revealing what looked like a fresh burn on her forearm.

"What happened?" I exclaimed, wincing as I leaned in to inspect the wound, at least four inches long and two inches wide. A large red *X* was branded in the center.

She quickly pushed her sleeve back down, mumbling, "I got too close to the wood stove."

I winced again. "Do you want Leo to look at it? I'm sure he could help you." I started to rise, ready to fetch the warlock for his magical healing powers.

"No, I'm fine!" She vigorously waved Caden's picture in front of my face, forcing my focus away from her arm. "Who's he?"

I smiled shyly. "That's Caden."

"Is he a vampire?"

I hesitated, then nodded.

"He's really good-looking. Does he have a girlfriend?"

"Um . . ." *Yeah, me. Except he tried to kill me. Inconsequential point, really.* What was he to me now? A boyfriend-in-waiting with a bad habit he needed to kick before he could be anywhere near me? *How pathetic.* I felt my cheeks flush.

"Oh . . ." She smiled knowingly. "Too bad for me." She leaned back on the couch, crossing her arms behind her head. Her wound didn't seem to bother her and she certainly wasn't acting like she'd just found out her parents had been murdered, even if shock was numbing her reaction. She seemed . . . triumphant.

"Are you sure you're okay?" I asked again.

"Yup! Hey, do you know why we're here?" Valentina shifted in her seat. "I'm assuming that witch, Sofie, is involved, but I have no idea why." I heard bitterness as Sofie's name touched her lips, but it was so brief that I barely noticed it.

I grimaced. "Because of me."

Valentina's thin, perfectly-shaped eyebrow arched.

"I'm so sorry," I blurted under a wave of guilt. "It's my fault you're here and that your parents are dead. I was supposed to bring a vampire back for Viggo and Mortimer so they could—"

Hey! Max's sharp warning cut my words short. *Don't tell her a thing!*

I turned to regard the paranoid werebeast. "Seriously, Max, who's she going to tell out here?"

She's on a need-to-know basis and she doesn't need to know.

When I turned back, Valentina's eyes looked as if they were about to pop out of their sockets. I realized what I must look like to her. "I'm not crazy! I really can talk to him," I said.

"How? I mean, I knew he wasn't normal but . . . " she whispered, looking at the dog with a mixture of intrigue and concern.

Look who's talking, Max grumbled sarcastically.

"Telepathically. Well, only one way. I can hear him in my head but he can't hear me. I haven't figured it out yet. Anyway, no one can explain it. It just happened."

"But, you're . . . human, right?" She continued in a whisper, her brown eyes still wide.

"Yes." I added with a chuckle, "At least I think so."

"Wow. That's the coolest thing!" she exclaimed. "Does he have any other special powers? Is he magical?"

"I don't know if magical is the right word for him. But he does regenerate like a human vampire and he doesn't age."

Okay. Enough about me, Max interjected.

"What's he saying now?" she asked eagerly. "What has he said about me?"

Max's deep, sarcastic chuckle boomed in my head.

"Umm . . . " I squirmed, searching for a lie. "He thinks you're really nice."

And brainless. Don't forget brainless, Max added.

I ignored him. He wasn't normally this rude. *He must be really hungry.*

"Aw. That's so sweet." She leapt off the couch and skipped over to pat Max's head, earning a disapproving grunt. "What's he's saying now?"

"Nothing. He's purring like a kitten," I answered, cutting off the voice in my head and grinning at the big beast. I stood, afraid I'd have to use my body as a shield for Valentina any second. But Max clambered to his feet and walked to the opposite corner of the giant room to gaze out the window.

"So," Valentina continued, "you were saying this is your fault?"

"Oh, yeah." I hesitated at another sharp warning from Max. "I made a mistake and we were in danger. Sofie saved us."

"But why'd she send us here?"

"Because I have something Viggo and Mortimer want and I can't give it to them yet."

"What is it?" Her brown eyes widened with excitement.

"I . . . " I hesitated, glancing over at Max, who watched us intently. *Do not tell her. The less people who know, the better. Please.* I couldn't miss the pleading in Max's voice now. I decided to listen to him. "I . . . um . . . can't say. Sorry."

She sighed. "That's okay." But she sounded disappointed. As if deciding to probe from a different angle, she asked, "What do they need with the thing you have?"

"My, you ask a lot of questions," Leo interrupted as he strode back in to the great room. "More than Evangeline, and I didn't think that was possible."

My thoughts exactly, Max called from his corner.

Valentina gave Leo a tight-lipped smile.

"Why don't you go check on your brother? At least one of you is suffering appropriately," he suggested.

What is wrong with these two? I shot Leo a disapproving frown. Valentina had just found out her parents were dead. They could show a little more compassion.

"I'm sure he's fine. I'm going to take a nap." With that, Valentina took off, leaving me gaping at her slender back as she climbed the stairs.

"People sure deal with shock in different ways, don't they," I murmured absently.

"I'm beginning to think it would have been wiser to leave them with their parents in New York," Leo muttered, settling in one of the armchairs across from me.

At the mention of New York, something suddenly clicked. News of their parents' death and the guilt I felt for my part in it had distracted me—until now. "Wait a minute." My exclamation drew Leo's gray hawk eyes to me. "How did you know his parents were dead?"

Leo's lips twisted into a smile. "I was wondering how long your curious mind would take to pick up on that." He chuckled. "Remember the communication spells I told you about?"

I nodded, dropping back into my chair.

"Well . . . ?" Leo lifted an eyebrow and waited.

When I finally put two and two together, I gasped. "You've talked to Sofie!" I lunged forward and grabbed his withered hands. "What's happening out there? Is Caden alive? Is he mad at me?"

Leo gave me a reproachful glare. "Why on Earth would he be mad at you? Give your head a shake, silly girl."

I averted sheepish eyes. "Because I told him it would be fine, and it wasn't. Worse, I think he actually believed me." I looked back up into Leo's eyes, now full of pity. "Are they okay?"

The old man squeezed my hands. "Yes. They are fine. Struggling, as is expected, but still alive . . . so to speak."

"Have they . . . " I struggled to move my next words past a painful lump in my throat.

Leo continued softly, "They're doing whatever they need to, in order to survive. Let's leave it at that." He released my hand and patted my head, accompanying that with a sympathetic smile. Then he leaned back in his chair, pulled the wilderness magazine out from under his arm, and flipped it open, clearly signaling the end of the conversation.

Accepting that, I opened my own book, but savored a small burst of joy at the news that Caden and the others were still alive, that Viggo and Mortimer hadn't killed Sofie. *They're doing whatever they need to, in order to survive*, Leo had said. That meant drinking blood. But whose blood? Aside from Julian and Valentina's parents, of course. I shuddered at the vivid images that conjured. My choices, my needs, had left Julian and Valentina orphans. And what about Rachel? Was she still hog-tied by Merth, or roaming free? Free to murder my friends or Sofie, as soon as her psychopathic mind decided it was a good idea . . . Those lemon-yellow eyes flashed in my mind. My stomach tightened at the memory of her clawing at Caden, back when she believed they were a couple. Caden had told me she was the most dangerous vampire I'd ever meet. And now I had brought her to Earth, to leave plenty more orphans in her wake.

"Oh, muffins!" Leo exclaimed with over-exaggerated glee, yanking me from my fretting. My nose caught a delicious scent as Magda slid a tray of freshly baked muffins onto the dining room table, and I realized he was being literal. "Come, Evangeline. You must be starving."

"Not really," I mumbled.

He jumped up and, grabbing my hand, pulled me toward the mountain of warm, soft treats—no doubt hoping to distract me. Leo didn't wait for me to choose one; he handed me a chocolate chip muffin with a wink, knowing full-well it was my favorite kind. That same odd mixture of creepiness and flattery raised my short hairs. They'd catalogued my every like and dislike.

I wasn't hungry, but I knew who might be. Impulsively, I grabbed another and a bottle of water and headed to the staircase, certain that my peace offering would do little to alleviate the pain that I had caused, but needing to do it all the same.

"I wouldn't, if I were you . . . " Leo called, finishing with a cluck of disapproval.

I turned to answer him and jumped, startled, as a canine face appeared immediately behind me. Max, already on my heels. "I was just going to get changed."

"Sure you were." Leo smirked, shaking his head as he took a bite of his own muffin.

Max's razor-sharp claws clicked against the hardwood steps as he trailed me up the stairs. I breathed in the mingled scent of cedar and muffins. Under normal circumstances I would find the aroma comforting but now, as I headed toward the one person under this roof whom I should avoid—whom I'd been told to stay away from—my stomach churned.

None of this was your fault, you know, Max said.

"I know," I lied, then added, "He's just lost his parents, Max. No one should be alone." Perhaps I'd be proven wrong soon enough.

Don't expect a nice reception because you're giving him a muffin, Max continued wryly.

"He can't be worse than Rachel . . . Which room is his?" I asked, looking down the long hall with three doors on either side and one on the end, which I knew was mine.

With a loud, dramatic sigh, Max answered. *Last door on the left.*

I walked up to it and, holding my breath, knocked timidly. No answer. I knocked again, this time harder.

"What?" an angry male voice barked from the other side, sending waves of tension through me. I opened my mouth to speak but choked, no clue what to say now that I was here. *It was me who brought back the vampires who killed your parents. Here's a muffin . . .*

I warned you, Max sang.

"Back off, Max. You're crowding me," I snapped.

The giant dog grudgingly took three steps back but then set his stance, making it clear he wasn't budging an inch farther.

"And not so much as a snort out of you!" I whispered harshly as heavy footsteps approached on the other side of the door.

The door flew open. "What do you want?" Julian snapped, glaring at me with red-rimmed eyes.

Has he been crying? My heart swelled. *So he is capable of normal human emotions.* When I didn't answer, his jaw tightened. He stepped back and moved to slam the door in my face. "Here!" I blurted, thrusting the muffins and water toward him. "I thought you might be hungry," I added in a rush.

He paused and looked down at my offering, then up at me. Finally he accepted it. "I thought Valentina would bring me something. She usually does . . . " His voice drifted off and he frowned.

"She was acting really weird earlier," I agreed. "It's just shock. She went to rest."

We stood in awkward silence for a few moments. "I also wanted to make sure you were okay," I added hesitantly.

Despite my gentle concern, he lashed out at me. "I just found out my parents were murdered." The glower had returned. "So, no, I'm not alright. But you wouldn't know anything about that, would you?"

"Actually . . . I do." At least I had one thing in common with the

Colombian drug lord's son. *What a terrible thing to have in common.*

The stark shock on his face told me he hadn't expected that answer. My hands, now empty, fidgeted nervously as his eyes bored into me. When he spoke again, the hostile edge had dulled a little. "By *them?*"

I assumed Viggo could be categorized in the "them" group so I nodded, offering him a small, sympathetic smile. He stared at me in silence for another long, awkward moment. Then he stepped back into his room. I expected the door to slam in my face. Instead, he said, "You can come in, but not with that thing. And shut the door behind you."

A deep grunt behind me preceded Max's declaration: *You're not going in there alone.*

"Max, I'll be fine," I assured him in a whisper. "You need to let go of whatever issues you have with Julian and make peace. We're going to be in these mountains for a long time."

After a pause, Max relented. *I'm right here, listening. If I hear the smallest threat, I'll bust this door down and tear his head off.*

"That's very sweet of you, Max," I murmured sarcastically as I stepped into Julian's room and shut the door as instructed, much to Max's annoyance. This room was smaller than mine, but it had the same cedar-paneled walls, slanted ceiling, and chest of drawers in the corner. A small single bed was positioned under the window, with an oil lamp on a simple pine nightstand beside it.

Julian stood about five feet away from me. He placed his food on the chest of drawers, then turned to face me. He began unbuttoning his black and green-checkered shirt.

"What are you doing?" I blurted, averting my eyes.

What's going on in there? Max called suspiciously; I envisioned the dog's massive head pressed up against the door.

My embarrassment brought a chuckle to Julian's lips. *So he's capable of laughing, too.*

"Relax," he said. "You're not my type. I need to change into that." He jerked his chin toward the bed.

Still avoiding his bare chest, my eyes darted to a pair of long johns, several layers of warm clothing, gloves, and a balaclava lying on his bed. "Oh, you're going for . . . a hike?" I asked.

"More like as far away from here as possible," Julian confirmed, dropping his shirt onto the floor, giving me ample opportunity to see his tanned, lean torso. It didn't generate the same reaction I'd had when seeing Caden with his shirt off for the first time, but I had to admit, Julian was pretty attractive, even if he was a world-class jerk. He paused to pick up the half-eaten muffin on his nightstand and inhale the rest of it.

"Um . . . " I began, directing my eyes to the wall behind him, where a painting of a little blonde girl walking down a sidewalk hung. *Good God, I'm everywhere!* I gave my head a quick shake. "I don't think that's a good idea. It's dangerous out there, in the mountains. I'm pretty sure there are grizzlies," I added for embellishment.

"Can't be any more dangerous than staying here with that lunatic butler and those freak mutts." He leaned over to grab the long john top and began pulling it over his head.

"But we're a long way away from anyone else."

"Who told you that, Leo? I don't buy it. There's probably a ski lodge on the other side of the ridge. How else would all this stuff get up here?" With his undershirt on, he began pulling on a second layer— a blue wool turtleneck.

"No, there probably isn't!" I retorted, panicking as I realized that Julian was about to walk to his death for the simple fact that he had no clue what he was a part of. "You don't know Sofie. We are nowhere near anyone. I guarantee it. She made sure of it. She doesn't want us to be found!"

"Why?" He turned to look at me.

I faltered. "She . . . has her reasons."

He reached back to grab a black sweater. "Well, I'm not waiting around to find out what those reasons are." He added more sarcastically, "They'll all be lies anyway."

"But Julian, you have no idea where we are!"

"Yes, that's exactly my point, Ev—what's your name again?"

"Evangeline."

"That's my point, Evangeline." He continued to speak as he yanked the sweater over his head. "One minute I'm in Manhattan and the next minute I'm in the mountains in the middle of nowhere, my parents are dead, and no one will tell me a damn thing! Do you know what it's like to know you're being lied to?"

I burst out in a laugh before I could control myself. My hand flew to my mouth in an attempt to contain it, and knowing I must look like a complete ass, I glanced shyly his way. He was glowering at me again. "I'm sorry, it's just . . . I know exactly what it's like to be lied to by everyone around me."

Yet again, surprise flashed over Julian's face. He crossed his arms over his chest. "How are you involved in this?"

Evangeline.

I ignored the warning. "It's . . . a really long story and I can't tell you a lot of it." I saw disappointment flicker in his eyes and the sudden, overpowering urge to confess my contribution to his parents' death, even if not intentional, took over. At least I could tell him that much. "I'm so sorry about your parents. I didn't mean to bring all those other vampires home with me. It was just supposed to be my friends."

"Your friends?" Julian asked slowly, quietly. I nodded before his icy tone registered in my mind. "Your *vampire* friends?" When I saw his eyes narrow to slits, I knew I had made a mistake. "I thought you might be a hostage . . . but you're friends with those leeches!" Julian suddenly screamed, his face twisting with rage as he stepped toward me.

I don't know what his intentions were and I didn't find out because the door exploded into dozens of splinters and Max barreled through, sending me stumbling to the side before regaining my balance. When I had, I saw Julian pinned against the wall with Max's nose pressed up against his collarbone. Hackles raised, teeth bared, Max growled so low, he sounded more like a bear than a dog

"Max! Don't!" I screamed. Max didn't move away. In fact, I think he may have edged closer. His fangs were inches away from Julian's throat and I knew he would tear it out at the slightest provocation. I'd seen firsthand what this werebeast was capable of when protecting me. "Max, please don't!" I pleaded, tears welling in my eyes now. "There's been enough death because of me. I can't take any more!"

My words silenced Max immediately. He shuffled back to stand next to me, his eyes never leaving Julian. Not that there was anything to worry about—Julian remained pressed up against the wall as if Max's fangs still held him there, his face as white as the snow outside.

"Get out," he finally whispered hoarsely, eyes wide with terror and acutely aware of how close to death he had just come. "Leave me alone. Please."

I nodded, shoving Max none too gently ahead of me as I bolted out of the room. I scampered down the stairs two at a time.

"Did that make you feel better?" Leo asked when I re-entered the great room; I heard the "I told you so" in his smug tone. He stood in front of the bookshelves, leafing through a new magazine, this one with cheetahs on the cover.

I didn't answer him at first. I walked stiffly over to the dining table to grab a bottle of water. Only when I tried to unscrew the cap did I realize that my hand was shaking violently. It wasn't about feeling better, I decided as I took a swig of water. As disturbing as it was to admit to myself, I couldn't help but feel some sort of connection to Julian. We had so much in common—both lied to and both orphans at the hands of vampires. If there was ever anyone I could feel a kinship with in this world, it would be him. I swallowed my mouthful of water and wiped a dribble from my chin before answering Leo. "His parents were murdered and he's been thrown into a world he has no clue about. Sound familiar?"

After a long pause, Leo inclined his head in assent and said no more, instead scanning the titles of the magazines on one of the bookshelves.

I slowly walked over to stare out the bay window at the wintry abyss. I swore it couldn't be any later than mid-afternoon, yet it was getting dark. It would be nightfall soon. Treacherous for a human. "And he's thinking of running away," I warned, branding myself a tattler. "Out there!"

"That'd solve one of my problems," Leo mumbled.

"Leo! His parents are dead because of me! Yes, they may have been ogres, but still! And if Julian goes out there, he'll die too." A sudden swarm of emotions made my eyes burn. "Everyone's dying because of me."

Pity flickered across Leo's face. He walked over and patted me on the shoulder. "Sometimes I forget you're not accustomed to this dark world we've forced upon you . . . He's not going anywhere. The dogs will keep guard."

I'll guard him, alright, Max muttered indignantly. *I'll guard him right off a cliff.*

Now it was my turn to glower, at my guard dog. "Max, I'm having a hard time dealing with all of this. Can you stop being so . . . you?" I whirled away, stopping with my back to him.

"Why don't you go and get some fresh air, Max," Leo suggested, walking over to open the side door. I knew what that meant: go kill something. Probably a good idea. He hadn't gone hunting since we arrived.

In my peripheral vision, I watched Max slink out the open door, leaving behind an air of rejection and a brisk chill that had crept inside with his exit. Guilt drew creases on my forehead. *Toughen up, Evangeline.*

"Now, what set Julian off, exactly?" Leo asked as he pushed the door closed.

"I told him I'm friends with vampires," I mumbled, pulling my stack of pictures out of my pocket once again. I flopped down on the couch, no longer interested in conversation. Leo took the hint and focused on feeding the flames in the fireplace with more wood. I flipped through the entire stack, recalling the nights with my friends. They were the best days of my life. Now I had to be kept away from them because they'd kill me. Could I even call them friends anymore? As long as I was human, I would never be safe around them.

I flipped through the pictures three times before resting the stack on my chest and closing my eyes. I was far from falling asleep so I simply lay there, listening to the soft crackles of the fire in the silence of the cabin. My eyes were still closed when an eerie scratching sounded against the side door. I sat up immediately, my body rigid.

"Oh, not to worry." Leo chuckled, walking over to turn the knob. "It's just Max." He yanked the door open and a large black rump backed inside. It was Max, alright.

"What the . . . " Leo muttered.

Max was dragging something in with him. A body.

Julian.

I found him about a mile from here, waist-deep in snow, Max reported, gripping Julian's jacket in his teeth.

Leo rushed to grab Julian under his armpits. Together, they dragged the still body over to lie beside the fire. I jumped off the couch and dove to his side, peering closely at him. Not a moan escaped him. No movement. "How did—" I began, then scrunched my face up in thought. Had I fallen asleep after all? Had Julian snuck past us and left?

Or . . . I shot a questioning look at Leo, my eyes narrowing with suspicion.

He went out the window, Max quickly confirmed. *I found prints leading from there. He must have pried it open and scaled down the wall.*

"Determined fool," Leo murmured, crouching down to inspect Julian's pewter-colored lips.

"Is he . . . " I couldn't finish. A hollow bubble grew inside me. Another death.

"He's not well, that's for sure." Leo hovered over him, his hands floating inches above his face. "Not well at all. Go and get some blankets and a pillow."

I was on my feet and running up the stairs two at a time toward Julian's room. Sure enough, I felt chill air the second I rounded the corner. I stopped at the shattered door and looked into the bedroom. The window still sat open a crack.

I scrambled inside, scooped the duvet and pillows from the bed, and half-dragged, half-carried them out of his room. Only when I was running down the hall did I remember his sister. She needed to know! "Valentina?" I called, my eyes roaming the hallway, wondering which room was hers. No answer. "Valentina! You need to come quickly!" My voice faltered for only a moment. "It's Julian!"

"I'm sleeping," Valentina called groggily. *Where had that come from? Second door on the right.* I grabbed the knob and turned it, only to hear a thud and feel resistance on the other side. Something was barricading the door. "I said I'm sleeping!" Valentina shouted.

"But it's your—"

"Leave me alone!" she screeched, making me jump two steps back.

"Evangeline!" Leo bellowed desperately from below.

"Coming!" I ran back down the stairs, gripping the railing to keep from tumbling over the blankets.

I found Leo rolling up the sleeves of his shirt. "Make him comfortable and warm," he instructed.

Comfortable . . . He's unconscious and frozen. Possibly dead. Make him comfortable . . . I gently slid a pillow under Julian's head, then draped the duvet over him, covering every inch of his body short of his face. "I don't think this will help raise his body temperature," I murmured warily.

"Of course not. Give me some space now," Leo announced, kneeling beside him. "This will take a while. The trouble these bloody kids are causing me . . . " he finished in a quiet grumble.

I dove for the nearest couch, hanging over the arm to watch Leo work. He sat completely still, his eyes closed, appearing deep in thought, or as if he were meditating.

Max settled directly beside me, and the other dogs appeared out of nowhere to investigate the situation as well.

"Magic?" I whispered, intrigued.

Yup . . . You know, I could have left him out there. Max began in a gruff voice. *When I caught his scent. I went out of my way to find him. I figured you'd want to help him out.* I glanced over to see his ochre eyes staring at me, brimming with something I rarely saw in them—anxiety.

My guilt-ridden werebeast was trying to make amends. I reached over and scratched behind his ear. "You did good, Max. Thank you."

Not that he deserves it, Max said, earning a flat look. *But I did it for you,* he added quickly, leaning over to nestle against my neck.

"Do you think Julian will die?"

Max didn't answer.

We sat. We waited.

CR

I woke up to something warm and wet sliding across my cheek.

Max's tongue. Lifting my head from the arm of the couch, I groaned at a kink in my neck left by the awkward position. A colorful afghan draped my body. At some point, someone had tucked me in. I was thankful, given the draft that crept in from somewhere. I rolled my head to peer at the fireplace and saw only embers. The fire was Leo's department. *Where is he?* I wondered, rubbing my eyes with my palms.

"How'd I end up back here?" a male voice croaked, startling a gasp from me. Julian was propped on the opposite couch, his face paler than normal, but alive. And he wasn't scowling for once, which made his face pleasant to look at, his features dark and masculine.

I sat up to face him. "Max tracked you down in a deep snowbank." I made sure I emphasized who his savior was. "He brought you back and Leo helped heal you. The lunatic butler and the freak mutt," I added, repeating his words from yesterday.

Julian had the decency to look sheepish as he glanced over at Max.

"Are you stupid?" I blurted before I could stop myself. But then, after thinking about it for all of five seconds, I silently praised myself. He deserved it.

Julian smirked before dropping his gaze to his hands. "Yes, I suppose I am. I don't know where I am, what is going on, why I'm here. I don't know anything except that my parents are dead and I'm surrounded by . . . " He didn't finish, either because he lost his train of thought or he'd been about to drop another insult and decided against it.

I turned to look at Max. "Where's Leo?"

Resting for the day. That much magic drained him.

"Okay." I turned back to see Julian's wide eyes and the same "Is she crazy?" look his sister had worn the day before. "Yes, I can talk to him telepathically," I supplied. "I have no idea how. It just happened."

Julian's brown eyes shifted between Max and me. "Well," he said after a long moment, "tell him thanks for me. It was colder than I anticipated."

"You just did. He understands you," I said. I glanced down at the floor to see my pictures scattered everywhere. *I must have dropped them when Max came in with Julian.* Rolling off the couch to my knees, I started gathering them.

"Are those your . . . friends?" Julian asked.

Friends. That word again. It was sounding more odd as time went on. I only nodded.

Julian eased himself off the couch to crouch on the floor and help collect the photos. He held up a picture of Bishop wearing a goofy grin and one of Caden, his face typically pensive. "So which one are you in love with?"

I snatched the picture from his hand, heat rising in my cheeks. He chuckled and continued picking up pictures, pausing on one of Amelie and Fiona. I noticed his eyebrow arch. "Who's the blonde?"

Despite my dour mood, I grinned. "That's Amelie. She's really cute, isn't she? You'd like her." *Except that she's a vampire, and she'll likely kill you.*

"Yeah, I'll bet," he murmured wryly. I caught the fleeting look of disapproval before he consciously made it disappear. "I'm sorry about earlier," he said. "I've been a complete jerk to you. I deserved what Max did." Max let out a small grunt of satisfaction. Julian glanced over before continuing, likely a little disoriented by the dog's uncanny ability to understand him. "It's just . . . I know my parents were mixed up with some bad things. But they were still my parents and now they're dead. One minute I'm visiting them for a weekend trip away from med school and the next thing I know, I'm I don't know where and . . . "

"Med school?" Julian, the son of a Colombian drug lord, saving lives? Sofie hadn't mentioned that.

"Yeah, my first year. I fast-tracked my undergrad," Julian explained.

I watched him obliquely as we collected the rest of the pictures in silence, wary of this new calm, polite version of Julian. Had Leo magically fixed him to be . . . nice?

"Why aren't they here, with you, if they're your friends?" Julian suddenly asked.

"It's a long story," I muttered. I had no idea where to begin.

He handed me the stack he had collected, then prompted as he climbed back onto the couch, "Well, I'm clearly not going anywhere."

I glanced at Max, who only shook his head. Not surprising. This world of secrecy was all the big dog knew. Lies and manipulation. Of course he didn't trust a soul.

"Please?" Julian coaxed, staring back at me with earnest brown eyes that looked more like those of an innocent seven-year-old than a twenty-something med student from a corrupt family. It was probably the same look I had in my eyes when I begged for the truth from Sofie. For once I held the answers, and I couldn't bear to leave an innocent person in the friendless darkness where I had dwelt.

For the next hour, I gave Julian the Cole's Notes version of my life as I had learned it over the last month, much to Max's mortification. Julian sat cross-legged on the couch and listened quietly, all signs of his previous offensiveness gone, replaced with a mixture of appreciation and sympathy. Once in a while he asked a question, querying the venom issue or where Veronique was hiding, but otherwise he just listened, seemingly absorbing my words. He was a wonderful listener, I had to admit. Once I started, I found it effortless to talk to him. It was easier than talking to Caden—but that was likely because I couldn't focus on any thought for too long around that face . . . Though Julian was becoming more appealing with his new demeanor, it was different.

I spoke briefly about Caden, stumbling over my words and blushing furiously. I left out anything that sounded like "love" and "soul mate" but the knowing look in Julian's eyes revealed that he'd quickly deduced what Caden meant to me.

At some point, a servant set a tray holding weak tea and lightly buttered toast on the nearest end table for Julian, which he accepted with a polite nod. "It sounds like you've forgiven them," he said, his face incredulous as he stirred sugar into his tea. "After everything they've done to you?"

"I wouldn't say I've forgiven them," I began slowly, feeling foolish again. I couldn't even answer that truthfully. I had in fact forgiven Sofie. Completely. And there was nothing to forgive on Caden's end. "Being angry won't change anything. It will only turn me bitter. Maybe it will surface later and I'll go on a psychotic rampage."

"But . . . " Julian paused, searching for words, "they tried to kill you and you still call them friends. You don't see there being anything wrong with that?"

"It's complicated," I mumbled, shrugging. "There's plenty wrong with everything that's going on. I hope that by the time I see them again, they'll have learned to control themselves."

Julian leaned forward, his elbows resting on his knees, his hands folded. "And when will that happen? How long? Are you—are we— stuck here until then?"

"Not long. Hard to say . . . " I worked hard to hide the lie from my face but, by the crestfallen look on his, I knew I'd failed miserably. I couldn't bring myself to tell him the full truth, that Sofie, an over-protective, borderline stalker, had locked us up here to keep me safe from a pack of vampires until they could be trusted around my blood.

We could die here.

3. THE SENTINEL

"Soon," I murmured softly, sliding my hand over the smooth white marble of my baby sister's tomb, knowing my promise was a blatant lie. One hundred and twenty years ago, she accompanied me, hand in hand, into a dank, dusty room in this very building—then a factory of sorts. One hundred and twenty years ago, I had stared straight into her anxious green eyes and sworn that I'd release her the second I fixed my magical blunder. As tears rolled down her rosy cheeks, I'd chanted the freezing spell, my voice masking her last sobs until the spell paralyzed and preserved her body, and I felt my heart break. I witnessed the magic marble winding around her body, encasing her in her glorious tomb, swallowing her beautiful, curly brown locks. And here she was, tucked away inside the atrium's focal point when she could be free. All it meant was that Evangeline had to die. *Damn the Fates and their twisted sense of humor.*

No. While Veronique was locked in her magic-induced coma, my lies couldn't hurt her. They would torture me, but I'd endure. I would keep her under this spell for as long as it took to outsmart the Fates. Just as Evangeline would remain in her own protective cocoon—for years, decades, a lifetime. I would keep her safe.

"I guess the others are in the cellar?" I said to no one in particular as

I strolled away from the statue, my eyes drifting over the twenty or so Ratheus inhabitants who lingered in the ruined atrium, huddled in circles, whispering amongst themselves. Likely still in shock over this otherworldly transportation. The other half—including Caden and his posse—were busy gorging themselves on blood bags in the cellar. Like unruly teenagers, they had broken into Viggo and Mortimer's stash within an hour of arriving and had stayed there since, satiating their thirst, dooming their previous moral convictions. All of the Ratheus vampires had spent a considerable amount of time in the cellar, but it seemed Evangeline's friends couldn't get enough.

Those four had also foiled my desperate plan to corner one and dissect their intentions. I needed to isolate one of them just long enough to infiltrate their souls and minds. Only thirty seconds, someplace where I knew I wouldn't be attacked by Mage for using magic or by Viggo for appearing to conspire against him. I would be breaking two parts of the truce by doing this and therefore would likely earn the wrath of both ancient vampires. I had no idea what Mage's wrath entailed; I wasn't sure I wanted to find out.

But it didn't matter because I could never get close enough. If Viggo wasn't around, then Mage was. Since she had some uncanny ability to sense my magic, I couldn't try anything with her in arm's reach. And if neither of them was around, then that bitch, Rachel, was—hovering, watching, poised to report back to Viggo and Mortimer. It was clear she had chosen to side with them in this power struggle, and appointed herself Viggo and Mortimer's eyes and ears. So I waited impatiently, and each hour that passed saw Caden and the others committing themselves more and more to their blood lust. My hope for something good to come of this charade was quickly thinning.

"Damn it!" I heard Viggo mutter, voice low. I whipped my head around in time to see him tucking his cell phone into his Armani suit pocket, his jaw clenched. *Bad news?* I felt a small smile curl the corners of my mouth. I knew exactly what that message was about. One of his compelled minions had informed him that their search for Evangeline had come back empty. No doubt there were a hundred such packs running loose around the world at this very moment, the brutes storming every location tied to my past. Both Viggo and Mortimer had been glued to their text pads, sending directives out to their vultures. I had expected as much.

His steely blue eyes locked on mine when Viggo realized I was watching. The hard look of frustration instantly vanished, replaced by his typical smug grin. "So Evangeline's little 'friends' refuse to pry themselves from our blood reservoir." He sauntered over to stand beside me, a smile of satisfaction tugging at his lips. It was just like him to find that amusing. But he didn't wait for me to answer, instead changing the topic completely. "Do you really believe we'll see Ursula again?" He added with thick sarcasm, "Assuming you were telling me the truth before."

I realized we were standing in the exact spot in the atrium where my nemesis had fallen to her death—or her host body's death. *Good question.* One I didn't have an honest answer to, other than what I had already told them—the death was too clean, too calm, to be permanent. I had no idea how that jealous witch had reincarnated herself once, let alone over and over again to stalk me through the years. She had no doubt made her own deal with the Fates. Of course, telling Viggo any of that was useless. He wouldn't believe me. So I simply shrugged. Ursula was the least of our worries.

The sound of a lock clicking set the tiny hairs on the back of my neck on end, erasing all worries. The exterior door release. Someone was entering. My shoulders tensed. I had sent every staff member away from here, with no hope of finding their way back! So who could . . . My nostrils caught a whiff of human blood. "Mortimer!" I hissed, my eyes glued to the gaping hole where the first security door had once existed.

"It's Monday. The gardener," Mortimer whispered in response. Not that there was any point to secrecy. The twenty Ratheus vampires in the atrium were well aware of the small Portuguese man entering to prune and weed the urban jungle as he did every Monday and Thursday. By now his blood was tantalizing their nostrils.

"What do we do?" I asked, hearing the panic in my voice. The words sounded foreign, coming from me. I wasn't used to asking Mortimer—or anyone—for advice.

But it was too late. Like a pack of super-speed bees—Rachel in the lead—twenty vampires swarmed toward the door to ambush the quiet, polite gardener the second he stepped through the gaping hole, the horror of the atrium's present ruin distracting him from his impending doom. He didn't even have time to scream.

I averted my eyes, unable to watch the massacre of the gentle, innocent man with whom I had shared a laugh on several occasions. *How could I have forgotten about him?*

"That's too bad . . . He knew how to prune Veronique's azaleas in just the right way," Viggo murmured with the empathy of Hannibal Lecter. I turned to see the hunger in his eyes, an arrogant smile of satisfaction on his lips as he witnessed the innocent man's death eating away at my core.

I dug my red-painted fingernails into my thighs as I fought the urge to gouge Viggo's eyes out, my promise to my baby sister becoming harder to keep by the second. I needed to distance myself. Spinning on my heels, I stormed toward my haven, throwing back over my shoulder with spiteful satisfaction, "The only way you'll find Evangeline is if you pry it out of my head." *And that will never happen.*

CR

Evangeline's delicate human scent lingered everywhere. The same delicate human scent that had enticed me for eighteen years, since the day I'd first laid eyes on her tiny pink form, swaddled and asleep in a bassinet. She had barely lived in this hideous blood-red room—the décor a twisted joke of Viggo's—and yet I could find traces of her on every surface. On the crimson silk bedding of the four-poster king-sized bed; on the taffeta drapery; clinging to the crystals of her nightstand lamp where her wrist had grazed them while switching on the light. Everywhere. It was why I had spent most of my time here, since the Ratheus vampires' arrival. It was why I warned everyone to stay out or suffer my wrath, truce be damned. So far, no one had tested me.

I wandered around the room now, clutching Evangeline's pink sweatshirt to my chest. She'd been wearing it the night of Ursula's attack. I shuddered, thinking back to that night, the raw pain visible in her eyes when she first learned the truth behind her mother's death. I'd wanted to run to her, to hug her, to protect her. And I couldn't. I couldn't allow Viggo and Mortimer to comprehend the depth of my love for that sweet girl. They would have used it against me. In the end, Ursula's attack was a blessing. Evangeline finally saw Viggo for what he really was: a conniving monster.

Passing by a full-length beveled mirror, I faltered. Sallow green eyes gaped back at me. My hair, naturally smooth and silky, drifted in disarray. Awkward creases riddled my fitted black and silver tube dress. Strange, for me. I didn't need to work very hard to turn the awed heads of every man, woman, and child I passed. I never looked like this . . .

I sighed. Evidence of my current frazzled state over being separated from my girl. For eighteen years, until the first night her curse sent her to Ratheus, she was always within a minute's reach, always under my careful watch. And now she was thousands of miles away.

I hated it. I hated Viggo and Mortimer for making me do it. *All I have is a picture,* I thought bitterly as I pulled a folded four by six from the only pocket in my dress. I had swiped it from the stack of prints I developed for her. In it, she was sitting on a bench, gazing off to her left and smiling. Likely at Caden. My finger traced the lines of her face, memorized long ago. How much like her mother she looked, with her blonde hair and dimpled smile. Longing tore at my insides. If I was honest with myself, I missed her more than Nathan. I missed her more than my sister.

I sensed his entrance a split second after he appeared in the corner of my eye. "I thought I made myself clear," I began, taking time to fold the picture and slide it back into my pocket. "No one is to enter this room." I turned to level Caden with a flat gaze. *Perfect. We're alone. Finally. Now's my chance. Except he's too far away.* I took one step forward, then another, slowly edging in without rousing suspicion. He wouldn't take kindly to being violated like this if he knew what I intended to do, I was sure. I just needed him to remain unaware for thirty seconds so he wouldn't bolt or attack me. And, if his motives for Evangeline proved wicked . . .

Caden suddenly and unexpectedly appeared inches away from me with speed to rival Viggo, his powerful hands tightly gripping my biceps. "Where is she? I need to see her," he whispered, desperation in his voice. His thumbs dug painfully into my flesh.

I had to tilt my head to meet his eyes. *God, he's strong. How am I going to do this without him knowing?* He certainly was a darling, I had to admit as my eyes roamed his features, delicate and masculine at the same time. I could see why Evangeline had fallen head over heels for him. "Why would I tell you?" I began, mentally plucking several helixes and readying them, wondering if I could carry on a conversation while dissecting him. Doubtful, but I'd have to try.

"I need to see her," Caden forced through clenched teeth.

"You used her and then tried to kill her," I spat.

Raw pain flashed in his eyes. He cocked his head to the left, toward the door. Checking for eavesdroppers. When he looked back at me, it was with grim determination. "Why don't you find out for yourself? I know you can do those kinds of things, witch," he grated, his own suggestion clearly an unpleasant one.

Did I hear right? Is he . . . volunteering to be explored? I felt my mouth twist with doubt. *No . . . he couldn't be.* What vampire in his right mind would—

"Do it now!" he urged, his voice breaking, despair shining in his jade eyes. "Quick! Before they find us!"

I didn't need any more prompts. With reckless abandon, I drove magical tendrils into his body, infiltrating his thoughts, his emotions, his pain, everything about him. I navigated through his past, through his human life, downloading his every hope, his every fear, his every desire as if they were all part of a computer program, the visions flashing in my mental eye, the emotions swarming my heart.

I felt my eyes widen as Evangeline's angelic face appeared, as I rifled through his memories of her, from the unconscious, frail creature lying on the cave floor to the moment her pendant locked within the statue's grasp in Ratheus. And then the atrium . . . Evangeline stood smiling at me. No, at Caden. Her smile faltered as Caden's overwhelming desire to kill her took control, as he lunged. The images ended with a mix of unruly desire and raw pain. Caden's.

He'd lied to Viggo. He truly loved her.

I gasped as my magic released him. "She's safe," I whispered breathlessly, relief flooding my soul as my hands flew to his cheeks, suddenly the cheeks of an angel in my eyes. He may want to kill her, but he wouldn't break her heart—perverse but comforting. "You need to get out of here now, before they find us together," I whispered in a rush. Now that I knew his love for Evangeline was pure, I was that much more desperate to protect him. I couldn't give Viggo a reason to try to kill him. "I left Rachel in the atrium with a body, but who knows how long that will keep her occupied. And God only knows where Mage is." At least I knew Viggo and Mortimer wouldn't be lurking. They had been all but glued to the atrium, to be near Veronique, their erratic paranoia that she was in danger growing tenfold.

Caden ignored my warning, scooping my hands from his cheeks to clasp them between his instead. "Does she hate me?" he whispered.

I chuckled, shaking my head. "Quite the opposite. The silly, sweet girl is busy worrying about everyone else, as usual."

Recognition sparked in his eyes. "How do you know? Does she have a phone? Can I talk to her?"

I shook my head. "Leo. I can communicate with him." Where only minutes ago I was ready to string Caden up and torture him mercilessly, now I was freely sharing my most protected details. Details that Viggo and Mortimer didn't and needn't know. "I didn't have a chance to set up phone towers where she is. And it's safer this way. Viggo's likely tapped into the phone companies."

"Where is—"

I cut him off. "No," I said, shaking my head. "It's better for everyone if I keep that to myself."

Caden nodded in assent, pausing only for a second. "When can we see her? I need to explain. I need to apologize."

"When you're ready . . . when I'm ready."

"Can't you do something? Isn't there some way to protect her?" Caden pleaded, tearing at my heart.

"Keeping her hidden is the best protection right now. You'd better go. Now!"

But it was too late. A familiarly serene voice interrupted us. "Has your magic given you what you needed?"

We were so engrossed with each other that neither of us had sensed Mage's approach. Now I slowly turned to face her, instantly arming myself with helixes, unsure of how she would react to my direct violation of the truce, of her specific requirement. To my surprise, the ancient vampire's coal-black eyes appeared . . . satisfied.

"It was necessary," I answered cautiously.

"Good." She turned to Caden, a small smile touching her lips. "I suggest you depart now and keep your distance from Sofie. The truth—however obvious it is to you and I—should be kept muddied for everyone's sake."

My eyes darted to Caden to see the same shocked expression on his face that had to be sitting on mine. Was the supposedly evil, sadistic Council leader . . . helping us?

"And you'd best wipe that affectionate grin off your face when you look at him and his friends," Mage continued, her words directed to me. "That's why I didn't allow you to do that thing with your magic earlier. One flash of that, and Viggo would see the truth. He needs to remain in doubt." She waved a hand dismissively at Caden. "Run along, now. And don't forget, you have a debt to repay, given you were going to leave me behind."

Caden hesitated with that last comment, bowing his head guiltily. Then he turned to whisper, "Tell her nothing makes sense without her."

I nodded once, squeezing his hand.

And then he vanished, leaving me alone with the ancient, magic-sensing vampire.

Mage's dark eyes settled on me. "I understand that he is important to Evangeline and I am in her debt. I will not allow any harm to come to them. Ever."

Her left eyebrow arched when a snort escaped me. "You don't believe me?"

"No. I'm sorry, I don't. For the life of me, I can't understand why."

Mage's red lips curled back in disdain. "I don't know when our kind became such treacherous, conniving fools. I remember a distinct shift within the last five thousand years."

It took every ounce of energy to keep my face from displaying my shock. *She's five thousand years old—at least!* No vampire had lived that long on Earth, as far as I knew. Of course, I didn't know much. Viggo was tight-lipped about our world's vampire history. I only knew that he wasn't the first vampire to exist, but now he was the oldest. My gut told me he played some role in that first vampire's demise, especially since the handful of others left roaming the world threatened to kill me for my association with him. He hadn't made a lot of friends.

"So this is Evangeline's room?" Mage asked, her eyes roaming the décor as she moved farther into the room.

I said nothing, studying her intensely, wracking my brain for a possible motive to her interest in helping Evangeline. The fact that I couldn't guess one had me on edge—more so than if I could definitively say Mage was evil. If only I could magically dissect her as I had Caden . . .

She stopped in front of the fireplace to study the painting—the one I had moved from Evangeline's previous room to here. It was the one I had painted of her as a little girl, picking daisies at the playground. "This is Evangeline."

"Yes."

"Charming." She stood in silence for a moment before speaking again. "You love her as if she were your child. I envy you for that." Those black eyes fell on me again, so peaceful, so reserved, so . . . unreadable. "I came here to tell you that the cellar is bone dry."

I felt my eyes bug, the sudden change of subject jarring, the news shocking. "There was enough to last weeks, at least!"

She shrugged. "What can I say. Obviously not. The incident in the atrium earlier should attest to that. Surprise guest?"

I cringed at the reminder of the gardener. "Yes, a complete

surprise," I answered, adding, "I'm not a fan of surprises."

"It will be a long time before you can trust any of them around humans," she continued, her tone tinged with rebuke.

"I'm well aware of that," I snapped, her condescension sparking rage. "This wasn't exactly planned."

If my tone bothered her, she didn't let on. "No. Of course not. Can you change the security code so no one else can get in?"

"I, uh . . . " I faltered, her suggestion flooring me. Why hadn't I thought of that? It was brilliant and simple! And something I would normally think of in half a human heartbeat if I wasn't so preoccupied. Yet, here Mage was, offering sage advice to *help* me.

That was it. I'd had enough. *Time to see what you're made of, Mage.* I turned to regard my concerned advisor, loosening my upper body, ready to spring. "Let's not dance anymore, shall we?" I began, my voice deliberately calm. "I prefer my dance partners taller and more . . . masculine."

Mage's long black tresses swayed as her head tilted back, a musical laugh escaping her lips. "Whatever do you mean?"

She finds this amusing. Great. I had a female version of Viggo on my hands. I sighed heavily. "What game are you playing, Mage? You would appear to be concerned about Evangeline and Caden's well-being, you're offering advice to avoid the chance of humans being killed. I don't have time for this. I play enough games with Viggo. So what is it that you want?"

The amusement vanished from her eyes, replaced by a hazy stare, as if she was no longer looking at me but into her own distant memories. "Does it not bother you that my world and your world are so similar?"

I paused to register her words, her sudden change of topic sending me reeling. "Yes," I answered truthfully. "It has bothered me greatly since the minute Evangeline began describing it."

"Because you wonder if your world is fated to the same demise as

Ratheus." Mage picked up a small figurine from the fireplace mantel. I watched quietly as she rolled it back and forth between her fingertips. "I worry about the same. The planets are identical, you see. There is only the venom issue."

Something in her tone, something in her words, stirred a gut feeling that a deep, dark secret lingered on her tongue, one that existed now as it had before, in the atrium.

"From what I—" Mage's eyes flicked to the door and she sighed. "Prying ears, as usual." I frowned, not sensing anything. Normally my senses for such things were keener than even Viggo's, due to my sorceress abilities. "You can create sound barriers with your magic, can you not?"

"While keeping the truce?" I smirked.

She smiled in return. "There are exceptions to every rule."

She was giving me permission to use my magic. Fury sparked, but intrigue quickly doused it. She wanted to tell me something that the others could not hear.

With a few carefully chosen words, I conjured a purple-hued bubble around me. Mage's eyes followed it as it expanded to touch the walls of Evangeline's room. *So she can see magic as well!*

Satisfied that the room was protected from listeners, Mage began again. "Now, where were we . . . yes, the venom issue. From what I gathered from Rachel, it was your fault?"

A derisive snort escaped me but I followed it with a nod. It was one hundred percent my fault. I had toyed with the Fates in my attempt to join Nathan in eternity. I was the one who had fried everyone's venom. I was the one who had killed my love. Never had I tried to shirk blame.

She smirked. "Well, you single-handedly changed the fate of your world. But by how much? Really, who can say. Was it enough?"

Enough for what? I wondered.

"We had no issues with our venom. So that's one difference

between the two worlds. And from what I gather, Ratheus is running on a different clock, as well; it's approximately seven hundred years ahead, based on the technology I've seen here," Mage waggled a finger at the digital clock and the built-in stereo system beside the fireplace, "and what I recall of our world before the war."

"Seven hundred years," I repeated, my stomach plummeting, the significance of the number unmistakable. "Didn't the war on Ratheus begin seven hundred years ago?"

"Yes, that's right. Around the same year as the one Earth is in now." Mage began pacing, her arms crossed over her chest. "So really, other than the time difference and your venom issue, the worlds are identical."

"Well, still. The worlds are not the same. There are the geographical names," I reminded her. "That's a big difference. Ratheus instead of Earth. And this New Shore; we never had a city named that."

Mage pursed her lips, then relaxed them to heave a loud sigh. "Have you ever heard of a seer?"

Changing topics again . . . where is this going? Aloud, I answered, "Cousin to the witch. Yes, I've heard of them, though I can't say I've ever met one."

"They're incredibly rare," Mage confirmed. "I had one at my disposal for a short while. A servant seer." Mage opened the door to Evangeline's closet, scanned the racks upon racks of brand new designer clothes, and arched her eyebrows. Finally she closed the door and turned back to me. "When the human world ended, she prophesized that someone of a parallel world in a parallel universe would come to us. She couldn't tell me why or when, but she felt the strong urge to hide the identity of our world."

"But . . . no." I frowned. "You're from Ratheus! That's not parallel!"

Mage paused for only a second. "Have you ever looked at the letters in the name 'Ratheus'?"

No. I closed my eyes. *R-A-T-H-E-U-S.* "Oh God . . . " I murmured.

Mage had lifted a figurine from the mantel and studied it as she continued, her tone conversational. "I played around with the words 'our Earth,' but couldn't find a name I liked with those letters. So I eventually came up with 'Ratheus,' using 'Earth' and 'us' as a base. And 'New Shore' was so named because it was the shore we landed on in our new world." Placing the figurine back on the mantel, she smiled sadly at me. "Ratheus is Earth, Sofie. Our worlds are parallel . . . as the fates of each may be."

Mage may as well have punched me in the stomach. The Fates had left the part about the planet being parallel out of their details. Deep down, I had toyed with the idea, wondering if it were possible. Then, when Evangeline told me it was called Ratheus, I'd relaxed, assuming they were only eerily similar. Mage had just crushed that with her admission. But something still didn't add up. "How is this possible?"

"What, parallel planets?" Mage shrugged, holding her hand up dismissively. "How do vampires exist? How do witches and magic exist? I learned long ago that there's no logical thought to all of this. You can't rationalize that which defies all logic. Don't even attempt it. You'll only leave with more questions."

"Do all the . . . Ratheus vampires know this? Does Caden know?" I frowned as I wracked my memory of what I had seen with my invasive spell.

Mage denied it with a small shake of her head. "My seer was adamant that it be hidden from everyone. It makes sense—had Evangeline known the real risk, would she still have agreed to it? Would you?" She paused. "So I had every single one of them compelled. I wiped it clean from their memory. All they know is Ratheus."

I felt my eyes bulge. *Vampires compelled? And so powerfully? Impossible! Only humans could be compelled.* "How . . . " I sputtered but Mage was already walking toward the door, straight for the sound barrier. Walking through that would break the bubble and end our conversation when I needed so much more info.

"It doesn't matter. I suggest you not mention any of this to the others yet."

"Mage, please!" One burning question needed to be asked. "What started the war?"

She stopped just before she reached the magical barrier and turned. "Well, for one thing, a group of fanatical humans who made it their mission to kill vampires and witches." *The Sentinel.* Further proof of our worlds' similarities. Nausea again churned my stomach. "They hid underground for years, until we were sure time and common sense had eradicated them. We became complacent, and they suddenly appeared, allied with the witches and stronger than ever, with their sole goal, outing us."

I frowned doubtfully. The Sentinel despised the witches as much as they did vampires. So many of my previous kind had been burned at the stake by the zealous Sentinel that an alliance seemed impossible. Sure, Ursula had used several Sentinel members in her plot, but that was the work of an insane woman offering her wiles in exchange for brute force, I was sure of it. "And then what?" I pressed. "The Sentinel and the witches attacked and started the war? Just like that?"

Mage hesitated. "Yes, they attacked. It may have been kept under wraps, had it not been for one imprudent vampire who executed an entire faction of them in front of a television camera."

"That would do it," I answered dryly, then muttered, "I hope you punished the idiot severely."

As Mage reached out to turn the doorknob, effectively breaking the sound barrier, a sad smile touched her lips. "I've punished myself every day since."

CR

"We need reserves!" Viggo exclaimed in exasperation the second I stepped into the atrium, still dazed by the devastating knowledge Mage had imparted to me—entrusted only to me. Until I could evaluate the risks of the others knowing, I would keep it to myself.

Viggo and Mortimer sat at their bistro table, guarding Veronique, as usual, oblivious to the real danger threatening us. The Ratheus vampires—if I could even still call them that—were milling about, now that they'd drained their supply of human blood. Their eyes darted furtively around the atrium and the balconies, as if searching for a human hiding amongst the charred leaves. My eyes rolled over Caden and the others, off in one corner, and rolled on as I intentionally avoided eye contact. Mage had been smart to stop me from reading Caden, that first day. Viggo would have spotted the truth, had it flashed in my eyes for even the briefest of seconds.

First things first, though. I bolted for the exterior doors, side-stepping the few vampires still trying to pull blood from the gardener's drained corpse, and stopped in front of the security keypad on the wall. *Thank God Leo gave me the pass codes to do this.* I quickly reprogrammed the passwords, a small giggle escaping me with the knowledge of how this would infuriate them. There. Both the exterior garage and the exterior walk-through door were locked down. No one would enter. No more innocent people would die.

I walked back, more light-hearted than when I had left them, smiling my satisfaction as I watched understanding dawn in Viggo and Mortimer's eyes, before fury narrowed them. Mage stood nearby. Our eyes touched, and my lips tucked up at the corners in appreciation of her suggestion. She acknowledged with a barely perceptible nod.

"Why would you do that?" Viggo yelled. "I have blood trucks ordered and on their way! Are you going to let them in?"

"We can't have Red Cross trucks pulling in here, with the Sentinel hovering," I threw back, adding after a snort, "And I won't have innocent truck drivers massacred for your entertainment. No. I'll take care of it."

CR

"Hey, Reg," I said when Reggie's deep voice answered, using my friendliest pitch. Reggie was a supervisor at one of the city's Red Cross blood banks. Two weeks ago, he had loaded a utility truck with blood and smuggled it inside for me—a gold mine when shoring up supplies in anticipation of four vampires. Of course, I had compelled him to do all of this, and had him at the ready to respond to future needs, leaving me with an open source of blood when I needed it. Like now.

A long pause, then, "Sofie."

Something isn't right. I had expected a much warmer reception. "I need more blood, Reg."

Another long pause. "Um . . . Okay." His voice quavered with fear. "Be at the receiving dock in thirty minutes." The phone went dead.

He shouldn't be afraid of me. I must have messed up the compulsion, forgotten to script it properly. I was normally so good at it! I hung up the phone, sighing my annoyance. Gone were the days where entire trucks could go missing without anyone being the wiser. Now, in the age of computers, every drop was accounted for. I could alter numbers, but then I'd have to follow the trail of information to cover a dozen different threads of evidence to hide my tracks. I didn't have time for that. I needed human blood.

I headed straight for the garage, a spacious concrete room two floors below the ground level. Nearly three dozen pristinely maintained cars and trucks lined the walls within, some of which had never seen the open road. They were merely part of a collection, another one of Viggo's material weaknesses.

My eyes drifted over the silver-blue Mercedes, with its dented and bloody front bumper—Viggo had used it to run down Evangeline's mother. He kept it as a memento. *Please choose Mortimer, Veronique,* I prayed. Viggo would be as good as dead for what he did to Evangeline.

I climbed into the shiny black Navigator, the largest vehicle available for carting back a supply. As expected, the keys were in the ignition; Viggo didn't fear break-ins. The tires squealed as I peeled out, taking the winding ramp up to the atrium at high speed. As I crossed the threshold and pulled into the atrium, curious vampires quickly put two and two together: *Truck going out means doors to outside world opening.* Excitement flared in their vibrant irises. They began flocking toward the car entrance. "Great," I groaned as I slowed the truck to a halt. "This won't attract attention." I pressed my hands against my temples.

Mage suddenly appeared in the passenger seat, the act of opening and closing the truck door happening too fast for me to even notice. "What can I do to help?"

The concerned vampire citizen again, are we? I leveled a stare at her. "Look, let's get one thing straight: I don't trust you, and you sure as hell would be smart not to trust me." An amused look crossed her face as she nodded. I sighed heavily. "I can't have a crowd of hungry vampires in the tunnel when I drive out the exterior door. People will see them—see what they are—even if they can't get past the Merth."

"Consider it handled. Be on your way." With that, she vanished from my passenger seat and reappeared outside the truck, standing in front of the crowd. I inched forward, the low rumble of the big truck's engine drowning out whatever Mage was saying. It had the desired effect, though; the crowd dispersed to the opposite end of the atrium.

A rap on my window stopped me. Viggo. I rolled down my window, curious.

"Which bank?" he asked.

I studied him, suddenly on edge. "Why do you need to know?"

He rolled his eyes in exasperation. "So we know when you'll be back and we can move everyone from the gates again! You'll need to open them to get back in, won't you?"

"Oh . . . " I hadn't thought of the trip back. "Same place as last time."

"Okay. So we should expect you back here within the hour. Call us when you're near."

"Yup." *Strange. Too helpful. What do you have up your sleeve, Viggo?* My head was beginning to spin, trying to keep up with everyone's various motives.

Mortimer appeared behind Viggo. "Keep a look out for *them*." Mortimer's bitterness with the People's Sentinel was long-standing and obvious.

You have no idea, Mortimer. I rolled my eyes, but anxiety flooded my body. They were out there, watching. We had been careful not to react, not to hunt them down, wanting to sort out this mess with Veronique first. But now, with what I had just learned from Mage, I didn't know if it was better to exterminate, or continue in silence. To be . . . complacent. That was the word Mage used. Had we become complacent? Was this another step down our predetermined path?

I waited as Mortimer punched in the code to open the interior garage door—I hadn't changed that one. Throwing the truck into gear, I pulled into the tunnel, checking in my rearview mirror for any desperate vampires. None moved from the far side of the atrium. None attempted to defy Mage. It was as if she had power over them. Maybe she did.

I made it to the blood bank dock with two minutes to spare, after a small detour through the city to shake any tails. Normally I could tell when I was being followed, but today was not the day to take chances. The delivery entrance for this bank was in a wide alley, the tall brick buildings on either side providing some privacy from the street. I backed the Navigator up to one of the delivery doors and threw it into park to wait for Reggie. My fingers strummed the steering wheel as I watched various trucks at different stages of unloading through my black-tinted windows. Guilt fluttered as I thought of the generous people who had unwittingly donated to feed forty hungry vampires. It took the meaning of saving lives to a whole new level.

I sensed the approach a second before the white knuckles wrapped against the window. My finger on a button rolled the window down and I regarded my blood dealer, an unusually pale, blonde man who reeked of terror. "Is something the matter, Reggie?" I asked in my sweetest tone. Apprehension tightened my insides. He shouldn't be frightened of me . . .

"There's an unmarked delivery truck on its way from a drive," he answered in a rush, ignoring my question. "I've deleted it from the main system so it's free for the taking."

Unmarked. That meant I could leave the Navigator here. Much easier than unloading and reloading. I flashed him my most appreciative smile as I pulled a thick envelope full of cash from the glove compartment and handed it to him. Viggo had cash stashed everywhere. "For your troubles."

His eyes widened briefly as he took it, then he looked quickly around to check for witnesses before stuffing the envelope inside his lab coat. I heard the loud rumble of an approaching truck. "There it is," he confirmed, turning to leave.

My hand shot out to grab his forearm. "Thank you, Reg." He glanced down at my hand, then up at my face, giving me the chance to lock eyes with him. I needed to strengthen the compulsion for the next time I needed blood. "There's no need to worry, Reg. I'm harmless. I would never hurt you," I crooned, waiting for the hypnotic trance to kick in. "I may come back for more blood in a few weeks. Please be ready and willing to help me out."

He nodded slowly, as if listening, but the haze of a compelled person did not register in his blue eyes. *That's strange . . . am I losing my touch?* The second I let go of Reggie's arm, he bolted into the building.

If I had time, I'd follow him in and try again. But I didn't have time, I decided as a hospital-green cube truck parked beside me. No telltale blood-donor markings. *Perfect.* Hopping out of my Navigator, I opened the truck's passenger side door and swung smoothly into the seat, earning a pleasantly surprised look from a balding delivery man in his sixties.

"Hello, sir. I believe you have a delivery for me?" I crooned, focusing in on his watery irises, pulling his mind toward mine as I had just attempted with Reggie. This time it worked.

"Do I?" he slurred.

"Yes. Please step out of the truck and begin walking away. Go home and take a nap. When you wake up, you'll remember nothing about this truck or me. Right?"

"Right," he drawled. Still mesmerized, he pawed absently at the door with his left hand, finally opened it, and spilled out of the truck. He staggered down the alley toward the street as if drunk.

"Okay. Now," I murmured, sliding into the driver's seat. I studied the truck's gearshift. "At least it's not a rig," I muttered under my breath. Those were a pain to drive. I threw the truck into drive and began rolling forward.

Two black Dodge extended-cab pickup trucks pulled in front of me, blocking my path. I slammed on the brakes as four burly men hopped out of each, a mixture of fear and determination in their eyes as they peered up at me. My attention flew down to their hands. There it was, the Sentinel tattoo. That meant they knew this red-headed, green-eyed woman was no ordinary woman. This was no accidental encounter.

Rage flared within me. They had gotten to Reggie, used him for an ambush. But how had they broken my compulsion? "Oh," I murmured, the puzzle pieces fitting together into a hideous picture. There was only one way to break a vampire's compulsion: witch magic. That meant either Mage's prophecy was coming true and the Sentinel was allied with the witches, or Ursula was back in action as a thorn in my side. I hoped for the latter at this point but, either way, I didn't have time for this.

I briefly considered ramming the trucks but decided against it. The damage might stall the delivery truck. Plus, the noise would most definitely attract the attention of curious passersby. I couldn't cause a scene in broad daylight in front of a blood bank.

I sighed heavily and rolled down the window. A gust of frigid November air struck me. "Hello, gentlemen!" I called cheerily.

The one closest to my door—a heavyset, brown-haired man of six feet—edged forward. He wasn't getting too close, though. *Smart.* "You don't look like the typical truck driver," he answered with a nonchalant grin, trying to play up his ignorance of my identity. He was a decoy, of course, meant to distract me from the two men to the right who were busy readying a flamethrower drawn from a compartment in the back of one truck—the Sentinel's weapon of choice against us. It was stupid, really, given the speed and power of a vampire, yet they still did manage to catch us unawares sometimes. But they hadn't been dealing with the likes of me.

I couldn't let this go any further, knowing they'd torch the truck, destroying the blood supply. I gave him my sweetest smile, all while plucking helixes of magic from my body, arming myself. I'd paralyze them. *Simple.* "Oh, but I'm not. You know that . . . don't you?"

The grin slid off his face as his eyes darted to the others; he gave the slightest nod.

I laughed aloud. "Seriously? Haven't you guys realized who you're up against?"

With that, I sent a bolt of magic out to seize the flamethrower clean from the man's grip, letting it fly back and smash through the passenger side window to rest on the seat next to me. Glass rained down everywhere but I barely noticed. "I've been looking for one of those," I said conversationally.

As the words left my mouth, I heard a faint click. I whipped my head up to see two men stepping out from behind a truck fifty yards away; one held a bazooka. It was pointing at me. And its rocket had been launched.

With no opportunity to weigh my options, I sent another bolt of magic out—this one a thousand helixes strong—to block the rocket and send it back to its launching point, trying to contain the blast. The truck rocked with the explosion, bricks, metal, and body parts flying in every direction.

"So much for keeping a low profile," I muttered, silently berating myself for being too cocky to notice their plan unfolding. *I need to get out of here. Now.* I wrapped magical threads around both trucks. With a flick of my wrist, they were swept aside like a minor inconvenience, crumpling against the brick walls and taking four more men with them.

I revved the truck engine and threw it into gear again. It jerked forward. The decoy man stepped in front of the truck to stop me. He disappeared under my truck as I drove over him, the back tires jolting over his body. I peeled out of the alley, speeding up as I passed various pedestrians running toward the commotion, some eyeing my truck suspiciously and a few of them jotting down the license plate number. I had no time to stop and do damage control. Looking in my rearview mirror at the fiery, body-peppered scene I had just left, I knew I needed a new blood supplier.

Not until the heavy iron door slammed against the ground behind me and I coasted into the atrium was I able to relax. I watched forty pairs of bloodthirsty eyes immediately lock onto the truck, the scent of this much human blood sending their senses into overdrive. The moment that back door rolled up, they'd turn into wild, blood-crazed demons.

"Take it easy. It won't come as easily next time," I called in warning as I hopped out the driver's side, on my way to Mortimer. Their ocular veins began pulsating in response.

My expression must have been grim because panic flitted across Mortimer's face. "It's safe to say they're onto us," I said dryly, scanning the crowd—for Mage, I realized. I had an overpowering urge to talk to her. She was the only one who could appreciate the coming disaster.

Mortimer's jaw tightened. "We managed to hide from them for a hundred and twenty years and yet now, at the most critical time, they decide they're going to have their little revolution."

"I'm beginning to think they've had some help," I replied, intent on explaining the link to the witches, but Mortimer's plea interrupted me.

"Please, Sofie. Just bring Evangeline back so we can be done with this and move on. We can lose the Sentinel."

I set my jaw stubbornly. "You know I can't do that."

"You'd risk everything for one human girl?"

I glared at him. "Yes." I sounded insane, but I didn't care.

"Well, that's just brilliant." He slammed his fist on the bistro table so hard that the metal legs snapped like twigs.

A shrill scream disrupted his tantrum. I turned to see a petite, mousy blonde girl of no more than fourteen step out from behind the truck. The body of a male Ratheus vampire lay on the ground beside her, chin smeared with blood, jerking in convulsions before it stopped and lay still. Dead.

"What the—" I began, but then I looked at her neck, where blood ran from two puncture wounds. The other Ratheus vampires hissed at the young woman but slinked away, their comrade's body keeping them at bay.

"Ileana!" Viggo exclaimed, rushing over to her, his arms wide for an embrace. "How lovely of you to come!"

The hairs on the back of my neck rose as Viggo led the young girl, her face full of fear, away from the throng. It wasn't until she moved away from the truck and the overpowering scent of blood that the wave of recognition hit me.

Magic.

She was a witch.

"How did—" I began, then cut myself short as I answered my own question, eyeing the garage door. Of course! She had hitched a ride on the back of the truck while I waited for the garage to open, and I was too frazzled after the attack to notice. That was why Viggo seemed so concerned with when I'd be back—he was planning her entry. "Are you insane?" I shrieked. "Plotting with another witch? Because the first time didn't teach you enough, you moron," I grated through clenched teeth, my hand flying up to my forehead. "You're inviting the Sentinel in!"

From the corner of my eye, I saw Mage's eyes—not transformed by blood lust, surprisingly—narrow as she studied the girl. Good. She wasn't impressed either.

"Oh, that's preposterous." Viggo dismissed my concerns with a wave of his hand. "That mess with Ursula was a fluke."

The frown on Mortimer's face told me he wasn't a part of this plan. He leaned in close to Viggo, whispering, "We didn't discuss this."

"I don't need your permission," Viggo responded arrogantly.

The two of them turned to face off.

"But this . . . after the fiasco with Ursula and that one—" Mortimer jerked his chin in my direction "—I thought we were washing our hands of these treacherous creatures."

"Oh, I know." Viggo patted the air soothingly. "However, Ileana is more than willing to remain quiet. For the sake of her dear mother, right?" He looked at the woman. Pain flashed in her cornflower-blue eyes.

Of course. I exhaled in disgust. Viggo had hired thugs everywhere. This was obviously a well thought-out contingency plan on his part. The young woman's mother was likely chained up in a basement somewhere with a bunch of sweaty, hairy men eyeballing her, appalling intentions running through their illiterate brains.

"I can't guarantee your witch will be safe here," Mage began, regarding the woman with disapproval, "among this crowd."

"Oh, we've taken care of that! Show them, Ileana," Viggo said. Ileana lifted a shaking hand to her neck and pulled a tiny vial on a chain from her collar. "Isn't it lovely?" Viggo crowed. "She stole it from one of her teachers. It makes her blood toxic. Anyone who bites her will die."

My attention shifted from the vial—a powerful weapon that the Fates must have played a part in creating—to the girl. Her trembling knees knocked together and she wrung her hands, clenching and unclenching her fingers constantly, clearly terrified. And her young age made her practically useless to Viggo; she would have just learned how to find the magic threads within herself, and she would have few spells in her repertoire—and no idea how to bend the laws of physics to create new spells. There was no hard and fast set of rules around sorceress magic. It took years of experimentation; the more cautious witches never truly figured it out. And this witchling was weak, judging by the tiny glow of magic radiating from her. The smug fool in front of me didn't know that, though.

"Viggo. She can't break the Merth's curse. She can't get Veronique out. She can't undo anything I've done. So let her mother go," I pleaded. The child would be lucky to tie her own shoes with her magic.

"Gladly! As soon as you release Evangeline." Viggo turned to the young witch. "This is Sofie. This is all her fault, you know."

The young witch turned to regard me, contempt flashing in her eyes. I sighed heavily. Great. Yet another enemy within these walls, thanks to Viggo.

"I hope you're not planning on having her toy with magic," Mage called, "considering we have a truce."

"Yes, I recall *Sofie* couldn't use her magic, right?" Viggo answered, smiling. "Sofie," he repeated. Mage's lips tightened, his emphasis not lost on her. "Ileana is not Sofie. I have done nothing to break our agreement. And what was that other part? Oh yes, no killing of anyone. That includes Ileana, here."

"She killed Tanner!" Mage threw back, glancing over at the corpse on the cobblestones.

"In self-defense! You can't hold that against her!" Viggo was testing her honor, seeing if she would back out of the truce she'd imposed. It was silly, really; she could tear both Viggo and this witchling to shreds in seconds, if she chose. But from what I could read of Mage—which wasn't a lot—her honor, or the impression of her honor, held sway.

Her mouth twisted and she nodded, and I knew Viggo had won.

"If her magic causes anyone any harm, I will strike her down." I glared at Ileana. "Dead."

"Agreed! She's not here to harm anyone!" Viggo exclaimed, throwing an arm proudly over Ileana's shoulder. She remained rigid, terror-filled eyes looking everywhere but at me now.

With an angry shake of my head, I turned and stalked off.

The glass panes of the French door rattled as I slammed it. I marched straight over to study Veronique's portrait, as I did every time I stepped foot inside the grand mahogany- and leather-filled parlor. "I hope you'll understand, Veronique," I whispered, anticipating the tales painting me as a wicked sister that those two monsters would spin. And she'd likely believe them. As lovely and sweet as my sister was, no one would ever have described her as clever.

I heaved an exhausted sigh. For over one hundred years, I had waited for the Fates to fix this mess and release my baby sister from her tomb. And then, for the last eighteen years, I had spent my days in a bipolar balance of bliss and dread as I watched Evangeline grow up, knowing what I had brought down on her, what my deal had condemned her to. I was exhausted, tired of the magic, of the unknown, of the constant fighting with Viggo and Mortimer, of the hatred boiling inside of me. I hadn't always been so angry.

Yes, I had a temper—Nathan had always been quick to point that out. I was his fiery redhead. But that fire had evolved into rot, deep within my core. The only saving grace, the only reason the rot hadn't fully consumed me, was Evangeline. And I would lose her if I didn't get that damn pendant off her, something I could not for the life of me figure out how to do. Each day I poked and prodded the boundaries of the spell's weave inside my head, delivered to me by the Fates in a hard, marble-sized packet of magic. But it was impenetrable.

And if that wasn't enough, now I had the fate of Earth on my shoulders. How would I manage to keep the end of the human world at bay when I couldn't even control the mess within these Fifth Avenue walls? For God's sake, I had just unwittingly helped Viggo bring in the enemy! A useless witch, but an enemy, nonetheless.

I pressed my fingertips against my temples, trying to ease my tension. I needed to focus on the more immediate task, the one I could handle: an update for Leo. He needed to know about the Sentinel and the truth of this parallel world. But more importantly, I needed to know how my Evangeline was coping.

Opening my mind up to the portal into Leo's mind, one of the simplest yet most useful spells I had designed over all my years, I reached out, following my mind's eye as it sailed down the long, blue-tinged tunnel to the link in Leo's head. The link I had planted the night I healed his wife. At the time, I had no specific plans for him; I just recognized an opportunity to call on a favor in the future, if needed. Boy, had I ever taken advantage of my dear friend Leo's debt to me!

I reached the portal in the old warlock's head within seconds. Oddly enough, it looked like a solid little wooden door at the end of a tunnel. I prodded at it, and sensed it open. *How is Evangeline?* I sent in greeting. And then I sensed something slither up behind my message. Like a tiny anchor affixed to my words, something was trailing them there, through the tunnel, to Leo. An invader.

I slammed the portal shut and sailed back into my own head, forcefully breaking off the communication before Leo could send out a probe to reply. Someone had tagged onto my message! Few had the skill to pull that off. There were only two possibilities within these walls: the five thousand-year-old vampire who had powers I couldn't grasp yet, or the meek witchling who couldn't meet my gaze. Both seemed impossible. Either way, someone would pay.

With shock and rage driving each step, I crashed through the French doors to the atrium, unwilling to take the time to open them. Shards of glass and wood flew in every direction. I didn't even flinch.

Only a few Ratheus vampires remained in the atrium. The rest, including Caden and friends, were either chasing the blood to the cellar or hiding out—away from the new witch, no doubt. Mage was nowhere in sight. I marched over to where Viggo and Ileana stood. The little witch-girl slipped behind him, her guilty eyes going wide. I had my answer. *Her? Seriously? That tiny wisp of a thing, her magic immature and weak? How?*

"Oh! I forgot to mention," Viggo began, his chest puffing out, "Ileana is something of a genius in her circles—decades ahead of where she should be, and extremely powerful." He reached over to lift the chain of her necklace. "This thing serves a dual purpose; it masks the power of her magic." He smiled knowingly at me. "I thought it best. I didn't want you feeling threatened by a witch more powerful than you in here."

So I wouldn't suspect her of being able to tap into my communication spell. His words only fed my rage. I stalked toward her, my intentions likely clear as day in my blazing eyes. Had she been able to locate Leo through her probe? No, it would appear not. Viggo and Mortimer would be furiously dialing coordinates to rush their henchmen to Siberia at this very moment.

"Now Sofie," Mortimer began, stepping forward.

"What? You're on his side now?" I spat.

"I've never been on Viggo's side," he answered bitterly. "I'm on Veronique's side. Unlike you, it would seem."

My words caught in my throat with that comment. When I spoke again, my voice was even and cool. "So, Viggo, you seem to have found someone who can tap into communication spells. How clever of you. And quick." My eyes darted over to Ileana's face, peeking out from behind Viggo's broad shoulder. What else could she do? I knew she couldn't undo the tomb spell without the pendant, so Veronique wasn't going anywhere. I was pretty sure she couldn't unwind the Merth I had so intricately woven through these walls in an impenetrable barrier. But I wasn't a hundred percent sure anymore.

"What can I say, Sofie? You're the one who gave me the idea when you said I'd have to pry it from your head!" Viggo replied with a smug grin. "So, you've been keeping close ties to Evangeline through that bastard traitor."

Fool, I silently admonished myself. But there was nothing I could do about it now, except not allow it to happen again. "Lucky I caught on so quickly," I murmured.

Viggo's mouth twisted with displeasure. "Yes, well . . . I guess you'll have to cut all communication to Leo now, won't you?"

I struggled to keep my expression calm as panic hit me. He was right. I had to sever my link with Leo, which meant with Evangeline. I would have no way of checking up on her, of knowing how she was doing. And Leo wouldn't send any messages my way now. He would have sensed me shutting down that connection so abruptly, and I had strictly instructed him not to reach out if he sensed anything "off." How long before I could connect with him again?

Viggo and I squared off, his smug smile of satisfaction inciting in me the urge to claw off his face. He needed to pay. I wanted him to hurt. I never could punish him before, on account of Evangeline. That wasn't an issue anymore.

I didn't have a vampire's strength that would match the two thousand-year-old vampire, but I had my magic. Magic that could shatter every bone in his body at a steady rhythm that gave them enough time to almost heal properly before rebreaking—over and over again. I felt the evil grin stretch across my face as I glared at him. His cobalt eyes grew cautious, likely glimpsing my intentions, wondering if he had pushed me past my breaking point.

But first, I needed to establish the pecking order. I turned to regard Ileana. "Rest assured, you won't have another opportunity. And if you try anything on me again, you will die a painful death."

"I don't think you are in any position to threaten such a powerful sorceress," Viggo began, adding sarcastically, "especially with our iron-clad truce."

But Mage isn't here right now, is she. I met his warning with a sadistic smile. "You want to see powerful?" I murmured. I had always been a powerful sorceress, even before transforming. Since then, though, my magic had compounded a hundredfold. These two idiots had no idea what I was capable of. It was time they found out.

I raised my hands and thousands of bolts of purple magic shot out of me in every direction with a ferocity I had, until now, hidden from them. Glass exploded from every window and door. Five stories of balconies came crashing down, the concrete and brick pounding the cobblestones and gardens into dusty heaps, sending the Ratheus vampires scuttling for cover. Every plant and flower previously untouched now shriveled. With a flip of my wrists, entire rows of cobblestones tore themselves out of the ground and spun in a tornado-like funnel before torpedoing in all directions. In only seconds, I transformed Viggo's cherished atrium into a war zone. Only Veronique's statue and the glass ceiling enclosing the atrium remained unscathed.

Viggo and Mortimer may not have understood the power behind the apocalyptic destruction, but Ileana certainly did; her face paled to a corpse-like pallor. *Let that be a warning to you, little girl.* "I am in exactly the position I need to be," I said evenly, then focused on my sister's vying suitors, "and while I can't kill you two for my sister's sake, I can certainly make every day you wait for her a living hell. And those days will stretch for a long, long time if you get in my way again."

Mortimer had the decency to remain quiet. But Viggo tutted and added, "Temper, temper."

Strangling a cry of fury, I whirled and stalked off toward the red doors, before I burned him where he stood. Mage was waiting for me in the doorway. *Damn it!* Of course my destruction of the atrium wouldn't go unnoticed. I held my hand up as I walked past her. "I know! I'm sorry. It was an exception. None of it was directed at anyone. I needed to prove a point. There will be no more." I hoped my brush-off would be enough to mollify her. No such luck.

"It's unsettling, wouldn't you say?" she observed, her voice soft. "Someone probing your brain, looking for information?" Clearly she had heard the entire confrontation.

"Can you blame me?" I continued up the stairs.

She said nothing in response.

"If she does it again, she's dead," I warned with conviction as I threw open the red doors, adding stubbornly, "And no truce will hold me back. I don't care what you do."

"I would help you."

Her words stopped me, not so much because they came as a

surprise as because they seemed suspiciously truthful. They left me believing I could trust her, something I knew I most certainly could not. I turned to face her, towering over her petite frame even though I was of average height. "Is there something else you need?"

My tone didn't seem to bother her. "You had troubles getting the blood?"

Troubles . . . I groaned as my palm flew up to my forehead. With the witchling and the tap into my head, I had forgotten about that disaster. I was dealing with so many different messes, my head spun. "Yes, yes. Of course." Mage needed to know. I wondered if the attack was on the news already. She joined me and we walked side by side into the building, me detailing the grim reality that was unfolding to my untrustworthy new ally.

4. ENEMIES AND ALLIES

"Of all the gin joints in all the towns in all the world, she walks into mine," Leo recited in a startlingly authentic American accent as we watched the movie credits roll on the flat screen, the reflection glinting off the window glass against the backdrop of night. It was after eleven now, but darkness had fallen many hours ago. "*Casablanca* is my favorite movie, you know," he added with the excitement of a child arriving at a fair.

You don't say? Max muttered from his spot on the floor beside the sectional I shared with Julian. The sarcastic comment earned a snicker from me before I could stifle it. It was the fourth time Leo had made that announcement.

"I can't believe I'm only seeing it now," I said as I leaned over to grab another fistful of buttery popcorn from the ceramic bowl. I stole a glance at Julian and caught his eyes on me. I smiled. He smiled back but said nothing. He seemed tired. His olive complexion hadn't completely returned yet.

We had spent the entire day in the great room, sprawled out on either side of the gray sectional couch as Julian recovered from his near-death trek. The servants quietly swept through several times during the day to bring snacks and hot drinks, which we readily accepted, Julian surprising me with the manners of a well-trained schoolboy. Otherwise, no one said two words to us.

After I had divulged the secrets behind my connection to the vampires, Julian must have felt the need to reciprocate, because he gave me a summary of his life, from his early grade school days in Colombia to his American all-boys private school to being accepted into Harvard medical school just this year. It was a fairly normal—if privileged—life for the son of a Colombian drug lord and slave-monger and it helped strengthen my sense of connection with my human companion in this isolated part of the world. We may have come from very different backgrounds, but we were equally confined by vampires.

As the day progressed and Julian's chattiness waned, I plugged in one of the seven hard drives sitting beside the forty-two inch plasma screen. No one could say Sofie hadn't prepared for years of entertainment. We settled on a marathon of goofy sitcoms and movies. Julian and I seemed to have the same tastes in shows. That was a good thing, given we would likely be watching a lot of them together.

It was dinnertime when Leo resurfaced from his room, his skin chalky, supporting himself on the furniture as he shuffled into the great room. In a burst of energy, Julian sprang from the couch to rush over and pull out a chair at the dining table for the old man, then offered to fetch some of Magda's delicious broth, if the beef goulash was too heavy. His attitude toward Leo had changed drastically since the old warlock had saved his life. Watching the exchange quietly from my nook on the couch, I smiled. Perhaps living here together would work after all.

"Oh, I'm not surprised it took being exiled to the middle of nowhere by a vampire for you to sit down and watch this classic. You young folks and your MTV and video games—or whatever the newest thing is," Leo muttered as he pointed the gray plastic remote at the television and shut it off. "No appreciation for the arts."

He struggled to rise from his chair. Julian threw his blanket off and slid for his corner of the couch to rise and reach for Leo's arm, but Leo waved him off, adding grumpily, "I'm not a geriatric!" Julian flinched as if struck. "But thank you for your concern," Leo quickly added, his tone more civil.

The old Irishman managed to get to his feet and hobbled over to the fire. "Can't seem to keep the warmth in this drafty place," he murmured as he leaned over to grab a log, bracing his other hand on the stones of the fireplace. Testing the weight of the log, he changed his mind and grabbed a smaller log. With some effort, he heaved it into the fire.

A twinge of worry nagged at me, seeing such crippled movements where only days ago he'd been a spry seventy-eight-year-old, practically bounding around. It was as if he had aged twenty years overnight. The exertion required for that spell to transport me here, followed by healing Julian, was proving too much for him. *He should be resting.* "Leo, why don't you just use your magic for the fire?" I suggested.

He chuckled. "I enjoy stoking the fire." He demonstrated by poking the logs with the iron prod to kindle the flames. "And if I used my magic for everything I could, rigor mortis would have set into this old corpse by now."

Leo a corpse. Dead. The very thought brought a pang of grief to my stomach. He was my ally, my magical guardian, along with Max. More, I felt a strange kinship to him, finding his sympathetic pats and gentle nods so . . . grandfatherly. I had never met my grandfather. I had no idea what it was like to have one. Yet, if I closed my eyes and tried to picture my mother's father, Leo's weathered, smiling face was the first to appear. I couldn't have him dying while protecting me. Maybe Sofie could heal him . . . if I could just get her here, somehow. "Have you heard anything more from Sofie?"

Leo opened his mouth to speak, then clamped it shut as his eyes darted to Julian.

"I've told Julian everything," I blurted, earning a loud grumble of disapproval from Max.

Leo's grim face indicated his agreement with my disgruntled canine. "Of course you have, silly girl," he muttered, exasperation in his voice. "You've learned nothing! I think you may be allergic to secrecy."

"Yes, I *have* learned!" I retorted, defiantly thrusting out my chin. I certainly had learned about the advantages of keeping secrets from vampires and witches. "But look at him!" I threw my hand out to point at Julian, who now squirmed uncomfortably on the couch as we discussed him. "He's a human. He's harmless."

Leo's mouth curved in a condescending smirk. "You assume humans are harmless?"

"No, but . . . " I stumbled over my words. In the end, there was only one answer I could give: the one that made sense. "He has a right to know. Just as I did."

Sympathy smoothed Leo's frown. With a slight nod, he settled into the tawny leather chair beside the fire. Julian and I waited in silence as he pulled his pipe out from his vest's inner pocket. He took his time unraveling the small burgundy packet of tobacco and tapping the corner of it on the edge of his pipe, filling its bowl.

My patience finally ran out. "So, about Sofie. Have you heard from her?" I pressed.

Leo paused and finally shook his head, concern filling his gray eyes.

"Well, can't you send her a message?" I turned to Julian, now sitting on the couch. "They can talk to each other through some sort of communication spell Sofie set up years ago when she was helping—"

"No. I can't," Leo cut me off, scowling his annoyance.

I bit my lip, silently admonishing myself. Leo and Sofie's relationship was a private story that Leo had entrusted me with, I realized. *Maybe I am allergic to secrets! Only I didn't know it was a secret . . .* "Helping him with something," I finished vaguely.

Leo held a match to his pipe, then spoke through a cloud of smoke as he puffed it alight. "A few hours ago, Sofie reached out to me, only she slammed the connection shut before I could get a response to her."

I frowned. "Why would she do that?"

He lifted an eyebrow. "And you finally ask an interesting question. Why, indeed?"

"Well, ask her!"

Leo shook his head. "There are rules, my dear Evangeline. Rules imposed by Sofie, and I dare not cross that fiery woman. Sofie's extremely paranoid, especially when it comes to you. I learned long ago never to question her." He took another puff on his pipe before he continued. "She warned me not to communicate to her if anything seemed suspicious. Abruptly cutting off communication like that is suspicious. Under no circumstances am I to initiate a message chain now. I can only respond once she's reached out to me."

"Well, did you guys agree on a schedule, at least?"

"Of course."

"So can't you . . . " I trailed off. What could he do, given the limitations Sofie had imposed? I felt my shoulders slump with disappointment, then tense as panic set in.

Leo sighed heavily. "Look . . . I'm going to tell you everything I know because I think you can handle it and because you've been lied to enough for one lifetime." He paused again as he fumbled with his pipe. "If she hasn't sent a message by now, something's very wrong."

His words lost no meaning with me. Not just wrong; *very* wrong. That brought me from lying lazily on the couch to perching on its edge, my blanket forgotten on the floor. I barely felt the draft in the air though; my stomach had dropped to my feet. "What does that mean? Is she dead? Are *they* dead?"

"That would be too easy," Julian mumbled.

"They're my friends!" I snapped at him, his callous remark pricking me. I had no valid reason to expect his compassion for them, but he could show me some.

Julian's brown eyes softened and he bowed his head. "Sorry."

I turned back to see Leo vehemently shaking his head. "No, I'd know if she were dead. I'd feel the connection break."

"And what about Caden? Is he dead? And Amelie? What about Bishop and Fiona?" My voice rose in pitch as I fired names at him. "They are! She doesn't want to tell me!" Up until now, knowledge that they were safely in New York City, on the same planet as me, had brought me a security blanket of comfort. But Leo's ambiguity was wrenching that blanket from my grasp.

Leo's forehead creased as he shook his head. "No, no. Don't get all worked up. I don't think that's it."

"Well, then why?"

"Like I said, I don't know, Evangeline," Leo repeated calmly.

I gripped the edge of the couch and stared at Leo, my stomach twisting with near-hysteria. "So send her a message!" I demanded. "How mad can she get?" The wrinkles on Leo's forehead twisted as he arched an eyebrow at my insistence, and I dropped my gaze to my hands, feeling like a child being scolded. "What's the big deal, anyway?" I muttered defiantly. "It's not like they can find me here, right?"

"Who? Viggo? No." Leo shook his head, then dropped his voice. "But I'm sure towns and cities all over the world are being scoured at this very moment as he hunts for you. There are people turning over every location connected to Sofie. And they will not stop. Not until they've found you or they've all died off from old age."

The buttery taste the popcorn had left in my mouth suddenly turned rancid as I absorbed the implications of Leo's words. Viggo was hunting me like an animal. And the end result would be much the same, if they found me. Suddenly this mountain was not remote enough. The trees were not numerous enough, the snow not deep enough; the cabin was so brightly lit, it was a shining beacon, visible from outer space. I had the urge to take an ax to the cables connecting the generators to the cabin and throw us into medieval times—anything that could help hide us from a two thousand-year-old vampire on his eternal mission to get this pendant off my neck.

My horror must have been written all over my face, because Leo rushed to calm me. "Not to worry, dear girl. They can't possibly find you here unless they somehow . . ." Leo's voice drifted off in a chuckle that faded as a thought struck him. His expression suggested impossibility had become possibility. "Well, not unless they could trace the link to the spell." He stroked his chin with a wrinkled hand, deep in thought.

A chill ran down my spine. "And who would help them do that?" I asked slowly.

Another puff of his pipe, this one long. I noticed that Julian was hanging off the couch beside me now as well, his attention riveted to Leo. We locked eyes for a moment and he offered a sympathetic smile.

The old man finally spoke. "My kind. A highly skilled sorcerer. Or sorceress."

I swallowed around a painful lump suddenly filling my throat and asked weakly, "You can do that sort of thing?"

Leo chuckled. "Me? No. I can't. But . . . I wouldn't put it past someone to figure it out." He snorted. "And of course Viggo would find that witch. He's resourceful, that one."

I remembered Sofie's earlier words about witches and vampires. "I thought your kind hated their kind. Where does Viggo keep finding these witches to help him?"

He nodded. "They do hate vampires. Yes. So much that they'll do anything to rid the world of them." He leaned forward to inspect the fire. I recognized it as a sign that he was going to launch into a story. "Don't you ever wonder how vampires were created?"

"I haven't gotten to that point yet. I'm still stuck at the fact that they exist," I answered dryly. I heard Julian's low chuckle beside me.

"Fair enough." Leo's head bobbed in understanding as he leaned back into his chair. "We created them. My kind. Vampires are the result of a Causal Enchantment."

I don't know why this shocked me, given everything I'd seen lately, but it did. I realized my jaw was hanging open and slowly closed my mouth. Julian leaned forward beside me, his elbows on his knees, hanging on the old warlock's every word. Words that so few would ever hear.

Leo grinned, clearly enjoying our reaction. "About five thousand years ago, a sorceress was searching for eternal youth and immortality for herself. She started messing around with that dark magic. The Fates. Nasty business, I tell you. Anyone who gets involved with them is absolutely crazy." Leo scowled. "Anyway, they granted her Causal Enchantment. They gave her eternal youth and immortality." The ghost of a smug smile touched Leo's mouth. "All she needed to do was drink blood. She became the first vampire, the most unexpected outcome of a spell. And the witches have been trying to correct that mistake ever since." He added under his breath, "Creating all kinds of other disasters along the way."

"The first vampire was a witch?" I whispered in disbelief. "So was she like Sofie? With powers? What happened to her?"

"Oh, my kind isn't privy to that much detail. She was ostracized as soon as the transformation happened. It's said she held on to a few of her powers, but I don't know. We think Viggo knows, but he won't tell Sofie. It's his one secret over her."

Of course he knew. Viggo was now the oldest vampire, but he hadn't always been the oldest vampire. I didn't doubt that he had something to do with this first vampire's death. He was such a conniving monster. I shuddered, imagining him storming through the side door at that moment. If I never saw him again, I'd be happy. Mortimer . . . I didn't fear him as much, not since he'd dropped his mask for that millisecond in the atrium that day. I knew without a doubt that he'd still kill me to get to the pendant, but I also knew he wouldn't take sadistic pleasure in it. That brought me some small level of comfort. "So do you think they'd actually trust another one?"

He shrugged, sighing loudly. "Who knows? I should suspect not, given the last 'arrangement' Viggo made, but who can say, with that psychopath? When he's desperate, he gets reckless." Bitterness tinged his voice.

I thought a moment. "So if he did find a witch to help him and Sofie doesn't send you messages, then no one finds me and everything's fine, right?"

Leo's laughter rang hollow. "Yes. For us, everything's peachy."

I frowned. I didn't understand this old man's sense of humor sometimes.

Leo sighed. "There are a few other issues that could be . . . distracting her."

My stomach did another sickly dive to my feet. "Other issues besides witches?"

Leo nodded. "Remember that day in Central Park? When you were attacked?"

"Yeah, I seem to recall something." I glanced sideways at the dogs as another memory flashed in my mind—this one of the mutt Badger's decapitated head. I shuddered.

"Those men with Ursula . . . they weren't just hired thugs," Leo explained. "They were hired 'People's Sentinel' thugs."

I felt my forehead crease as I wracked my memory for something to link to the name. No bells. "Have you mentioned them before?"

Leo groaned heavily. "Why must I be the one to explain everything? The People's Sentinel is a long-standing secret society of humans fighting for humankind against vampires. Against anything nonhuman, actually. Even against witches. They've existed for thousands of years now. You heard of women burned for being witches?" Julian and I nodded in unison. "The handiwork of the Sentinel. In the past, their society numbered in the thousands. Then they fell into the background like a sleeper cell, where they've remained for several hundred years. Only now they've resurfaced and they're stronger than ever. We're not sure how many are involved. Mortimer and Viggo had been lying low for years while this mess with Veronique was getting settled—hence the Foreros' involvement. However, we've started seeing them around again."

"Well, if they hate the witches so much, why would they have been working with Ursula? Are you sure it was them? Maybe you're mistaken."

Leo leaned over and gestured to the meaty part of his hand. "Because they brand themselves with tattoos on their hand. The markings look like deformed crosses."

Leo's words jarred forth a memory. A deceptively nice old gentleman's hand. And on it, a curved cross tattoo. "I saw it!" I confirmed.

"They all have them. Stupid, really. It marks them immediately for what they are. Vampires can spot them a mile away."

"What happened to these people who attacked you in Central Park?" Julian asked.

"Oh, Max and the others got hold of them." My eyes closed and I shuddered, trying to shake that gruesome bloodbath from my memory. "But these Sentinel people would have killed me otherwise."

"Oh . . . " Julian murmured. He looked at Max. "Good."

Maybe he isn't a complete nitwit after all, Max grumbled, earning an eye roll from me.

Leo continued. "The only reason Viggo and Mortimer have

restrained themselves from hunting down the Sentinel up until now is because of Veronique. The moment she is out and transformed, they will go on a mission to rid the world of every last one. I guarantee you that."

And I'll be there with fangs on! Max chirped eagerly in my head. *Not one of them will survive.*

"Easy, Max. That won't be for a while."

"What'd he say?" Julian asked, his brown eyes shifting between me and Max.

"Oh," I reached over to scratch behind Max's ear, "anyone with a Sentinel tattoo pretty much has a death warrant with Max, here."

Julian hesitated, watching the dog. "I don't blame him." He looked back to Leo. "So . . . do you think they can win? This Sentinel group?"

"They're only human. What could they possibly do against an army of vampires?" I answered before Leo could.

When I glanced at the old man for confirmation, his eyebrow arched. "Oh, I don't know," he drawled. "How about starting a war that obliterates all of humankind? Sound familiar?"

My eyes went wide and I gasped. Ratheus. A war between humans and vampires. He was right. How could I have forgotten about that? I was so wound up with my own situation that I hadn't connected the dots.

"They likely wouldn't," Leo continued, trying to mollify me. "The easier thing for the Sentinel to do is bomb the Manhattan building. That would eliminate ninety-five percent of the vampires on Earth. They'd just have to pluck off a few more . . . "

I felt the blood drain from my face as a vivid image sprang into my mind of Viggo and Mortimer's palace exploding—with Caden and the others trapped inside. If Caden died, if Sofie died, I'd have no one left. The very thought forced tears to my eyes.

"Oh, Evangeline, I'm sorry," Leo exclaimed, softening at the sight of my distress. "I don't mean to sound blithe. I highly doubt that'll happen. As long as the Sentinel is left in the dark about what's going on inside those walls and about the venom issue, there's no reason they'd do something so drastic."

"But what if they find out?"

"Who's going to tell them? No one," Leo assured me, adding sarcastically, "You're here. Otherwise I'd be worried." I answered with an irritated scowl. Now was not the time for teasing.

"Is that what happened on this Ratheus?" Julian asked me softly. Despite the detail I had gone into earlier that day, I hadn't gotten into specifics about Ratheus with him. I wasn't in any mood to explain those details now, with my body numb, my heart aching. So I simply nodded. "Humans against vampires. The humans lost. They can't win," I said, my voice hollow.

The room fell quiet as we all absorbed the full weight of the situation. Well, what we thought may be the situation. Julian shifted around on the couch as if unable to get comfortable. He likely wouldn't be able to—most people become overly sensitive when words like "war" get thrown around.

Finally Julian did speak. "So, how do we stop this from happening?"

"We can't do anything, up here in the mountains. Absolutely nothing." Leo paused. "Sofie needs to keep the Sentinel calm and the witches uninvolved, for starters. We can't let any of them know what's going on inside those walls. Nothing about the venom issue."

"Right," Julian murmured, adding slowly, "because if they can kill all these Ratheus vampires in New York in one blow, no more could be created."

"Right," Leo confirmed. "They'd likely attack with full force, trying to eradicate the lot of them before they could create more."

"In fact, from Earth's standpoint, it would be best if they did do it. Because then there would be no retaliation. The general population would likely never even find out vampires exist," Julian surmised.

No wonder he's in med school. He's catching on way faster than I ever did, I thought, even as despair flooded into me. They were talking about my friends and Sofie and why killing them would save the world. No . . . that couldn't happen. There had to be another way.

"And what happens if this Sentinel and the witches don't find out? If everyone's all happy and quiet, no one kills anyone?" Julian asked Leo.

"The Sentinel isn't going away. Not unless they're all hunted down and killed. The witches certainly aren't going anywhere. Whether they fight now or fight later, it's . . . inevitable. But if they fight later . . . once the vampires are released and able to breed more vampires to build an army . . . " Leo shook his head. "Not good."

"Ratheus will happen," I whispered. I dropped my forehead into my palms. This conversation had gone from horrible to catastrophic. My friends were never going to live in quiet peace, even after they conquered their blood lust. After everything they'd been through, after a war and seven hundred years of waiting, the course of their lives could now possibly repeat itself. "Are we doomed, Leo? I mean, is this our fate? Are we destined to end up like Ratheus?" I asked, barely above a whisper.

The lines on Leo's forehead deepened as he frowned. "I'm not a fan of fate. It breeds concession—a nasty human weakness. Besides, there are clear differences between Ratheus and Earth, the biggest one being Sofie's magical blunder. Now, if they were parallel planets, on the other hand . . . " He took a haul on his pipe. "Doom would likely be the operative word."

"Right." *Earth is not Ratheus,* I repeated mentally, the reminder helping calm my racing heart. A tiny shred of hope, but something I desperately needed. If Caden could just hang on until Sofie released them, they could go into hiding, somewhere away from the Sentinel.

Even here. And if we could get Veronique out of their tomb, Viggo and Mortimer could leave New York, vanish from the radar. Then this Sentinel would have nothing to hunt. Or wouldn't they? I recalled Leo's words. "You said ninety-five percent of vampires. Not a hundred percent."

Leo winked.

"Ugh! Leo, you said no more secrets. There are more? I thought those three were it! Where are the other vampires and why don't they help?"

Leo tapped his finished pipe into an ashtray. "Viggo has made enemies. They won't come within a thousand miles of him."

"Surprise, surprise," I muttered.

Leo barked a laugh. "That's right. You're not the only one Viggo has screwed over."

"What'd he do?" Julian asked.

"Like I said before—Viggo was not the first vampire, but he's now the oldest."

"That means he killed off an older, more powerful vampire? Why?" Julian asked. "So he could be the oldest?" When Leo answered with a noncommittal shrug, Julian asked, "How?" Leo's head was shaking before he answered, his eyes widening momentarily, as if strained. Our barrage of questions was starting to annoy him. "I haven't the slightest clue. It took some extraordinary manipulation and acting on his part, I'm sure. But he is one devious creature." Leo stood with an exaggerated stretch. "Let's save the rest of this talk for another night. We'll have many of them yet. Max, you'll walk Evangeline upstairs?" Leo didn't wait for an answer, of course. He shuffled by, lightly patting my head. "Get some rest, Evangeline." He nodded once to Julian. "Night."

Julian nodded back, and his eyes followed the old man all the way to the stairs. We sat in silence in the great room, brooding over the possible end of the world.

Suddenly feeling the cold, I tugged my blanket up to wrap it around myself. I burrowed into the corner of the sectional and pulled my feet up so I was curled into a tiny ball, even then wishing I could just disappear. Julian, who had moved to sit beside me while talking to Leo, leaned back until he was half lying, half sitting and threw his own blanket over himself, but he didn't return to his corner of the couch. Yesterday's awkwardness had completely vanished between us, leaving us comfortable with one another. I rested my cheek on the cushion behind me and quietly studied Julian's profile as he stared ahead into the night, deep in thought. All traces of his scowl were gone. He was good-looking; *really* good-looking. And yet there were no sparks as I gazed at him now. Nor did I feel anything from him toward me, given his earlier proclamation that I wasn't his "type." Nothing hung between us and I was happy for that. *I wonder what Amelie would think of him?* I smiled to myself.

Julian turned to catch me smiling and frowned. "I didn't expect smiles after that news."

The reminder wiped any trace of happiness off my face. I shook my head. "I was just thinking about . . . something unimportant."

"Well, what are we going to do?" Julian asked.

There was that word—*we*. Not "you," but "we," as if he were joining me in this struggle, sharing in my fears and pain so I didn't need to bear them alone. I had another ally. "I don't know. You heard Leo. We can't do much here. We just have to hope the secrets remain hidden, that no one who could use this information against them finds out. And then when we get out of here, we find a new life. You're welcome to come with us. Sofie made sure I had lots of money." I wasn't going to tell him how much. That would just sound like bragging.

"Right." Julian snorted. "Live with a bunch of vampires? How exactly do you do that . . . " His voice drifted off as understanding slackened his face. "You're not going to . . . turn yourself into one of them? I mean, I guess that would make the most sense, but . . . " His tone betrayed his disapproval.

I shrugged noncommittally, as Leo had earlier, averting my eyes. I knew the answer. So did Julian. He didn't need me to say it.

He wouldn't let it go, though. "How can you even think of doing that? Choose to kill humans, to drink blood!"

A tremor ran through my body. "I don't want to think about any of that," I muttered.

"Well, you need to! You need to think about what kind of life that is!" He was no longer talking quietly but almost yelling. Max's head lifted, cobra-like, and he eyed a warning at Julian. "I'm sorry, Max," Julian said, lowering his voice as he addressed the dog—a strange thing to watch from a different perspective, "but she needs to think about what she's giving up before she goes and does something stupid!"

"It's not stupid!" I retorted, but my voice was unconvincing. Maybe Julian was right. Maybe it was stupid. Maybe it was downright insane. All I knew was that the idea of becoming one of them wasn't half as scary as the idea of losing all of them, an idea that had just come to life, thanks to Leo. I wasn't sure I could live as a vampire, but I was now one hundred percent positive that I couldn't live the rest of a human life without my vampire.

A touch on my calf made me look—Julian's hand on top of my blanket, patting my leg soothingly. "Please don't cry. I hate it when girls cry. My sister always cries. It'll be okay."

I hadn't noticed the tears streaming down my cheeks until now. I lifted my hand to rub them away, but Julian's thumb was already there, gently erasing one as it rolled down the bridge of my nose. "I just feel so . . . trapped."

Julian smirked. "Yes, I know the feeling."

Of course he did. His life had been irrevocably changed as well. He had lost his parents, he had by all accounts nearly frozen to death, he had listened to the same devastating possibilities as me. And yet here he was, trying to make me feel better. *Poor Julian. He's stuck in here with me—a sniveling, self-pitying crybaby.* Suddenly I felt foolish. There was nothing we could do about the outside world while we were here. Sofie would have things under control. She would protect Caden and the others. She would keep the peace. My only job was to stay sane until I did see Caden again.

"At least we're trapped here together." Julian gave my leg another pat. "It'll be alright, you'll see. Nothing will happen. No witches casting spells. No Sentinel attacks. Right now, boredom will be our worst enemy."

I nodded firm agreement. "You're right. We'll be fine." I swallowed the painful lump in my throat. *God, I hope you're right, Julian.*

I turned in soon after, craving the comfort of my pillow, and privacy, but I was far from sleep. My mind spun in ten different directions, replaying parts of the earlier conversation that I had forgotten until now. "Hey Max, what other nonhuman things are out there?" I asked as I crawled into my double bed. The sheets held the cold, even with a fire blazing in my hearth.

Oh, this and that. The bed creaked with the weight of Max's body as he leaned up against the frame.

"Stop being evasive, dog," I grumbled, knowing my reference to his original species would prick his ego.

I'm not. I'm protecting you from unimportant information that will unnecessarily frighten you. You sleep poorly as it is.

"Well, I want to know! I'm ordering you!"

Warm air puffed onto my face as Max snorted loudly. *On the grounds of protecting you and myself, I choose not grant your request.*

Max had figured out the loophole for denying my order; he was now basically pleading the Fifth. "Since when did dogs start following the Constitution?" I muttered. He answered with that funny grunting sound I recognized as dog laughter. With a huff, I rolled over to put my back to him, pulling the covers up over my ears to shut Max out. I spent the rest of the night trying to fall asleep. And failing.

5. TRANSFORMATION

"Thirty-two days, Sofie!" Mortimer groaned. "Thirty-two days, penned up in here." He waved his arms around the atrium, now an urban war zone, thanks to my temper tantrum. "How much more of this can we bear?"

Thirty-two days and counting since the day Evangeline had returned with an army of vampires. It felt like thirty-two years. I had done six more blood runs since the first, all at night, all uncoordinated, all old-fashioned thievery. The several trucks that had gone missing had made it to the news, only building on the speculation regarding the explosion and multiple deaths outside Reggie's Red Cross. I couldn't do much about it. Compelling and erasing paperwork took time and required the freedom to move about. I had neither. Not that it mattered anymore. That first run to Reggie had made it clear that the Sentinel was aware of us, and they had at least one witch—likely Ursula—helping them. They had to be wondering what was happening within these walls that would require so many trucks of blood. Maybe if we stayed in here long enough, they'd get bored, I thought sardonically. Fat chance. That group had lingered from generation to generation, passing on secret truths and missions, breeding hatred for us. They knew how to lie in wait.

Ileana was locked in the parlor, quietly working on her spell casting, Viggo driving her to exhaustion daily. I couldn't see what she was doing. The clever little witchling had learned how to mask her weaves well. But just having someone's magic so freely circulating through the building set my neck hairs on end. I could see it bothered Mage as well, showing daily in her strained features. But as long as Ileana caused no one any harm, she wasn't breaking the truce. Mage's diplomacy wouldn't allow her to kill the little girl out of personal displeasure.

For now, the Merth's powers still confined the vampires to the building, so things were okay. Tense, with a jealous and volatile Rachel lurking at Viggo and Mortimer's side, with me ignoring Caden and his friends while keeping watch twenty-four hours a day, but okay. They spent most of their time in the cellar, feeding nonstop. Mage seemed to think it was a good idea; that, if they could hold their resolve, feeding more would help them. It was counter to everything I knew, but I wanted so desperately to believe her that I readily supplied it as needed.

And they needed it. Again. I would be making another trip any night now—another random truck hijacking. The spontaneity was safer in one regard—it made it difficult for Viggo to execute any of his clandestine plans. Who knew what else he had up his sleeve? He had become so distrusting, so secretive, that even Mortimer appeared uneasy around him.

I recognized the soft footsteps approaching on my right as Mage's graceful glide without looking. We had spent much of the last thirty-two days together. I wasn't sure what was happening—were we becoming friends? Friends who openly declared their distrust for each other; who were prepared to strike the other dead for any reason. Yet a mutual, unspoken respect seemed to be growing—downright sinister for any other species and yet for us, a requirement. I hadn't had a friend in over a century, aside from Leo.

Our closeness was driving Viggo insane, I could tell—me allied with someone far superior to him, to the leader of a horde of dominant vampires. Several times, he stealthily slid a comment or question into conversation, fishing for information on Mage. He seemed determined to know about her lineage, where she sat in the pecking order. Was she the original vampire? The one whom the witches on Ratheus created just as the witches had created Earth's? For some reason beyond my understanding, it was important to him.

Mage remained civil but tight-lipped, divulging nothing. So now Viggo kept his distance. Mortimer and their snaky sidekick, Rachel, followed suit. I was fine with that.

"I think it may be time to time to test our venom," Mage stated.

Everywhere in the atrium, vampire ears perked up. Viggo and Mortimer, previously flanking the statue, suddenly appeared beside us.

"It's only been a month," I reiterated.

"Yes, but they've been feeding nonstop."

"On plastic bags. Bags don't run away." The chase of a warm, flowing body was as much the addiction as the end result. Just talking about it stirred excitement within me.

"We may find ourselves short on time soon," Mage said softly. Unlike me, she was convinced the Sentinel were already planning something big. "Wouldn't you like to know that this was all for something?"

I was secretly desperate to find out. I wanted to witness a transformation, something I had never done. But I wouldn't turn this place into a slaughterhouse. "How many people will we go through in trying?"

"Who cares!" Viggo exclaimed.

"I am capable of resisting the urges," Mage continued, ignoring Viggo as she typically did. "I will be the one to do it."

I caught a flicker of contempt in Viggo's eyes and couldn't help but pause for a vindictive little smile. But then I quickly brought myself back to reality. "And what about the others?" I retorted, my eyes roaming over the group of vampires listening to the conversation, their eyes wide with anticipation. Caden and his friends had resurfaced from the cellar and now stood off in a corner, as usual, listening without appearing to care too much about anything.

Mage turned an icy glare toward those milling around the ruined atrium. "They will listen."

So sure of her authority over them. Why? "And if they don't?"

She chuckled. "They will listen to me. And if they don't," her voice turned hard, "burn them."

℣

The dramatic gong of the doorbell announced that our guinea pig had arrived on time, ignorant that the invitation from Viggo was in fact his death sentence as a human.

"Now remember, none of you are to so much as step toward our guest," Mage called out in a stern schoolteacher-like voice, her eyes on the door. "And if you do, you will die where you stand."

A chorus of hisses and grunts rose from the cowering group, who likely feared that their lack of control would inadvertently get them torched. My eyes flicked over Caden and the others. *Please don't be the ones to test Mage's threat.*

The doorbell rang a second time. Our guinea pig was impatient. Reaching the exterior door as only I could, I punched in the code that only I knew. The door lock released and the door creaked open. "Good afternoon, Mr. Adesina." I shot one of my flashiest smiles at the towering Nigerian.

He peered over his sunglasses to appraise me from head to toe, intentionally keeping his expression indifferent. But I knew otherwise. Lewis Adesina—his first name wasn't really Lewis but that's what he went by—was very much interested in what this address had to offer him. Lewis was an astute businessman and a high-end drug dealer now residing in the wealthier part of Queens, looking for ways to expand his enterprise. He had piqued Viggo's interest years ago and Viggo kept tabs on him, silently channeling business his way, watching the man's wealth grow. That was how Viggo worked. He nurtured the up-and-coming, all while extorting pertinent information needed to swiftly clean out accounts—both local and offshore—once his subject amassed greater wealth. Doing this for two thousand years had garnered an obscene return on Viggo's investment and efforts. Lewis was now valued at somewhere around eight digits. He made the perfect victim.

"Right this way," I said warmly, gesturing down the tunnel.

He removed his trench coat and folded it over one arm of his custom-tailored navy pinstripe suit. "What's this about?" His eyes roamed the tunnel as we walked.

I chuckled. "Do you normally accept invitations to strange places with no idea why you're going?"

He threw a contemptuous glare my way. "When the address is Fifth Avenue, I'm willing to be surprised."

That earned another sadistic laugh. "Oh, you'll be surprised, alright."

Wariness edged into his aura. Not fear. Guys like this didn't scare easily.

But soon it would come.

Lewis nervously adjusted his draped coat and the sparkle of a diamond-encrusted watch caught my eye. I couldn't help myself. "So the meth business is quite profitable for you, I see."

Lewis pursed his lips and shot me a look of smug disapproval, but said nothing.

"It takes an exceptionally revolting kind of person to nurture fourteen-year-olds into addicts and prostitutes," I prodded, thoroughly enjoying the moment. It was like poking a cornered rabid raccoon with a long stick.

Lewis sneered. "I don't know who you are, lady, but don't mess with me . . . " His voice faded as we reached the gaping hole that opened onto the destroyed atrium. And his death. His eyes widened with surprise. "What the hell happened in here?"

"Someone messed with me," I answered flippantly. His deep laughter filled the tunnel. *He thinks I'm joking.* He lifted long legs over fallen bricks and followed me into the atrium. A new wave of his wariness filled my nostrils.

Mage was waiting. "Hello, Lewis."

I glanced to my left, where the others huddled in a far corner, shifting their weight from one foot to the other as they watched intently, their eyes morphing. It was as if they could sense the blood pumping through millions of vessels nearby, but they couldn't figure out how to get to it.

Lewis gave Mage the once- over, as he had done to me. "I'm a busy man. What can you do for me?" he answered, peering arrogantly from his greater height at the diminutive woman before him.

Her coal-black eyes lit up. "Oh, something very important. We can give you immortality." Mage smiled sweetly as she glided forward. "You're here to test our venom, so let's get started. I'm going to inject my venom into you and we'll see if you survive or not." Mage's announcement was so simple, it was as if she were explaining a basic dental procedure.

But Lewis wasn't distracted from her words "What the—"

Mage was instantly beside Lewis, her leg flying out to knock him to his knees, her dainty hand seizing his chin and effortlessly forcing his head back. Hideous, pulsating veins engulfed the whites of her eyes as she leaned forward—and sank her fangs into his neck.

A wave of terror hit me as Lewis's fear overwhelmed his aura, followed closely by the unpleasant scent of urine. He jerked wildly, attempting to fight off his tiny assailant. In response, Mage's left hand moved to his spine and twisted. I heard a sickening snap and his body slackened. There was no more fight from Lewis.

Mage took her time, slowly draining him of his blood. His face grew chalky, his eyes glassy. He would die if she didn't complete the process soon.

"Mage," I warned. Bloodshot irises rose and locked with mine. "The test," I reminded her in a slow, even voice.

She blinked. And then her lip curled slightly—a sign of the pain that came with the release of her venom.

Lewis Adesina's limp, unresponsive body dropped to lie in a heap on the ground as Mage retracted her fangs, finished. Now sated, her eyes quickly reverted back to their normal coal black as she called, "Someone—a towel, if you please?" Blood covered her chin and hands.

Neither Viggo, Mortimer, nor I moved, our focus riveted on Lewis. Luckily, whatever had kept the Ratheus vampires pinned in the corner no longer held them; Jonah instantly appeared beside her with a white cloth.

"Thank you, Jonah." She dabbed at her face. "It's been so long since I've changed a human . . . I forgot what it felt like." With a black high-heeled boot—one of Evangeline's that, though two sizes too big, I had grudgingly given her—she nudged Lewis in the ribs. A feeble moan escaped him but he remained motionless. Intrigued, I moved closer to inspect our test subject.

"Ah, that's right. Our Sofie is a virgin!"

I shot an annoyed glare at Viggo, who returned it with a smug grin. He was right, but he didn't need to announce it. I had never witnessed a transition and, having not experienced the typical method myself, I didn't know what to expect. Mortimer had described the stages to me once, about seventy years ago. If it worked as planned, Mage's venom was snaking through every vein in Lewis's body, spreading like wildfire to infect every inch of him . . .

Suddenly his body spasmed. Like a skittish cat, I jumped back several feet, earning a chorus of chuckles from the audience. I giggled nervously, embarrassed at being surprised so easily but also filled with exhilaration. Few things surprised me. I crouched and crept in slowly again. His eyes were still closed.

"It's beginning," Viggo whispered, pointing to a bead of sweat running down Lewis's forehead. Ten more beads followed in quick succession. Then, with another violent spasm, the half-digested contents of his stomach shot out of his mouth, barely missing me.

"Thanks for the heads-up," I muttered dryly, deciding to observe from a safe distance. Was it really working? *I wonder if* . . . With one eye on Mage, I plucked a magical helix and let it slowly float toward Lewis, ready to probe. Coal-black eyes flew to me instantly. She could see it! Would she say anything? Would she complain that I was going against the truce? The slightest nod and the shadow of a smile told me she wouldn't. It would be our little secret.

My magic invaded Lewis, burrowing through walls of tissue and muscle without reservation to reach his vital organs. Like microscopic probes, the strands found his kidneys, his liver, his heart, all shutting down, hardening into ornaments without purpose. I tested his body temperature. It was plummeting. I flashed the smallest smile back to Mage, my only indication to her that things were going as planned. One step closer . . .

For the next hour, a ring of vampires circled Lewis's corrupting body, watching the violent spasms and shivers with interest. An hour that felt like ten. The shivering finally stopped. The color began to return to his dark skin, bringing with it a more youthful, healthy look, wiping away blemishes and imperfections—subtly, the awkward bump on the bridge of his nose smoothed and his left nostril, wider than the right, evened out. It was mesmerizing, watching the birth of a true predator.

Lewis's eyelids suddenly flew open. Rich hazel irises rolled as he gazed around the atrium, studying the smallest movements and details. In a split second he was on his feet, taking in the audience who watched him as if he were a prize animal at a zoo.

Mage's venom had worked. We were no longer an endangered species.

"It worked!" Viggo whispered, echoing my thoughts. He gave Mortimer's shoulder a friendly slap. Normally Mortimer would shake it off, but today he was too busy sharing his rival's cheer to even notice.

Mage smiled triumphantly. "Satisfied?"

"Oh, immensely!" Viggo exclaimed. I had never seen him this genuinely giddy, ever.

"Good." Mage's hand shot forward. Loud gasps and cries erupted from the onlookers as it drilled into the vampire Lewis's chest and wrenched his heart out. His body dropped straight to the ground. She tossed the bloody, unbeating thing to the cobblestones beside me. "Sofie. Would you mind? We don't need another mouth to feed right now," she explained as I gaped at her, caught completely off guard.

I realized she was right—callous, but right. With a pull of a magical thread and a flick of my wrist, the former New York City drug lord and his detached heart were engulfed in flames. Every vampire, including Caden and his friends, scattered to the far corners of the atrium, leaving behind only a silence bred of fear and shock. For me, this was so much more than one new vampire. This was my one hundred and twenty-year-old blunder, finally corrected. This was the fear of spending the rest of eternity with Viggo and Mortimer breathing down my neck—gone. It wasn't over until I got that pendant off Evangeline's neck, but it was one enormous step closer. And when I got that pendant off . . . I could keep her.

For the past eighteen years, I had dreaded the day Evangeline's mortal human body withered and aged, the day I was forced to lower her into the ground—a mother's worst nightmare. But now, I could keep my sweet little girl with me forever. Once I figured out how to get that pendant off her, she was free to become one of us. And as long as Caden survived, I knew there was nothing she'd want more.

Mortimer's booming voice disrupted my reverie. "Do you know what this means?" His tone was heading in a direction I knew very well: fury. He moved to tower over me. "Veronique could be released right here—right now!"

"If it meant Evangeline wouldn't die then yes, that's what it would mean," I answered coolly, meeting his glare. "But that's not possible and so you will wait."

He wasn't backing down. "You can't keep us within these walls forever."

"Oh, but I can," I answered with cold certainty.

"You have to give in soon," Viggo's voice joined Mortimer's like an echo. "You can't protect everyone all the time." His calculating eyes flitted toward Caden, who only glared back. "Accidents happen."

He's planning something and it involves Caden dying. My stomach tightened. The very idea terrified me. "Give in?" I repeated, feeling my lips stretch into a malicious smile. I would not allow him the satisfaction of rattling me. "Never," I hissed.

"We'll see," Viggo sang, pulling out his cell phone. "Until then, I have some money to move . . . Ileana!" he bellowed, heading toward the library.

ᆺ

The grandfather clock gonged once. *One a.m.* "Where are you, Caden?" I whispered, wandering aimlessly, the size of this palace more daunting than usual. Since Viggo's overt threat earlier today, I was especially vigilant in knowing the whereabouts of Evangeline's friends at all times.

Viggo would have to be insane to do something to Caden or the others, I reminded myself. He needed me to get out of this building. He needed me to free Veronique. If he killed Caden, he was as good as dead. He realized that, didn't he?

The truth was, I suspected Viggo was in fact insane. And now I couldn't find Caden. Not in the cellar. Not in Evangeline's room. Not in the atrium.

I wove in and out of rooms, stumbling upon Ratheus vampires everywhere as they inspected technology, rooted through closets, soaked in Jacuzzis, or otherwise distracted themselves with luxuries long since lost to them. It had taken almost a month of constant feeding, but finally they had ventured out to other parts of the building besides the cellar and the atrium, their thirst somewhat sated. Now most lingered in the inner rooms, keeping as far away from the paralyzing Merth boundary as possible. I was fine with that.

I pushed open the solid mahogany door leading into Leo's quarters, a large room decorated with eighteenth century masculine flair. It sparked renewed frustration. I hadn't talked to him since Viggo's witch showed up a month ago. I had no idea how Evangeline was doing and it was driving me nuts. But at least I knew she was safe from this mess.

Leo's room was empty. I turned to leave . . . and froze, my eyes noticing a pair of man's black dress shoes poking out from the edge of the bed. A nauseating wave of déjà vu washed over me and I had to grab hold of the door frame for support. *Please, no . . .*

I ran and dove over the bed, coming face to face with flat, death-filled eyes. But not jade eyes. Not Caden's eyes. They belonged to one of the other Ratheus vampires. A small sigh of relief escaped me. Only a small one, though, because I now had a new problem, I realized.

Rolling off the bed, I squatted beside the male vampire and spotted two gaping holes in his neck where fangs had entered.

Murdered by his own kind. His own kind, who was now a mutant.

"Why would someone do that with all this human bl . . . " my words drifted off.

To escape.

Oh, God. A mutant running loose in New York! Could it be? Had it gotten out yet?

Eyes wide with panic, I bolted out of Leo's suite. How could I stop it? Where would it make its escape? *Oh, God. I don't know what to do.* Overwhelmed by desperation, I did the only thing I could think of. "Mage!" I called out in a harsh whisper, hoping it wouldn't attract Viggo or Mortimer's attention. None of the Ratheus vampires would come—they seemed happy to keep their distance from their Council leader after witnessing her ruthlessly ending Lewis's life.

No response. "Mage!" I called, a little louder.

"Yes?"

I whirled, teetering slightly as I lost my balance. I never lost my balance. Mage frowned as I stumbled. Jerking my chin toward Leo's room, I grabbed her arm and led her to the body, afraid that any words would be overheard.

I watched the fire of rage alight in Mage's black eyes as she stared at the body. "Jonah. He's behind this," she whispered hoarsely, adding, "I was afraid of this!"

"What? Why? Jonah's already a mutant," I said, confused. "He can already get out and you promised he wouldn't try!"

"No, he wouldn't defy me on his own. But if he could coerce a group to join him—"

"A group?" A new wave of panic hit me. "You mean there may be more mutants?"

"There most certainly are," Mage answered. Her voice held no room for doubt.

"I have to find Caden." What if someone targeted Caden? Or the others? Now it wasn't just Viggo after him. It could be anyone!

"They're in the theater," Mage said. "Go find them and bring them back. We need all the help we can get. I'll check around the building to see if there are any more bodies. I hope we can stop them before they escape." I nodded, glad that Mage had swiftly and expertly taken control of the dilemma. She crouched down and shoved the body under the bed. "We'd better keep this under wraps for now. Who knows what Viggo and Mortimer will do when they find out."

I knew. It would set them over the edge. It would be an excuse to break the truce, a way to force me to drop the Merth wall. Viggo would blame me for all this. He would punish me. He would attack.

I had to get to Evangeline's friends before anyone else did.

I ran for the theater, bursting through the heavy black doors to see a curly blond head in the front row, giggling hysterically at the comedy on the screen. Three others flanked her. "Oh, thank God!" I exclaimed.

All four were instantly up and facing me, their eyes wide with concern. "Sofie! We're not supposed to be talking to each other!" Amelie whispered. It was the first time she had spoken directly to me.

I took a deep, calming breath. "We have a problem."

CR

The icy breeze of a chilly December night caressed my cheek as I stood in the third floor room, staring at the gaping window. The wrought iron grill had served as nothing more than a minor inconvenience; the two center bars had been torn free.

The mutants had escaped.

"How many?" I asked, my voice hollow.

Beside me, Mage let out a heavy sigh. "Five."

Five bloodthirsty, hideous mutants running loose in New York City. "What a disaster," I moaned, rubbing my temples with my fingertips as if soothing a headache. If a vampire could actually develop a headache, this nightmare would certainly cause one. "I should have killed him when I had the chance." I shot a reproachful glare at Mage.

"I agree. This is my fault. Jonah's allegiance to me over the years was unwavering, which is why I protected him. But now . . . I'm sorry."

Sorry wasn't going to cut it. I threw my hand toward their escape route. "But now I have to go out there and hunt down five mutants before they wreak havoc on the city. Before the Sentinel finds out about them!" I was practically yelling now. "How the hell am I going to do that?"

"Get me past the Merth and I'll help you," Mage answered calmly.

I snorted. "Are you nuts? I'm not letting you out there!"

"You don't have much choice, Sofie," Caden murmured from his spot in the corner, where he'd been quietly observing our exchange. All four of Evangeline's friends were there, their backs against the far interior wall as if lined up for a firing squad, their faces a row of grief-stricken masks.

"I think I have proven that I can control myself." Mage folded her arms over her chest, her expression turning icy, eyes as dark as night holding mine. "Get me past these walls and I'll help you. You have my word."

"And what value is your word, exactly?"

Rage froze her face. "It is binding and unbreakable."

I believed her. Instantly. And that terrified me. In the month that I had known her, she had exuded nothing but integrity. And I wasn't easily fooled. Not like my naïve, sweet Evangeline, who would approach a mewing lion caught in a trap. But still, to let Mage out . . .

"You can't take on five mutants, Sofie," Mage added softly. "You will fail. And you will die."

And then none of you would see the outside of these walls and Veronique will sit in her tomb forever. She was right. Even with my magic, I'd be an idiot to think I could take on five desperate mutants, born from vampires each at least seven hundred years old. I had no choice. I had to take her with me.

I opened my mouth, about to concede, when the door suddenly flew open. I turned. *Great. Stalker Barbie,* I thought as Rachel stormed in.

"Quite the party in here!" Rachel exclaimed, tossing lush, jet-black hair over her shoulder. Her citrine eyes drifted over Amelie and Caden, oozing raw hatred as they touched her former lover. "Viggo will be happy to know you're conspiring together. Breaking the truce—"

Fabulous. Another volcanic mess to clean up.

Luckily, the gaping window distracted her from spinning on her heels and running to tattle. She hesitantly stepped toward it, careful not to cross into the Merth perimeter. "I knew that bastard would get out eventually," she muttered.

Was I the only one surprised by this?

"Rachel," Mage began, stepping slowly toward the volatile vampiress, her head cocked innocently. "You should take a seat over there. Relax for a bit. Viggo has you working too hard." Mage pointed to the red and burgundy-striped chair in the far corner. The one within the Merth boundary.

I studied Rachel's pinched face, expecting to see her throw her head back, waiting for the cackle to fill the room. Instead, Rachel's eyes drifted over toward the chair as if contemplating the idea. I watched her take a dozen steps forward—directly into the Merth. She dropped to the carpeted floor to lie in a heap, like a wet towel.

Dead silence followed as five vampires gaped at Rachel's still body, shocked. Five vampires gaped. Not six, I noticed as I looked over to see Mage eyeing me guardedly. She wasn't shocked that Rachel had taken her suggestion. She had expected it.

A strangled gasp escaped me, the answer suddenly so obvious. There was only one reason why Rachel would do something so stupid. She had been compelled. *Compelling a vampire! That's unheard of!* "My, someone's been keeping secrets after all, haven't they?" I hissed, shifting my stance, suddenly on the defensive.

Mage's mouth twisted. "I didn't tell you because you wouldn't trust me."

"No shit," I spat.

"Didn't tell her what?" someone asked from the corner, either Bishop or Caden; I couldn't tell. It didn't matter. My attention was glued to the treacherous vampire who had just turned more deadly in the blink of an eye.

Mage answered with an exasperated groan. "We don't have time for this. Viggo and Mortimer could be following any second—"

"Well then, you can just compel them into the Merth as well, can't you!" Gasps of comprehension came from the others. My eyes remained locked on Mage's. "So they don't know what you're capable of." *Interesting.*

Mage pressed her lips together. "We're wasting time."

I crossed my arms over my chest and planted my feet firmly to the floor. I wouldn't get another chance to force the truth out of Mage. It was now or never.

She exhaled in annoyance. "There are things I can do that no other vampire can. It's because I am the first one. The vampire created by the Fates."

"Things like what, exactly?" I pressed, silently muzzling my shock over her admission.

"Well, I can see and sense magic. You already know that, though." There was that crooked little smile again. "I can also compel vampires." Her black eyes roamed over to the others as they stifled exclamations. "I don't do it often, though. I prefer not to."

"No, you can't," Bishop said confidently, as if calling her bluff.

As a response, Mage waved her hand toward Rachel. It quashed further rebuttal.

"How could we not know this?" Fiona asked. Close beside Bishop, she clung tightly to his biceps.

Mage smiled again. "That's part of the magic. You can't feel it. It's not like a human coming out of a daze. You feel perfectly normal. You feel as if the idea is yours. It's a different type of compulsion. It's more like I'm . . . originating . . . an idea in your head. One that becomes yours that you can't possibly ignore. You have no idea that it's actually mine."

All five of us shuddered in unison.

"So all this time . . . " I wracked my memory of the last month, searching for anything I had done out of character, choices I had made that may have been planted by Mage.

Mage was already vigorously shaking her head. "No. I stayed out of your head."

"Bull!" the retort flew out of my mouth faster than even I had intended.

"I did!" Mage insisted. "Partly because it's harder to influence a cross-breed such as yourself and Jonah. Partly because I knew you'd never trust me if I did."

"And you think I'm going to trust you now?" I snorted mockingly.

"It doesn't matter now."

"How does you being able to insert thoughts into our head not matter?" Caden interjected before I could ask, his tone low, threatening. To say no one in the room was happy would be an understatement.

"Because . . . " Mage paused, resignation settling on her face. She wasn't used to divulging her secrets and it was clear she didn't enjoy doing it. "Once you're aware of what I can do, it's no longer possible for me to do it without you seeing it for what it is, rendering it useless."

Did I believe her? I wasn't sure . . .

Mage smiled. "Why do you think Viggo has been so anxious to find out if I'm the original vampire? He knows what the original vampire can do."

It made sense . . . Viggo evaded any questions I had about the first vampire, including what had happened to her. *That sneaky bastard.* He knew what Mage might be able to do to me and he didn't warn me! I'd pay him back for that one.

"Speaking of Viggo," Mage pressed, "we need to get going. Now. Before this mess gets any bigger than it already is."

As usual, Mage was right. There were bigger issues to deal with for now. We both turned to stare at the window. My attention couldn't help but drift over to Rachel lying on the floor. "You know I could leave you in limbo, caught within the Merth's hold. Powerless," I murmured.

"Yes, you could. But you won't. You're not an idiot. You realize having me as an ally is a better position to be in than otherwise," Mage answered without missing a beat.

Check mark. Another right answer, Mage. "Fine." I glanced back at Evangeline's friends. Viggo could stumble on this at any moment, as Rachel had. If they duked it out, one of them would die. I couldn't risk it, I decided. *I guess it's time to test out your blood theory, Mage.* "We're all going."

CR

"If I so much as think you're getting out of line, I'll instantly have you bound and gagged with magic," I warned the five vampires standing in a row behind me, dressed head to toe in black to blend into the night like cat burglars. Purpose and exhilaration shone in their vibrant eyes. And fear. Such an uncommon emotion for a vampire, but we were all acutely aware of the consequences if we failed. Mage and I more so, given we knew the real truth behind Ratheus. I'd have to tell the rest of them eventually. Now was not the time.

"We'll be fine!" Bishop assured me, waving away my concern. "Let's go! I'm ready to kill some mutants."

"I hope that's all we kill," Fiona muttered from his left side, not nearly as confident as her partner.

I glanced back at Caden and Amelie. "We're good, honest!" Amelie exclaimed with a nervous smile. Caden attempted a reassuring grin but it came out looking like a grimace. No one was sure of this—except Mage. She seemed to hold confidence in them. They had been feeding nonstop for weeks now, gorging on enough blood to last most new vampires a year, at least, and that paralyzing lust that first consumed them did seem to be slowly vanishing. Now I glimpsed Amelie's bubbly personality, Bishop and Fiona's affectionate nuzzles, Caden's gentle smile—the vampires Evangeline had fallen in love with. It was heartening to see what I thought forever gone now suddenly here and real. But could they handle what lay outside these walls?

Impatient, I glanced at my watch. *Only a few hours until the city comes to life.* The darkness would help hide the mutants. But with the sunrise . . . We needed to stop them. Tonight.

"How long before Mortimer and Viggo discover this window?" Mage asked.

I shrugged. "Soon. Or never." They rarely toured the building. But now, with others wandering about, it was going to be hard to hide. "They will notice we're gone as soon as they decide to go looking for us. Let's get out before they start looking. Okay . . . you guys ready?" I asked Caden and his friends, feeling oddly elated. Hunting did that to me.

"Hell, yeah!" Bishop grinned boyishly.

"Yeah!" Amelie cheered, earning a groan from Caden.

"We're not going clubbing, Amelie!"

Her plump lips turned down in a pout. "I know. It's just . . . "

Caden wrapped his arm around her shoulders and gave her an affectionate squeeze, smiling wickedly. He would be happy to see Jonah dead. Their pasts held a secret, I was sure of it.

I stepped to the edge of the Merth boundary. Rachel lay unmoving on the tiles nearby. *Exactly how I should have left you from the beginning.* I glanced back at Mage. She nodded and moved to stand beside me. Like two amiable women, we clasped hands and stepped forward.

A prickling sensation like a thousand tiny electric shocks instantly permeated my skin as I entered the Merth barrier. It wasn't comfortable, but I knew it was nothing near the agony Mage was feeling right now. Like razor blades cutting into skin—that's how they all described it.

The power of the Merth overwhelmed Mage's body and it slackened and crumpled to the floor. I looked down at her frail little body. I could leave her here. It was a once in an eternity chance, and for a short second, I considered rolling the powerful, manipulative vampire over to lie beside Rachel. She'd never have the chance to insert anything into my head again.

Instead, I leaned forward and grabbed hold of her slender waist, heaved her up, and tossed her tiny body over my shoulder. I stepped onto the window ledge and paused, inspecting the dark alley below for any witnesses. None. Thankfully the mutants hadn't busted out of a room facing onto Fifth Avenue.

At three storeys up, it was a long way down. For a human.

I jumped.

The heels of my boots cracked against the pavement beside a dumpster, the impact jarring my knees. Almost immediately, Mage was fully functional, pushing free of my grasp to stand beside me. She smoothed her black, mock turtleneck sweater. "Thank you for not stabbing me in the back."

Despite myself, I grinned. "Anytime."

Her eyes scanned the dark alley. "No bodies here. Good start."

"Okay, wait right here. I have to get the others." I hesitated. I had just unleashed a five thousand-year-old vampire with unique powers upon New York City and was about to leave her unchaperoned.

Mage rolled her eyes, such an uncharacteristic act for her. "Stop wasting time!"

I nodded once, then scaled the wall to get Evangeline's friends.

True to her word, Mage didn't abandon me while I transported the others down. Soon they stood with me in the dark alley, the ability to satisfy their insatiable thirst lying open ahead of them. No Merth held them back; nothing kept them from bolting. And yet each stood frozen in place. In control.

Fat snowflakes began floating from the sky to speckle our clothes and hair. The temperature was dropping rapidly. It was December, after all; almost Christmas. It would have been beautiful, if not for the situation. But at least the streets would be relatively quiet.

"Okay, so now what?" Amelie whispered, her large, emerald-green eyes widening as a late-night reveler passed the entrance to the alley.

"If you'd just escaped prison and were looking for fresh blood, where would you go?" Caden asked.

Great question. I began walking toward the street, the five of them trailing me like shadows in a V-pattern. I stopped when we reached the sidewalk and scanned the vicinity, analyzing every structure, every object, every movement. Across from us stretched Central Park. The trees along the edge were lined with thousands of twinkling lights to mark the holiday season but beyond them, the heart of the park was vast, shadowy, and concealed. The perfect place for a massacre. Would there be one there tonight? There had already been one small massacre in Central Park recently, the day Ursula and the Sentinel attacked Evangeline.

My stomach instantly twisted into knots, remembering the day I almost lost her. Had it not been for Max, I would have. I was busy appeasing Viggo and Mortimer, toiling with my magical weaves to give the illusion that I was trying to solve Evangeline's next steps on Ratheus. I wasn't doing that. I already knew the answer to that. I was busy trying to dismantle the entire spell when the normally obedient girl hoodwinked Leo, turned Max's allegiance, and snuck out.

Would Central Park appeal to the mutants? Every direction one turned was crawling with fresh, warm blood. Did the mutants have the sense to hide their faces? I pricked my ears, listening for the bloodcurdling screams I expected to come from any human encountering those demonic white eyes. Nothing. That was a good sign. But it wouldn't last long.

"Let me try something," I murmured, calling on my magic for a spell weave I had discovered in my regular witch years. It was the result of a moment of madness, after I'd accused Nathan of cheating on me because he refused to convert me. He had taken off in a huff. In a fit of fear-filled rage, I'd concocted a tracker spell and used it to find him in the woods nearby, feeding on a coyote. I wasn't sure if it would work on mutants, but it was worth a shot.

I stepped back into the alley, not wanting to attract attention. Gathering a hundred helixes together, I held my hands out in front of me. The tiny purple coils appeared between my fingers for all to see. I began weaving them together in an intricate figure eight pattern until both sides were perfectly symmetrical. *There. Now for something to track.* To find Nathan, I had used his scent as the target—easy, because his scent lived on everything I owned. But now I had no scent to track the mutants. An idea struck me.

"Quick. I need blood," I called out. Mage's hand was there in an instant, a sharp piece of metal in her other hand. "On the links. Lots of it." She ran the jagged edge across her wrist without flinching, opening up a wide gash. Blood streamed out onto the magical links, saturating them before her wrist naturally healed over. "That's good. Thanks." I hoped it would work, given I had used vampire blood instead of human. There was a chance the links would pick up on regular human-to-human violence in the city. Still, it was the best option. I broke the figure eight in half, flinging one bloody, glowing half outward.

"Wow," Fiona and Amelie murmured in unison, watching it float away. The guys were busy surveying the streets, Caden with his arms folded tightly over his chest and Bishop with his hands deep in his pockets, rocking back and forth. Both looked anxious but completely in control. This was a good sign.

"It's a tracker," I explained. "Not exactly subtle, but anyone out at this time will be too drunk or high to be suspicious." *Unless they recognize magic.* My eyes shifted nervously to the trees across the street, watching for movement within the shadows. The foliage had long-since disappeared into a mass of blackness—perfect cover.

"Pretty, isn't it?" Mage observed, interrupting my paranoia. "Should you make a couple more, just in case?"

I nodded. A regular sorceress would be foolish to use her magic in this way, knowing she was going into battle. It took a significant amount of magical reserves. But I had more than enough helixes floating around my body. I went to work, sending two more tracker links out within seconds to do our bidding. "There. When the links find fresh blood, they send back a message to their sister-half."

"So, now what?" Mage asked, hawk-like eyes surveying the street.

I drew the three links from my hand around my wrist. To anyone without a clue, they looked like purple glow-in-the-dark bracelets, the kind teenagers wore to raves. Except they were covered in blood. "Now we wait."

Approaching heels clicked against the sidewalk. We all turned to see a young woman in a long dark trench coat and woven red beret hurry past, her furtive eyes glancing down the alley to see six people staring back. She sped up, casting a worried glance over her shoulder at us. That was the worst thing a person could do with a group of vampires behind her. I shifted my weight, ready to ground them with magical ropes if necessary. But they remained still, Amelie admiring the woman's leather boots. Not even one vein pulsated in their eyes. I began to relax. Maybe Mage was right . . .

Bright purple light began flashing in the alley. I looked down at the helix links. One's identical twin had found fresh blood; it was pulling me to the right. "Come," I hissed, magical bolts of fire ready at my fingertips as I set off at a brisk pace. The streets were nearly empty at this hour. *Thank God.* We passed ten people in the first block. Each time, my attention bounced from the passerby's face and hands— looking for signs of a Sentinel spy—to the five vampires traveling with me, assessing everyone's level of control. Each time, Mage turned to meet my gaze, to assure me, "They'll be fine." It wasn't much, but it was the support I needed.

As if we'd walked into a solid wall, all six of us suddenly stopped, hit with the pungent scent of freshly spilled blood. Both Amelie and Fiona let out cries of pain, the crushing urge to feed catching them unprepared. Caden and Bishop each threw their hands out to grab them by their shoulders.

"I'm okay!" Amelie cried, though her emerald-green eyes were morphing. I checked all of their eyes. They had all morphed, but none were quite so full of veins as before. That was a good sign. It meant they had some level of control.

I moved ahead, hugging the wall so closely that my shoulder grazed the bricks, gaining distance from the others as they hung back. The link was pulling me to an alley ahead. What would I find there? Jonah and his posse of mutants? No; trapping and disposing of them all in an alley would be too easy. I slowed to a creep, edging forward until I could peek around the corner into the darkness. No mutants, from what I could see. Two fire sparks instantly ignited at my fingertips, though. I wasn't taking any chances.

Caden and Bishop came up and flanked either side of the alley. With boyish, commando-like signals, they waved me through.

"How about we stay on guard out here," Mage suggested, her arms linked through Fiona and Amelie's.

I nodded and entered the alley alone, heading toward the dumpster in the back corner. My stomach sank as I spotted a trail of red leather, torn and bloodied. It led to the far side of the dumpster, to a pair of long, pale, female legs, lying in a pool of blood. Evangeline's precious face flooded my mind then, paralyzing me for a moment. I forced myself to continue to the other end of the dumpster and looked down. My teeth clenched so tightly, I thought they would crack.

There could be no doubt: this was the work of newborn mutants.

By the silky material around the woman's thighs, I could tell she had been out enjoying New York's nightlife. Her last night out. From what I could see of her face, she looked young, no more than eighteen. My heart instantly swelled for her parents. This girl was someone's Evangeline.

Mage suddenly appeared beside me to observe the body, but only lasted a second before turning around and stalking to the other side of the alley, the blood no doubt the cause of that. "We need to keep moving," she said through tight lips, adding, "fast. If anyone finds that . . . " She didn't need to finish. I knew what would happen. It would make front page news.

I sighed, then muttered, "We can't leave her here." We couldn't have this much attention this close to Viggo and Mortimer's place. The Sentinel would certainly put two and two together, if they hadn't already.

"Then you had better do something, and quick. They're likely still traveling in a pack. They wouldn't think to do otherwise right now. But soon enough, they'll scatter."

And then we'd have five mutants heading in five different directions. I brushed away the giant snowflake that had landed on my nose as I weighed my options. I couldn't burn the body; the smoke and flames would draw too much notice. And cloaking spells were temporary. I didn't have time to weave the spell that would mask the evidence properly. Those kinds of spells took more time than we had. I looked at the dumpster. A very unimaginative, human way of disposing of a body.

"I'm sorry for this," I whispered, throwing open the top of the large green bin. Delicately, careful not to soil my clothes—I enjoyed blood as much as the next vampire, but I didn't enjoy bathing in it—I hoisted the body up and tossed her in, rubbing my hands to get all evidence of blood off afterward. There. At least when she was discovered, it would take time to trace her back to here. I assessed the blood pool on the pavement. Perhaps I could lift it all—

The second link on my wrist began flashing brilliantly. *More fresh blood.* The third one went off immediately after. *A lot of fresh blood.* All thoughts of this crime scene vanished, driven out by fear of what lay ahead. I ran to the others.

"Where to now?" Mage asked, faint red lines still marring her almond-shaped eyes.

"This way. Quick," I ordered.

We followed the pull of the links for thirteen blocks, ending up in another alley, in front of a gray steel door, where the scent of blood infused the air. My tongue curled, the coppery taste filling my mouth. I turned to see five sets of eager eyes. "Whatever is behind this door could be hard to handle," I warned.

Fiona and Amelie clasped hands. "We're ready this time," Amelie said with stoic conviction.

Caden reached out to grasp the handle. "It's locked." With a nod to me, he swung his long leg at the door. It caved in with a loud creak, the frame twisting so badly that the door simply fell over. We stepped down a set of stairs and into a dank concrete hallway. The weak fluorescent bulbs shook violently with each beat of the music pounding in the underground club ahead. They illuminated four large, mangled male bodies sprawled on the dirty concrete, their freshly spilled blood splattered along the walls like abstract art. Their size identified them as the bouncers. The mutants had carved through them effortlessly.

"Keep moving!" I shouted, grabbing hold of Fiona and leading the way to a second set of doors at the end of the hall. I looked over my shoulder to find the rest following, struggling but somehow bypassing the bloodied bodies, Caden with steely eyes and a hand hooked around his sister's arm.

Swallowing the lump forming in my throat, I listened intently at the doors. I heard no screams, no moans, just hammering music. What would we find on the other side, a mass killing ground? These late-night parties held hundreds, if not thousands of young people. Thousands of fast-beating hearts pumping fresh, warm blood through millions of veins—could the mutants control themselves?

I squeezed the metal door handle. The door popped open, the previously muffled music now exploding through the crack as I peered inside—at a sea of moving, gyrating bodies. I breathed a sigh of relief. No mass killing here. Yet. It was a late-night rave in the giant, low-ceilinged basement of a building, complete with a smoke machine, kaleidoscopic light show, and a dense crowd of wasted revelers. The perfect plucking ground for a hungry vampire.

The six of us quickly slipped through the entrance. Bishop closed the door behind him, bending the door frame to jam it so no one could exit through that doorway and find the bouncers' bodies. I spent a few moments scanning the crowd for our repulsive targets but soon realized it would be impossible to find them while standing here, even with our abilities.

"We need to split up," Caden yelled, echoing my thoughts.

Mage gestured to Bishop and Fiona and pointed to the right. Caden and Amelie followed me as I headed along the left perimeter.

"See? We are going clubbing after all!" Amelie chirped as we wove through the edge of the crowd. I couldn't help but smile.

The place reeked of sweat, booze, and vomit but no one seemed to care; all were too engrossed in bumping and turning into each other. As a human teenager growing up in nineteenth-century France, my nights had consisted of reading books by kerosene lamp and the occasional ball or late evening picnic—nothing like this. I'd quite happily kept Evangeline away from this scene, not wanting her exposed to deadly drugs. Ironic, really, given all the other deadly things she was now exposed to, thanks to me.

A young girl of no more than seventeen, dressed in a tight, microscopic white dress, suddenly flew out of the crowd to throw her arms around Caden. "You are the most beautiful thing I've ever laid eyes on!" she shouted, her voice slurred.

Caden smiled politely while gently extricating himself from her arms. "I'm flattered, but I already have someone."

Unwilling to take no for an answer, the girl leapt at him. I think she tried to lay a kiss on his mouth but, in her drunken state, missed and buried her face in his shoulder instead. A tiny hand reached out and grabbed a handful of the girl's long, straight brown hair. "He said he's taken. Back off!" Amelie yelled. With a flick of her delicate wrist, she sent the girl flying backward into the crowd; she took several revelers down like dominoes as she plowed into them.

"Come on!" I grabbed them both and pulled them ahead of me, hoping to get away before a fight broke out. Only ten feet away, we passed a group of young men leaning against the wall, and I sensed their despicable intentions as their eyes appraised Amelie and me. I recognized their type immediately—they would lure a woman into a quiet location to have their way with her. Normally, I'd respond by batting my eyes—I enjoyed baiting my meal. But not tonight. Tonight I needed to deal with five other vile creatures, and it wasn't for pleasure. It was for survival.

Amelie read their lewd intentions as well and, unfortunately, she wasn't as focused. Lunging at one of the men, she easily pinned him up against the wall and bared her teeth in a snarl. Caden yanked her off before she could take a chunk out of the guy's neck; before anyone could see her eyes morph.

"Amelie!" I barked, pushing her forward. "We don't have time for this! I'll put you on a leash if you don't behave."

"Sorry," she muttered with a sheepish smile, her irises quickly reverting to their girlish green. We continued along the perimeter of the room, Caden now with one hand firmly locked on his feisty sister's shoulder.

My own eyes roamed the crowd, searching in vain for any sign of the mutants. Happily, there hadn't been an attack yet. They were showing restraint. But I knew they were here. There was no way they could pass up a thriving scene like this.

We passed a young blonde man and my eyes locked with his as he attempted a covert look-over while taking a drink. It was enough for me to catch the small mark on his hand—a deformed cross. The Sentinel were here, too. *They must be watching us. Too coincidental to be otherwise. Great.* Well, as long as they remained watchful and nothing more, we would have no trouble with them tonight. I continued shifting through the crowd, marking the Sentinel's location for future reference.

And then I spotted them—two people hunched over in the shadows of a dark corner, their black hoodies pulled up to conceal their faces. But their eyes couldn't be hidden. Demonic white eyes peered out from the darkness, delightedly studying the crowds, scouting their next victims. Mutants. There were only two, though. Where were the other three? I grabbed Caden's arm. "To your left. By the speakers." Caden's eyes quickly zoned in and his body jerked forward to attack. I squeezed his arm, stopping him. "If the others see us, they'll escape. We need to find them all first."

"I'll watch from here," Amelie offered, her eyes shifting over to the group of lewd guys by the wall.

"Amelie!" I warned sternly.

"I know, don't kill them," she drawled, rolling her eyes like a petulant teenager.

With that, Caden and I slid through the crowd toward the mutants, separating as we got closer and surveying the area around them for the others.

I was perhaps twenty feet away when the first waves of magic hit me. Someone was casting a spell. I searched the crowd for the source, and immediately locked eyes with Mage as she pushed her way toward me. Her panicked expression told me she could feel it too. "We have to get out of here," I mouthed to her. She jerked her chin toward the nearest exit. I nodded, and turned to locate Caden and Amelie.

I came face to face with cloudy irises. A man stood two feet away, average-looking and on the smaller side, staring at me with empty, dead eyes—not dazed as if compelled; dead.

I turned in a full circle, seeing the others closing in, encircling us— eight zombie-like men in total. I watched with odd fascination as three hands floated up to seize my shoulders and arm. The instant their fingers made contact, I felt it—magic, oozing out of them. No emotions. No intentions. Magic. They were under a witch spell. What kind, I had no idea. Something hypnotic and very powerful.

I reached up and picked off one of the hands, quickly scanning it for markings before I dropped it. No Sentinel cross. These were just plain old humans under the spell of a witch, obviously intent on getting to me. It had to be Ursula.

I twisted and shook my body to toss the other two hands off me. I began moving forward, trying to push through the circle. The man directly in front of me reached toward the back pocket of his jeans. His hand returned, brandishing a knife. I couldn't help it, I laughed. What did that idiot Ursula think a knife would do?

I prepared for the zombie's clumsy lunge, one I could easily outmaneuver. Only it didn't come. Instead, he turned the blade toward his own wrist and slid it across his flesh. Just as Mage had done earlier. Blood immediately poured out—fresh human blood. *Ursula's trying to get me to attack, cause a scene, reveal myself for what I am.* My control was too strong for that. But there were ten vampires in here who could not say the same.

"No!" I screamed, sensing someone rushing in from my left— Amelie, unprepared for the sudden rush of fresh blood. Caden was immediately behind her, and gripped her in a headlock to restrain her. Her arms flailed wildly, her clawed hands scratching the air as she screamed in frustration.

The crowd was moving back as people sensed the commotion, saw the man's wrist, the blood. If we could just get out of here . . . The glint of a new blade caught the corner of my eye. I turned to see the other zombies brandishing knives as well. With quick, intentional movements, seven more wrists were opened. The overpowering scent of blood hit me like a blow to the face. And then a shrill scream cut through the deafening music.

On the other side of the zombie circle, Bishop was holding back an equally ferocious Fiona. By the pained expression on his face, he was fighting his own urge. He wouldn't be able to hold himself off much longer. We had to contain this mess now.

And just like that, it was too late. Four mutants dove into the circle before me, the fresh blood luring them. They attacked the bleeding men like hungry wolves, tearing and slashing with their teeth and hands. Drunk and stoned patrons stampeded toward the various exits, crawling, pushing, and screaming the entire way. Most couldn't know what was happening, what with the strobe lights still pulsating and the music still pounding, the effects challenging their eyes and ears. But their human instincts told them to run and so they ran. Pandemonium had officially broken out.

Mage stepped in behind two of the mutants, too distracted by their victims to notice her. Her hands reached toward their backs, and their bodies arched, then toppled to the ground, leaving Mage with fists full of bloody hearts. Quick and definitive. Purposeful, that was Mage. Throwing the mutant hearts to the ground by my feet, she swiftly dispatched the other two mutants, equally engrossed and oblivious to what was happening. She tossed their hearts to join the others then, looking up at me, mouthed the order, "Burn it all."

So much for a covert operation. But it needed to be done. All of this evidence needed to disappear without delay. Pushing Caden and Amelie back, I pulled forward a few dozen helixes and wove a fire spell, one hot enough to incinerate bones. I blasted the pile of bodies—both mutant and zombie. In seconds, nothing but ash remained.

A vast, empty basement now surrounded us, the music and lights still playing but no humans left. Caden and Bishop had their arms wrapped around the girls, who had calmed considerably. Everyone observed the bonfire with faces filled with quiet worry.

The music suddenly cut off, and I turned to see Mage stepping away from the speakers, still gripping torn power cords. "Jonah wasn't here," she announced. One mutant was still loose. Better than four, but still. He was free to roam New York City, to be noticed. "Did you see the witch?" Mage asked me. "I couldn't find her anywhere."

I shook my head. I had assumed it was Ursula before, but something about this told me it was bigger than a jealous witch out to get me. Whoever it was, they were clearly intent on revealing vampires to the world. "It's time we got back home," I said. *Home.* What a strange term for our Fifth Avenue vampire asylum. But it was the safest place for us to be right now. We needed to strategize. We needed an escape plan. And it was time everyone learned the truth about Ratheus.

6. WEREWOLVES AND THE POSSESSED

"Are you trying to melt the snow with your super-powered stare?" Julian asked in a bored tone, his chin resting on his palm while he studied the game board on the small table between us. His other hand rolled a chess piece back and forth between its fingers.

"If I am, I suck at it," I grumbled. The snow may actually have gotten deeper in the five hours since I'd sat down in this chair, even with the hot sun beaming down on it. It felt sauna-hot when it streamed in through the bay window of the great room, but out in the midst of the mountains in the dead of winter, it was still probably deathly cold. I didn't know for sure, though. I hadn't stepped outside in . . . forever, it seemed. "It's Monday, right? Oh, wait—no. It's . . . Tuesday?" I could feel my brows pulling together in frustration as I realized I didn't even know what day it was anymore.

"Tuesday, I think," Julian murmured absently, his focus on his next move.

Saturday, Max called from his resting place in a sun spot beside the table.

"Saturday?" I echoed, feeling my eyes bug out as I did the math. That meant a month had passed since Sofie exiled us here. A month with no communication with the outer world, whether through normal human means or otherwise. A month of wondering if my vampires still lived. I assumed they did, but I couldn't shake that ominous feeling in the back of my mind that they were doomed, a belief that made me want to curl up in a cocoon and hibernate for the next several years.

That belief had also turned me into a wretched cabin mate. I didn't realize it until I hit rock bottom two weeks ago. Each night, Julian and I took turns picking out the movies to watch and it had been my night to pick. When I rhymed off *Old Yeller*, *The Perfect Storm*, and *Steel Magnolias*, Julian finally lost it. He grabbed the hard drive and flung it across the room, then threatened to provoke Max into killing him because he couldn't stand being trapped in this wooden hut with "Sulky Evie" for one more day.

Of course Max was on his feet and ready to oblige Julian just for the fact that he had raised his voice to me, but I quickly stopped the beast, realizing that I had become that whiny, miserable girl that I loathed. The girl whom I somehow had avoided becoming after my mother's death, when I barely existed because everyone had been compelled to ignore me. Even after I found out about the curse, my optimism held. But here, exiled in the mountains and worrying about Caden and my friends, I had finally broken. Now someone would rather die than be near me.

After that night, I tucked the pictures I had so desperately clung to into my nightstand, only to be pulled out for emergencies. I made a conscious effort to force all thoughts of Ratheus and vampires out of my head—I tried, anyway. It was impossible. Jade eyes and springy blonde curls crept into my thoughts with every silent moment, and there were a lot of those, in exile.

"I'm going to go nuts," I murmured, more to myself than anyone else. Rubbing my eyes, I turned away from the blinding glare of the sun reflecting off the snow to look at Julian.

Brown eyes glanced up at me before dropping back to the game board. "You and me both," he mumbled as he moved a piece—I wasn't paying attention to which one. "Your turn."

In the month since Leo brought the disagreeable Forero son back from death, he and I had become what some might call best friends, whether we liked it or not. We ate our meals together, we watched movies together, we swapped books when the other was finished. We did everything together that didn't require privacy. Sometimes we didn't even bother "retiring" to our rooms, as Leo called it, but instead slept buried under blankets on either end of the sectional couch, finding comfort in each other's presence. Those were the nights when the feelings of isolation were especially strong. I guess I didn't feel quite as alone with Julian around. Sure, I was never really alone with a three hundred pound werebeast glued to my heels, ready to protect and serve, but having Julian around was different. There was a soothing aspect to it. That was the word to describe being around Julian: soothing.

Every once in a while, I'd find myself studying Julian's face—usually while he dozed on the couch—wondering if I'd be this comfortable with him in different circumstances. If I'd talk so casually, laugh so freely, if I were sitting across from that face back in the real world, where we weren't orphans and exiled by vampires; where I wasn't pining over a jade-eyed Caden. With those full lips, olive skin, and chocolate-colored eyes, Julian was one of those guys a girl like me would probably fall hard for. But I hadn't, thankfully. It would just complicate an already thorny situation, especially since it'd be one-sided. *You're not my type,* he had said. That was for the best. Right now, I just needed a good human friend.

And so my new bestie and I sat in this chalet, day in and day out, looking for ways to occupy ourselves. The task was becoming more challenging with each sunrise. Our latest activity was chess. Julian had discovered a game board in one of the storage closets two days ago, and offered to teach me how to play. It quickly became obvious that chess wasn't my game.

"Can I move the horse over here?" I asked.

"The knight?" he corrected me. "Yes, you can move him there . . . if you want to lose this game."

My hand jumped away from the piece with his warning. I spent the next few minutes reevaluating my options while Julian took a turn staring vacantly out the window, deep in thought. "I wonder what summer's going to be like here," he murmured.

"Pretty. Long." It was my turn to sound bored.

"And then another winter," Julian continued, his tone flat.

"And don't forget spring and fall in between."

I glanced up to find him looking at me, defeat in his eyes. "Long," he agreed.

I lifted my finger to my temple and made a circular motion. "I'm warning you . . . cuckoo!"

Julian gave me a crooked smile. "Take bets on who loses it first, you or me?"

I grinned. "Maybe Leo?"

Julian shook his head, chuckling, his deep dimples appearing. "No way. Not Davy Crocket." Of all of us, Leo actually seemed to thrive here. Perhaps it was because he didn't have to answer to Viggo's demands at all hours of the day and night.

"Right. He's rock-solid," I said, thinking of the others. "Maybe Valentina?" My hand immediately to my mouth. "Sorry."

Julian's face turned solemn at the mention of his sister, who might already be nuts. We had seen little of her since arriving. She spent most of her time secluded in her room, her door barricaded with a chair. For protection, she said. I don't think she did much else but sleep, based on her head of matted hair. Every once in a while she'd come out to get some icy air or grab a bite to eat. Or stare at me with those big, chocolate-brown eyes, long since transformed from innocent into something wild and calculating. I always smiled politely but otherwise I kept my distance.

I'm going to go crazy listening to you two jabber on, Max grumbled, rising to sit on his haunches. Max was not enjoying his time in the wilderness, much to my surprise. He said it was because there wasn't a lot to hunt, this far up in the mountains. It meant traveling a bit, which meant leaving me for at least a day, a proposition he shunned immediately, even with the other dogs here as backup. As a result, he was starving and beyond ornery. Two weeks ago, his snark had reached unbearable proportions. I lost my patience, banishing him as I had the night he found Julian. He'd sullenly ventured beyond his comfort zone and stumbled upon a musk deer. When Max came back later that night, he was a much happier werebeast.

That was two weeks ago. Crabby Max was making a comeback. I said nothing, shooting a dirty look at the dog while I reached for my next chess piece. I shifted it over a few squares.

My move earned an exasperated sigh from Julian. "Do you intentionally go against every rule of this game?" he said.

"Sorry." It was the seventh or eighth time I had done something stupid. I slid the piece back.

Move your queen over two squares, Max instructed, his massive head now hovering over the board.

Great. Even the dog knew how to play. With a casual look at Julian—not that there was any reason since he couldn't hear Max—I followed instructions. I knew I was cheating, but I'd take that over looking like a complete idiot.

Julian's hand shifted to cover his mouth, where it sat for a long moment. When he reached forward to his piece, I caught the devious smile. "Checkmate. And there's no way you can get out."

Oh, thank God it's finally over! Can we please do something else now?

I'd rather have my fur set on fire than watch you play chess.

I gasped, my brow furrowing in shock as comprehension hit me. "You sneaky mutt! You tricked me!"

Julian looked back and forth between Max and I and then, realizing what happened, exploded in laughter. "You're taking chess lessons from the dog?"

Max snarled with displeasure at the dog comment but Julian didn't even bat an eye as he reached out to give the werebeast's forehead a rub. Since Max had saved his life, Julian was no longer the least bit apprehensive.

I held my scowl for a few seconds longer, but then I was laughing as well. Soon the two of us were borderline hysterical.

"What's so funny?" An annoyed, high-pitched voice called. We turned to see a puffy-eyed, sallow-skinned Valentina strolling into the room.

"Don't worry. Some people aren't meant to play chess," Julian said as our laughter quickly died down. "My sister couldn't win a game if her life depended on it," he added in a low voice to me before turning back to take in her disheveled appearance. He frowned deeply. "Are you feeling okay?"

"Of course," she mumbled as she wandered past us to the dining table, her arms swinging lazily at her sides. She grabbed a freshly baked croissant from a plate, folded it up, and shoved it into her mouth as I imagined a starving savage would. Flakes spilled from her lips to scatter on the floor.

I glanced back to see Julian gaping at his sister. She also noticed she had an audience. "What're you looking at?" she snapped. When neither of us answered, she strolled toward us.

What's the over/under on her insanity again? Max asked. I ignored him, my back tensing as she neared.

"Ugh. Chess . . . who's white, you?" Those wild eyes rolled over my face. I nodded, adding a grimace. She looked at the board for a moment as if analyzing it. "You should have moved your bishop there. You could have forced him to move his rook and then . . . " she named several other steps I didn't understand, ending with, "and then you would have won."

"Oh . . . thanks." I glanced at Julian to see shock. Hadn't he just finished saying she had no idea how to play?

Leo's voice drifted into the room from the back hall. "Take those boxes to Evangeline's room."

The property keeper with the white-blonde hair—Yeti One, Julian and I called him—marched into the room in snowy boots, arms laden with large, unmarked cardboard boxes. Leo trailed him.

"What are those, Leo?" I peered curiously at the boxes.

"Oh, some clothes and things for you. We had a delivery this morning."

Valentina whirled, her body going rigid. "Delivery?"

Leo's mouth curved into a tight-lipped smile. "We're not completely abandoned out here. Sofie made arrangements for regular provisions. Didn't you guys hear the helicopter come in?"

"No! Why didn't you tell us?" Valentina shrieked.

Leo's amusement quickly faded, replaced with a scowl of irritation. "I just did."

"When's the next one?" Valentina demanded.

Another smirk stretched across Leo's face. "Getting cagey?" The smirk vanished just as quickly. "It's a one-way delivery. No one leaves."

Something harsh flashed in Valentina's eyes—rage? She bit down on her bottom lip as if to stop herself from speaking. I couldn't blame her for her reaction. Everyone was getting cagey.

Yeti Two came in then, pulling in a wooden crate on a dolly. "To the cellar with that," Leo instructed. He turned to Julian and me, ignoring Valentina, and announced in a cheery voice, "That should do us until spring!"

"The helicopter's not coming back until spring?" Valentina cried. Her hands flew up to cover her face, and the sleeve of her blue shirt slid down her arm, exposing a red, festering gash on her forearm. The same place she'd been injured a month ago, on that first day here.

I gasped. "Valentina! Your arm!"

Her hand flew to tug her sleeve back down before the others could catch a glimpse, and she threw a scowl in my direction.

"What's the matter with your arm?" Leo asked slowly.

"Nothing."

"Nothing?" I exclaimed. "It's infected, Valentina! Leo can help you. Show him!"

Her jaw set. "No, I'm fine."

Julian, visibly worried, raised his hands in a soothing gesture. "Leo's alright, Valentina," he said, his tone calm. "He helped me. He can fix whatever—"

"No one is touching me!" she shrieked, her eyes crazed. "No one!"

I traded a look with Julian and Max before turning to Leo, to find him staring at the distraught Colombian girl. His face was unreadable. Finally he seemed to decide on something, because he shrugged. "Fine, one less person to feed soon."

My jaw dropped. "Leo!" I exclaimed.

Leo turned to us and winked. *Oh, thank God. He's kidding.* "Why don't you two get out for some fresh air? It's a balmy day compared to the last couple weeks. There are snowshoes in the front closet."

Julian and I glanced out the window and shivered in unison. It was true, the sunshine looked inviting, but . . .

"Out!" Leo shooed us with his hands. "You guys have been cooped up for too long. The fresh air will do your minds good. I don't need a bunch of deranged young folk in here with me!"

"You know, that's not a bad idea, old man," Julian piped up, eyes twinkling at his playful dig at Leo.

"That's why it came from me, little boy." Leo's riposte earned a smirk from Julian. "Max, go with them. Keep them out of trouble. The rest of you," he looked at the three other werebeasts, "I have need of here."

"You should come with us, Valentina," I suggested, earning disapproving glares from Julian and Leo.

Luckily Valentina wasn't interested. She answered with an exaggerated yawn, her arms reaching out behind her as if stretching. "I think I'll just stay here."

"Suit yourself!" Julian pushed his chair out and jumped up, no doubt wanting to escape before she changed her mind. "Come on, Evangeline."

"Enjoy the day. Dinner won't be ready for several hours, so . . . don't rush back," Leo said. There was a strange look in his eyes when he glanced at me.

"Is something wrong, Leo?" I asked, noticing his hesitation. My stomach suddenly churned—had he received bad news from Sofie and didn't know how to tell me?

He chuckled softly, as I imagined a grandfather would. "Oh, nothing at all. I haven't heard from Sofie, if that's what you're thinking. This cabin is just getting the better of all of us."

No . . . there was something more. I caught another flash of something strange in his eyes. Resolve . . . acceptance . . . what was it? I had no idea, but I knew I could threaten to pull the stubborn old man's teeth out and still not get any hints, so I didn't press. I headed up to my room to dress in a hundred layers.

℘

This way, Max instructed, trudging effortlessly through the deep snow as he wove confidently through the trees. Every so often his back would brush against a snow-covered branch, sending clumps of the white stuff cascading down and releasing the fresh, crisp scent of evergreen into the air. He seemed to know where he was going. I, on the other hand, had no clue. Every direction looked exactly the same: trees, snow, and rocky peaks, stretching as far as the eye could see.

Leo had been right. Swathed in long johns, layers of wool and fleece, and arctic outerwear, I found it almost pleasant outside. I could feel my nose hairs freezing together, but I was actually breaking a sweat as I trekked behind Max in my first pair of snowshoes.

"I've never done this before," Julian said, echoing my thoughts.

"You're doing really well."

"Thanks. So are you," he offered.

"Thanks! It's fun. A lot more fun than chess." I threw a mischievous grin over my shoulder at him. The sudden movement threw me off balance. Arms and poles waving, I toppled over to land butt-first in an ungraceful heap in a deep snowbank.

Julian doubled over in laughter. "I stand corrected."

Thank God I didn't take you the other way. You'd have ended up going over a cliff, Max muttered.

"Wouldn't be the first time, Max," I said, the memory of stepping off the cliff in Ratheus and being saved by Caden stirring an ache in my heart. But that was then and I was here now. I couldn't dwell on the past or I'd get pulled back into that dark place. I shook the memory away, giggling over my clumsiness instead.

Julian's laughter suddenly stopped. I looked up to see his brown eyes locked on something behind me, his face drained of all color. I followed his gaze toward a giant white wolf standing not twenty feet away, its beady eyes shifting between Julian and I. It made no movement. It simply watched, not the least bit bothered by us or the werebeast accompanying us. I couldn't say the same for Julian or myself.

"Max!" I hissed, my eyes glued to the wolf, terror paralyzing my body. I may as well have been trussed up on a buffet table and slathered with sauce, stuck in this snowbank. I couldn't believe my super-powered werebeast hadn't noticed a wolf slinking up behind us! "There's a wolf over there!"

Yeah, so? Max answered, his tone flip.

"So, kill it!"

If I kill it, then who will cut our firewood?

Who's going to . . . I screwed my face up in confusion. "What?"

"What's he saying?" Julian whispered, trying not to move his lips, his eyes still glued to the motionless wolf.

"I don't . . . " Frozen with fright, my brain struggled to make sense of Max's words and his lack of reaction to the giant wolf. *The wolf doesn't cut our firewood. The Yetis cut our firewood . . . Why would it matter to our firewood if we killed a wolf? It doesn't make . . .* Comprehension suddenly slapped me in the face. I gasped, studying the wolf's fur more closely. It matched Yeti One's hair color.

Finally. You're a little slow today, Max murmured, clearly enjoying this.

"What? Tell me!" Julian hissed, frustrated.

I normally always reiterated what Max said to Julian, so he didn't feel like an outsider. But this time I didn't answer, instead turning back to Max. "What is he?"

Oh, that's your run-of-the-mill werewolf, he answered dryly.

We had werewolves living with us? "Why didn't you tell me?"

There was a pause. *You didn't ask.*

I groaned my exasperation. "Max, why would I ask if people are werewolves?"

Well, maybe you should.

"Arggh, Max!" I cried, grabbing a handful of snow and throwing it at Max's head as hard as I could. I missed. "Stop keeping secrets!"

"Werewolves?" Julian whispered.

I turned back to see that the wolf had taken off. "That was Yeti One," I explained to Julian, adding bitterly, "Max forgot to mention that he's a werewolf."

I didn't forget. You just—

"Right!" I snapped, throwing my hands in the air. "I forgot to ask!"

"Great. Witches and vampires aren't bad enough. Now we're exiled with werewolves," Julian muttered.

I wasn't ready to let it go. "So, who else do we have here, Max? Who else have I *forgotten* to ask about? Is our Russian cook a unicorn? What about the others? Any of them moonlighting as a succubus or a shifter?" My anger with Max was at its highest peak now.

No. Don't be—

"No! Seriously!" I yelled at him, not caring that me screaming at this giant, menacing beast might concern an onlooker. "What about Valentina? Maybe she's . . . Ursula!"

"Who's Ursula?" Julian asked.

"Oh, no one." I shook my head, waving my hand dismissively. "I'm just being stupid. I—"

Max's murmur cut me off. *I don't believe it . . .*

I sighed impatiently. "What don't you believe now, Max?"

There was a long pause. *How could we have missed it!*

Max was rattled—such an uncommon thing that it sent shockwaves of panic through to my core. "Missed what, Max?" I asked evenly.

I have to warn him, Max muttered. *Stay here. Stay away from the cabin until you hear from me again!* Max raced past us and disappeared, galloping through the deep snow toward the chalet.

"What? Warn who?" I said aloud, replaying my last words to Max. I had made that insane suggestion about—I gasped, and threw my hands up toward Julian. "Help me!"

Julian had me on my feet in seconds. "What's going on?"

"I don't know," I answered abruptly, setting off toward the cabin. It couldn't be true . . . but if it was, then Leo was in danger.

"Yes, you do. You know something!" Julian pushed.

"No time to explain!" I called back, now several feet ahead of him. "We have to get back." The truth was, I couldn't explain this to Julian until I knew if it was true. How could I tell him his sister was—no, not until I knew it was true. How had she found us?

Thankfully Julian stopped asking and caught up to me. Walking in snowshoes was easy; running was impossible. I settled on speed-walking. By the time we got back to the chalet five minutes later—the longest five minutes of my life—I was panting.

The side door into the great room hung limply off its hinges, the victim of a giant werebeast's impatience. "I guess our werewolf will be fixing that?" Julian commented as we shook off our snowshoes. Julian carefully pushed open the broken door and held it for me to pass through.

We entered a war zone. Everywhere my eyes landed, they touched destruction. The antler chandelier once suspended over the dining table now sat in a broken pile on the floor beside my feet. Every piece of furniture was upturned, legs broken, torn material oozing stuffing. The fireplace looked as if someone had blown chunks of stone from it with a cannon. And the windows—every one on the far side of the room was smashed, leaving a deadly minefield of shattered glass to navigate through. Frigid air poured in.

All of that became irrelevant as soon as I saw Leo lying on the floor, a wide gash on his forehead making a bloody mess of his face. Valentina towered over him, her stance defensive. The dogs stood unmoving, watching her from various points in the room. *Get out of here, now!* Max screamed inside my head.

"No!" I cried, panic pinching my voice.

Julian stepped inside. "What the . . . " He fell silent as he took in the destruction.

"Julian," Leo called weakly, struggling to rise. "Get her out of here. Run!"

Valentina's foot landed on Leo's chest, shoving him back to the floor. A wicked smile touched her lips as she gazed down at the old man.

"Val! What the hell is going on? What are you doing?" Julian cried. When she didn't acknowledge her brother, he screamed, "Valentina!"

Her head whipped around to regard him curiously. "Oh, right." She smiled. "I guess I go by that name too." She turned and took two steps toward us, her icy gaze landing on me. "Though if you want my attention, you're better off using my real name. Ursula."

I felt my back hit Julian's chest as I stumbled backward.

"She's gone mad," he whispered.

"Not exactly," I whispered back, trembling. "That's not Valentina anymore."

Ursula responded with a throaty laugh.

Clever witch, Max said. *She was ready for us.* He still hadn't moved from his position. None of the dogs had. Surprising. I figured they would have quartered her by now.

"It was exhausting, using my powers and cutting my arm every day for the spell to mask my identity from those canines." She looked down to Leo and gave his ribs another forceful nudge. "And this relic."

Max had sensed it all along. He had sensed something "off" about her, but he couldn't figure out what it was. And I had chastised him for being unkind.

"And thank God this young little thing decided to come into that garden when she did!" Ursula gestured to her body. "I may have had to do housework here if I ended up in one of those maids' bodies."

I gasped at that revelation, remembering when Valentina had stumbled, that first day in the atrium. That hadn't been an innocent stumble; that was Ursula infesting her body! Ursula had been with us from the very beginning.

"Who's Ursula?" Julian whispered, his tone somber; he realized we were in real danger.

"A bad person," I whispered back, none too quietly.

Another throaty laugh. "I'm not so bad, once you get to know me. Sofie has filled your head with lies. That's what she does."

Run, Evangeline, Max warned again.

I locked eyes with my canine protector. *Do something!* I silently pleaded.

"He can't help you," Ursula said. "None of them can move. I've made sure of that."

"What do you want?"

Ursula chuckled. "Many things. For one, I want out of this godforsaken hellhole, and this bastard won't give me any clues as to how and when I can do that." She kicked him again, earning a groan.

"Please stop doing that," I pleaded, tears welling up in my eyes.

She continued on as if I hadn't spoken. "And then I want to see the pain and suffering in Sofie's ugly green eyes when she watches me kill you."

My breath caught in my lungs. I barely felt Julian's hand settle on my shoulder.

Evangeline, run—both of you. Get as far away as quickly as possible. She'll need to break her spell to stop you and then we'll have her. Run.

"Get behind me." Julian's voice was barely audible.

All we had to do was run and this would all be over. I shifted my weight.

"Stop!" The shrill scream froze me in my tracks. "Try to leave here, and this place goes up in flames. Everyone dies. Not as poetic as my original plan, but . . . " her lips curled into a bitter smile, "Sofie will suffer, all the same."

Everyone would die because of me. I couldn't have that.

I gave Max my best "what now?" look, wishing I could communicate telepathically to him.

I guess she's smarter than I gave her credit for. An exaggerated sigh followed. *There's one other way . . . Throw something at her.*

What? My confusion must have played across my face, because he continued.

Injure her, and whatever spell she cast will break. Witches can't hold their spells when they're attacked. I'll reach her before she can recast. I hesitated. *Look at Leo! He's too hurt to use his magic to protect himself! Hurry!*

My eyes darted to my gravely injured guardian. His eyes were now closed. Was he dead? Desperation washed over me. I scanned the area nearby for objects, and my eyes settled on a jagged antler by my feet. If I could impale her with the sharp end . . . Taking a deep breath and summoning every last ounce of courage, I psyched myself for the drop and the precise throw I'd need to execute, one I doubted I could do with accuracy. I tensed, preparing for the dive—

And went sailing away from my target to land several feet off to the side, broken glass crunching under my weight. I was now level with Leo, lying only ten feet away from me. I glanced back to see Julian charging toward Ursula, a jagged piece of the chandelier held out in front of him.

Her eyes widened in surprise, then immediately narrowed. With a quick glance down at the unconscious Leo, she decided something. Her hand lifted toward Julian, her lips moving.

Oh, shit! Max moaned. *Tell him to throw it. Now!*

"Throw it!" I shrieked, echoing Max's command. From the corner of my eye, I saw Leo's lids flash open, his eyes now bright, alert. His lips were moving quickly but I couldn't hear him over the sound of rushing blood in my ears.

Julian roared as he swung his arm back to launch the antlers at her—just as a purple light shot out from Ursula's outstretched hand, heading straight for his chest.

I stopped breathing altogether and squeezed my eyes closed,

waiting. Expecting the shriek of pain, the thump of a body hitting the floor.

Instead, I heard a drumbeat.

7. AND SO IT BEGINS

"Do you feel that?" Mage hissed as the six of us made record time back to our Fifth Avenue base, distancing ourselves from the ring of suspicious ashes and incoherent babbling of rave attendees at the underground club. It would certainly make the news later today.

I did feel it; it was impossible to miss. An awesome amount of magic was being channeled somewhere nearby, more than anything one witch could summon. It only strengthened my concern that this went beyond Ursula's meddling. "I don't know what they're planning, but we need to get inside now, and scaling the wall with each of you will take too much time." Everyone nodded their agreement. With that, we headed straight for the main door.

Getting back into Viggo and Mortimer's fortress was easy. I punched in the code—Evangeline's birthday in two different formats—and ran in, Mage's limp body draped over my shoulder. I didn't give a second's consideration to leaving her within the Merth this time. We had bigger issues than a vampire with magical abilities.

Mage was alert and dropped to her feet as soon as I stepped into the atrium. We found Viggo and Mortimer in their customary warding positions on either side of Veronique, but their normally controlled expressions gave way to shock as they watched us enter from the outside. It was such a rare sight. "What the . . . ." Mortimer began.

"Hold on a sec," I called, already on my way out.

In seconds I had Evangeline's friends safely inside. It took only that long for Viggo and Mortimer's shock to disappear. Now they wore glares that could have incinerated me, if they had any sorcerer magic in them.

"In private?" Mage suggested before Mortimer could explode. She accentuated the suggestion with a pointed stare at the horde of Ratheus vampires surrounding us.

The anger slid from Viggo's face immediately, replaced by a fake grin and a polite gesture toward the library door. "Certainly. Right this way . . ."

Mortimer uttered not a single word. He spun on his heels, jaw visibly clenched, and grabbed the elbow of a sickly-looking Ileana as he passed her. The six of us trailed behind them into the library, Mage shutting the French doors behind us.

Viggo turned to the witch. "A sound barrier, if you would be so kind, Illie?"

I caught the fleeting wince, likely due to Viggo's nickname, but she nodded and quietly went about casting the common spell. I watched Mage's eyes follow the purple-hued bubble as it expanded to reach the outer walls of the room. *I can't wait to sit down and learn about that vampire's uncanny sense for magic!* It was beyond annoying.

Only after Ileana nodded to Viggo did Mortimer react. I knew it was coming; I expected it—yet the vicious blow that instantly shattered my jaw caught me off guard all the same. The crushing pain dropped me to one knee where I remained, waiting for my bones to mend themselves. Five seconds later I was on my feet again, throwing a catty response at him. "Haven't you heard it's not nice to hit ladies?" I couldn't help it, though I knew I was only throwing fuel on already roaring flames.

"Lady," Mortimer grated through clenched teeth, "you belong in Hell."

"I have to agree with you on that one," Viggo murmured, his back to us as he gazed at Veronique's painting above the mantel. He turned, the fireplace poker gripped casually in his hand. He lifted it up to show a glowing point, as if it had sat within the flames.

"What are you going to do, Viggo? Brand me?" I joked, trying to defuse whatever panicked reaction he was hoping to get from me.

"What would be the point of that? You heal too fast and you're tough as nails, you old hag," he retorted with a condescending smile. Instead he grabbed Ileana by the back of the neck and pulled her close. Without pause, he pressed the poker to her cheek. The smell of burning flesh curled everyone's nostrils up in disgust. The young witchling's eyes began to tear up and she let out a howl of pain. "Quiet, now! You are here to be our eyes and ears, Illie. Your one task is to watch that devil woman over there. And yet somehow she managed to escape, unnoticed. And with five vampires! What do you have to say for yourself?"

Tears streamed down her cheek as she tried to muffle her screams. Finally her knees buckled from the pain. Viggo kept her on her feet.

"It wasn't her fault," I said. "You had her busy trying to break spells she can't break."

A wicked smile touched Viggo's lips. "You're right, Sofie. It was your fault. Much like every problem around here is. But—" With a flick of his wrist, Viggo forced Ileana's face to turn. He shifted the poker to her other cheek. "Since you obviously take some sort of masochistic pleasure in being beaten, I thought punishing someone else would be more effective."

"Please!" Ileana managed to sputter between sobs.

I glanced over at Mortimer to see him staring at Veronique's face, as if he couldn't hear Ileana's pained cries—or he was blocking them out. He was good at that. I was not. I so desperately wanted to level Viggo with my magic, but now was not the time to start a physical battle with him.

"When you're finished your pathetic display of dominance, we'd like to discuss the impending war outside," Mage said, her normally serene voice carrying a cutting edge. Her words made Viggo release his grip on Ileana's chin. She tumbled to the hardwood floor, her hair falling forward to hide the burned flesh marring both her cheeks.

"What are you talking about?" Mortimer asked, his tone doubtful. "My spies have said nothing about any signs of an army."

"Your spies are probably the Sentinel, working undercover to feed you lies," Mage spat.

Mortimer snorted. "Do you think I'm stupid? I checked their hands. No tattoos."

She cackled. "Did you check their entire bodies?"

"No, why would I?" Mortimer's face twisted with doubt. "They tattoo their hands. That's what they do. That's what they've always done."

Mage offered him a condescending smirk. "Near the end, before the war on Ratheus, we discovered they began marking their kind elsewhere on their bodies, so they could act as double agents with the vampires."

I turned to stare at her. *You neglected to tell me that, Mage.* That meant those eight suicidal zombies in the club could in fact have been the Sentinel.

She continued without batting an eye at me. "The witches would break the vampire compulsion spells and cast their own to protect the spies, so they couldn't give anything up if caught and interrogated."

"Well, that's your world, not ours."

"Are you so sure?" Mage taunted, smug in knowing what neither of them knew; what none of Evangeline's friends, standing quietly behind me, knew.

"What does she mean?" Mortimer asked slowly. "Sofie?"

I shrugged. *Let them chew on that.*

"Sofie?" Amelie's raspy voice called. I turned to see four sets of confused, scared eyes staring back at me. "What does she mean?"

I sighed, not so content with leaving them hanging. I looked to Mage. With a nod, Mage explained the seer and how she'd single-handedly retrained every vampire remaining into believing that the world they lived in was called Ratheus and not Earth. Six sets of wide, disbelieving eyes bored into Mage by the time she was finished. I didn't know how they would react.

Mage did, though, so she was prepared when Viggo attacked. In a split second, the two of them squared off against each other, Mage's hand firmly on the poker that Viggo had intended to drive directly through her skull. She laughed. "Don't worry, your suspicion was enough to protect you from being compelled—I've already tried." Viggo sneered. "Believe me, I can't!" Mage exclaimed in mock innocence. "If I could, you'd be lying in the Merth spell next to Rachel by now. I'm curious, though . . . do I look nothing like the original vampire from this Earth?"

Viggo's mouth twisted as he decided what to say. "No, I can't say you do."

So he knew the original, after all . . .

She released her grip on the poker and stepped away, unworried that Viggo might take another swing. "I don't think any vampire has ever disgusted me as much as you have. Bravo. Fine effort." Keeping her black eyes locked on Viggo, she said over her shoulder to me, "Explain to me again why this one needs to remain. Because unless there is a good reason, I'd very much like to be done with his melodrama."

Mortimer quietly observed the scene, clearly as unaware of Mage's abilities as I was, and likely wondering the same thing I had—had Mage influenced his thoughts?

Amelie and the others were unfazed by the power struggle, still in shock over Mage's confession. "It can't be! Everything I remember . . . " Fiona murmured.

"Is what I planted in each and every one of your heads," Mage answered softly. "I've met you all before. You just don't remember."

"So . . . we're going to end up back in the same kind of world?" Bishop asked, his voice full of grief.

"Not yet," I said, mustering as much confidence as I could and turning to regard Caden, who had his eyes trained on the floor.

"We wouldn't have come, had we known," he whispered distantly.

I reached out to rest a gentle hand on his forearm. "It doesn't matter. What matters is that we need to get out of here. Now," I stated.

"As soon as we get that damn pendant, we can run as far away as possible!" Mortimer boomed.

"Veronique will be fine. No one is getting to her," I assured him calmly, letting go of Caden.

"She can't be moved?" Mage whispered.

I shook my head. "No. That spell is bound to its location." I turned to Viggo. "As much as I'd love to leave you two here to rot, there is a war brewing outside." I gave them the rundown of what had happened, beginning with the mutants and going all the way to the force outside. "We need to regroup somewhere else until we can get a handle on what we're up against."

"All of us?" Amelie asked. "Even the others out there?"

"No." Mage's answer came quickly and firmly. "I can only compel them against killing humans for so long, and they don't have the resolution you four do."

"So . . . " Amelie prompted. Everyone looked at Mage.

"So, we leave them here."

To starve. They wouldn't die; they'd slowly wither to stationary lumps of flesh, too weak to lift their heads.

The room went silent as we each thought through the plan. Was it a good plan? I had no idea. At this point, running was the only option. "Okay, let's—" I began, but Leo's voice cut into my thoughts. *Valentina is Ursula. She's with the tribe now.* The connection died immediately, as if someone had taken a knife to it. "No!" I exclaimed before I could stop myself, at the same time that Ileana groaned. Had she heard it?

Seven vampires were instantly on edge. "What is it?" Mortimer hissed.

"Nothing," I answered before clamping my mouth shut, my eyes glued to the crippled witch on the floor, looking for signs that she'd received the message about Evangeline's new location. A location I had chosen only as a last resort and never in a thousand years thought Leo would need to use.

Unfortunately Viggo noticed my sudden interest in the witch who had the uncanny ability to trace communications. "Tell us what you know!" he demanded. When she didn't answer immediately, he grabbed her by her upper arm and, wrenching her up to her knees, he drove the poker through her right shoulder, just under her collarbone. It must have pierced a major artery, because a steady stream of blood shot out, eliciting hisses from those behind me.

I barely noticed, though, more concerned about what might escape her lips. Hairs lifted on my neck as I watched her open her mouth . . . but only a strangled croak came out. In response, Viggo roughly twisted the poker around. I winced, knowing from experience what pain that inflicted. Teeth bared and tears streaming down her cheeks, Ileana worked her mouth as if she were trying to get words out— words I couldn't allow. I dove for her, fully intent on silencing her permanently. Mortimer intercepted me, blocking my path long enough for her shrill scream.

"She's with the tribe!"

The sound of the poker and Ileana's battered body hitting the floor resonated through the suddenly silent room. Viggo looked at me, his blue eyes perplexed. "Sofie?" Normally I would enjoy that look, but not this time. "What does she mean by the tribe? Not *the* tribe; you destroyed them years ago."

Mortimer towered over me, glowering. "That's what she told us. We took her word for it."

"Who is the tribe?" Caden whispered.

"Shhh," I warned, eyes still on my two deadly adversaries, wondering how long it would take them to figure it out. Not long, apparently.

"Have you gone absolutely insane?" Mortimer exploded.

I stalled. "Whatever do you mean?"

"There's only one 'tribe' that bastard butler could be referring to. We should have known you didn't kill them!" Viggo hissed.

"Don't you realize they're just as likely to kill her as they are any of us, you fool?" Mortimer added.

"What?" All four of Evangeline's friends yelled in unison, Mortimer's words panicking them.

But I ignored them, still focused on the two vampires in front of me who now knew where Evangeline was. "Desperate measures," I answered coolly.

Viggo's lips curled back in a hideous smile. I hated that smile. "Well, at least we know she's reachable."

"Not while you're in here," I reminded him.

The smiled only grew larger. "If not by us, then by someone else," he taunted, displaying his cell phone.

Without thinking, I shot a helix out, knocking the thing into the fire. "I'll fry every phone line in this place, too," I added spitefully.

"No worries." Viggo grinned. "I'll just go get her myself."

It was my turn to smile. "How? You can't get past the Merth."

"Didn't we just discuss this? We need to escape from this

impending doom of which you speak."

"Change of plans," I shot back, not missing a beat.

"Sofie," Mage warned in a low voice.

"No!" I snapped. "They're not getting anywhere near her. I won't allow it. Ever. They can sit in here and wait for whatever is going to happen. They're more trouble to me out there than good."

A faint chuckle drew everyone's eyes to the frail little body crumpled on the floor. Her cheek resting in a pool of her blood, Ileana smiled and whispered, "Here they come!"

Alarm bells went off inside my head. Who was coming?

"I never did get along with my mother," Ileana murmured, her eyes closing. "She never accepted me with my powers. It was the perfect trap. And now you're finally all going to die." As if a cover had suddenly been lifted, magic began radiating from her body—not as if she had just now cast a spell, but as if the spell had always been running and only now could I see the tiny coils—hers were mauve—dancing around. What exactly had she been masking, though?

A split second later, the walls of the library shook as an explosion in the atrium rocked the building. Bishop and Fiona dashed out to the atrium with all of us close behind, crashing through the magical sound barrier and the glass into a maelstrom of thick smoke and bits of burning building.

That didn't concern me. What concerned me was the crowd of several hundred humans in dark clothing spilling through the gaping hole in the wall, all with those same dead eyes as the humans at the club. In their hands they carried machetes—nothing permanently damaging to us, but I had a feeling we weren't the weapons' intended targets. Sure enough, I watched them turn on each other and attack, hacking and swiping at one another, opening deep, bloody gashes in their flesh. In no time at all, rivers of red snaked over the cobblestones, too much to ignore, even for me. They were bait in a trap, meant to lure the vamps in, stop them from running or fighting intelligently. But to what end? Unless . . . My stomach turned in knots as I put two and two together. Viggo had led the real enemy right through our gates. Ileana's wicked giggle replayed in my head. *Here they come,* she had said. She wasn't talking about the Sentinel.

Bishop and Fiona tore off toward the crowd. My arms flew out to grab Caden and Amelie before they could follow. "Out of here—now." Easier said than done; their eyes were morphing into hideous veined orbs. Mine likely matched theirs.

"We can kill them all, easily," Caden growled, jerking toward them.

I tugged them back, hard. "Stop!"

"What are you doing?" Viggo hissed behind me. "Go on! Decimate them with your magic!"

"Them I can, yes. That's the point—they're a distraction." I watched the battle unfold. The Ratheus vampires had taken the bait, flying onto their victims, oblivious to the stabs from the machetes as they fed, assuming they'd heal after they gorged. But they weren't safe. Far from it.

"Here comes the cavalcade," Mage murmured beside me, eyeing the door. She had figured it out as well. "The witches. We need to get out of here."

"But, Fiona and Bishop!" Amelie cried, eyes on her two friends in the thick of it, unable to resist.

"I'll get them." In an instant, Mage was standing over a feeding Bishop. She wrenched him away and dragged him back to us. Distanced from the frenzy, Bishop appeared to snap out of the blood lust.

"We need to leave, Bishop," I yelled over the noise. "The witches are coming."

He nodded, eyes wide. "Fiona!" he bellowed.

"I'll go and get—" Mage began, only to stop abruptly, her black eyes on the tunnel entrance. I turned.

Like a wall of magic, a row of twenty-two women materialized in the chaos, fire at the ready, hands raised, pointed.

"Fiona!" Bishop screamed.

It was too late. The witches aimed for the group of vampires closest to them, Fiona among them. Fire shot out, engulfing the group. Fiona disappeared in the flames.

"No!" Bishop and Amelie shrieked, fighting wildly to break free and run to her. Luckily Caden and Mage had iron-strong grips.

"We need to go. Now! Or we'll be next," Mage yelled as the witches' attention moved on to the next cluster of vampires.

"We can't use the last escape route—they may be waiting for us there. Take them to the underground garage," I instructed.

"We can't get down there," Caden reminded me. "The Merth."

Damn it! I had to break the spell. I had no time for anything else. "Go!"

Bishop was resisting, woeful eyes on the circle of fire where his love lay. "Bishop, we have to go!" Caden cried "She's gone! We can't lose you, too!"

"Go! Now!" I screamed and ran back into the library without a second glance. With a last look at Veronique's portrait, I dove to Ileana's side. She appeared to be sleeping peacefully, but I knew better. And I knew she didn't need to protect her blood any longer. Running my hand along her neck, I grabbed hold of the chain and pulled.

Mortimer's hand clamped over my wrist with a vise-like grip. I turned to see fear in his chocolate eyes, such a rare sight. "Help us."

I gritted my teeth. They would die if they stayed here. They couldn't die, for my sister's sake. "She will be fine," I promised. "You two won't be." I began a whispered chant to reverse the spell, a chant that only I knew, for a spell that responded to only my voice. The words would release all vampires from the confines of the Merth, including Viggo and Mortimer. In seconds, it was done. "You're free. Get out of here."

"Veronique!" Viggo cried from the doorway. "I won't leave her!"

"Suit yourself." I shook free of Mortimer's hand. "When you smarten up, meet me at the Warehouse and we'll figure out what we're going to do." The Warehouse was an old, abandoned building by the city docks, where one could often go for an easy late-night meal on one criminal or another. With that, I left them, running as fast as I could past the line of witches and toward the garage. I had no intention of meeting Viggo and Mortimer there.

8. THE TRIBE

My eyes flew open to find Ursula and the snowy mountain chalet gone, replaced by a canopy of trees in the foreground of a night sky and the monotonous hum of people chanting. The source of that chant lay about forty feet to my left: a group of fifty or so people encircling an enormous fire, their hands joined, their lean, scantily-clad bodies swaying from side to side. They repeated a low, garbled mantra over and over again as a man with a strange headpiece sitting outside of the circle pounded a rhythmic beat on his drum. I squinted at the thing on his head. It looked like a . . . tiger's head?

A shout pulled my attention back toward the fire. This time I noticed the four tall wooden posts rising around it. My eyes drifted up their length, culminating in a platform-like structure at least fifteen feet above the fire on which sat a man wearing a large hat. It was dark, but I thought he was pointing at me.

Leo had transported me. Again.

"Evang . . . "

The weak groan drew my eyes to a body lying on the sandy ground behind me. Julian. The bonfire cast just enough light to illuminate the dark stain forming on the front of his parka. "Julian!" I shrieked, dropping to my knees beside him. Leo had sent him with me to save him from Ursula, but by the looks of it, Leo had been too late. With the lightest touch, I slowly unzipped his winter jacket, afraid any movement would hurt him further. "Please don't die!" I moaned.

I vaguely noticed that the incessant drumbeat and chanting had died, exchanged for gasps and words spurted in an odd tongue. I didn't pay too much attention, intent on seeing how badly Julian was wounded.

Evangeline, stand up, Max commanded in a flat tone.

A wave of relief washed over me. "Thank God you're here, Max! Julian needs help."

Stand up. Now, Max said a second time, now with an ominous undercurrent.

I ignored him, pulling Julian's jacket back to see the deep gash between his rib bones. Blood ran freely. So much blood.

I felt the low rumble in my chest as Max growled. *Too much blood. It was tempting a hungry Max.* "Help him," I cried meekly, knowing there was little hope. If only Sofie or Leo were here . . .

Something cold and sharp grazed my chin. I shifted to see a metal spearhead attached to a shaft that was a good seven feet long. Panic sparked in me. Leo wouldn't send us somewhere dangerous, would he? My eyes drifted up the length of the spear, over the pair of clawed, dark-skinned hands that gripped it, up along a nude male torso, to finish at a set of jaundiced eyes, the whites so sickly yellow that they gleamed like glow-in-the-dark stickers. In hideousness they matched the decaying teeth and disfigured nose, multiple heavy gold rings stretching out both nostrils in opposite directions. I cowered at the man's unsightliness. I wasn't sure if I should even call him a man. What were they? Glancing left and right, I found the others surrounding us were equally repulsive.

The spearhead pushed up under my chin, digging into my flesh. *Stand up,* Max instructed, and this time I obeyed. *Don't let them touch you.*

"I'm in no rush to let them do anything," I mumbled, my attention flitting from one set of jaundiced eyes to the next.

The man who sat on top of the platform—whose hat was made of colorful peacock feathers, I now saw—barked out something in that strange tongue that I didn't understand. A dozen spears were instantly leveled—most of them at Max, one at me. No one bothered with Julian. He was no threat to anyone.

"Wait!" I held my hands up in the most non-threatening manner I could. None of them moved. "What the hell do I say, Max?" I hissed.

I doubt it matters.

The man's eyes darted to Max, then back to me, his eyes narrowing as if he understood our ability to communicate and he didn't like it. He uttered another string of gibberish. One of the men lowered his spear and stepped forward, his arm outstretched toward Max.

Max's teeth bared in response. A warning. The reaction was several spears to his back and legs. His cry of agony pierced the night air.

"No!" I cried, watching in horror as they forced my werebeast to the ground. I dove to wrap my arms protectively around his neck, bracing myself for a painful stab to my back. "Fight back, Max!" I whispered in his ear.

No. They'll kill me.

Kill an immortal werebeast? Hopelessness washed over me. "Why would Leo send us here, Max?" I whispered, gripping the dog tightly and burying my face in his fur, sensing the crowd closing in on us.

The feather-capped man barked a word that sounded like an order. No one moved. Again, he barked.

He wants you to stand, Max translated.

"No! They may stab you again," I moaned.

If you don't, they will definitely stab the both of us. I like my odds better with you standing.

With that in mind, I scrambled to my feet. The leader descended from the platform and moved forward through the crowd, his sickly eyes scanning my face as if reading something on it. Suddenly he threw his arm out to the side, palm raised. A spear was placed in it.

I sucked in a mouthful of air, terrified.

Your necklace, Max whispered. *Show it to him.*

For a moment I didn't move, too paralyzed with doubt. Then my hand flew to my neck to fish out the pendant. The abrupt movement caused a commotion in the group and spears rose. "Wait!" I exclaimed, holding my palms out again. Featherman shouted an order and the spears immediately dropped. Moving slowly this time, I reached back up to my coat and tugged the zipper down. Sliding my hand inside, I grabbed hold of the chain and pulled the dull black pendant out from under layers of winter clothes.

My breath caught as Featherman's spear tip approached my chest. Without stepping any closer, he gently hooked the end of the spear around the chain and stretched the pendant toward him, his eyes narrowing as if to analyze it. With a look up at my face and back down, he nodded and mumbled something to himself.

Julian moaned then. Dropping the spear, Featherman turned to look down at the young dying man, then stooped to inspect the wound.

"We need to get him to a hospital," I said without thinking. Taking in their loincloths and mud huts, I realized how absurd that statement was. Yet I couldn't just let him die. "Help him, please."

Featherman waved his hand in a circular motion, then pointed to Julian. The crowd immediately parted to allow in men and women holding long sticks with loops of rope attached at the ends. They each hooked one around Julian's arm or leg without touching him. With surprising grace, they lifted Julian in unison, earning a gasp from him.

"Max, what are they doing?" I whispered anxiously as we watched them carry Julian toward the fire.

I don't know. Honestly.

Something dug into my back. Turning, I found one of the tribesmen nudging us to follow with the blunt end of his spear. I obliged, walking hesitantly forward. When we were about fifteen feet away from one of the little huts where the bearers had stopped with Julian, another spear suddenly appeared to block our path. *Close enough*, they were saying.

Max and I watched in silence as a woman appeared from the hut, pulling on a pair of dark, elbow-length gloves as I imagined a surgeon would do in preparing for an operation. Other tribeswomen followed behind her with wooden trays holding various objects—bowls, leaves, ominous-looking tools. The procession wordlessly circled Julian, whose eyes remained closed.

The woman with the gloves leaned toward Julian, a sharp object gripped in her hand. "Oh my God, Max!" I whispered, grabbing a fistful of Max's fur and squeezing. It earned a small grunt from him but I didn't care. What was she going to do to Julian?

We watched as she stretched the collar of Julian's shirt away from his neck with one hand. She then pulled the sharp object along the material, slicing it in half and spreading the sides open to reveal his chest and the worrying gash. I breathed the tiniest sigh of relief.

Next she took a wooden spoon and bowl from a tray, dipped the spoon into the bowl, and began gently slathering a pale gray, mud-like paste over the wound. When the area was completely covered, she dropped the tools and knelt down beside him to smooth over the application with her hand. Julian's face tightened briefly in pain, but no noise escaped him.

"Max!" I hissed. "What are they doing?"

I don't know, but as long as they don't touch him with their skin, they're likely trying to help.

"What's wrong with their skin?" I took a few steps closer, but a spear swung toward me in warning. I cautiously backed up again.

They're called Ambulans Mortem. Walking Death.

"Why are they called . . . that?" I faltered, watching as the four women assisting Julian's nursemaid joined hands around them and began chanting.

Their touch is instant death to all—humans, vampires, werebeasts. Anyone except their own tribe. And they have no qualms about using it. The death tribe hates our kind—hates all kinds, except their own.

"Just a single touch?" I repeated slowly, uncomprehending.

Contact with their skin. Yes.

My eyes widened. "Where did they come from?"

Sofie made them. Accidentally. She was supposed to kill them years ago, but decided not to. I think they fascinated her. She kept them hidden from Viggo, of course, who would have sent a nuke here if he had known she was crazy enough to keep them alive.

"How on Earth does someone 'accidentally' create something like that?" I wondered aloud.

It's that Fates magic. I don't know . . . Sofie can explain it to you one day.

Another, more concerning thought popped into my head. "Why on earth would Leo send us to these people?"

Because Sofie told him to, if the need ever arose. Of course she expected that it would involve Viggo finding you . . . It's probably the safest place for you to be right now. No vampire or sorceress in their right mind will enter these lands. Sorcerous magic doesn't work around them. They're like a black hole for the powers of vampires and witches. An anti-magic. They have their own kind of magic.

"But . . . " I was struggling with all of this. "How did she know they wouldn't kill me?"

Well . . . she didn't, for sure. She created them, so they show some deference to her. But it only goes so far. Several years ago, she approached them with an offer in exchange for help, if this day should ever arise. That pendant was the signal. Max chuckled. *That woman has more escape routes than an eel.*

"And of course you knew this all along," I said through gritted teeth.

There was no need to scare you. I never thought we'd end up here.

I angrily shook my head, but now was not the time to scold Max over his continuing duplicity. I needed information. "What did she offer them?" I whispered.

Tigers.

I screwed my face up. "What?"

Tigers. You know: rawr.

"But . . . " Thinking about the headdress that drummer wore, I didn't finish.

For some reason, tigers are immune to their touch. They think the giant fur balls are gifts from their fire god, so they surround themselves with tigers.

My eyes roamed the clearing, looking for the presence of these animals. "I don't see any."

Oh, they're there. Look harder. Behind the huts.

I followed his direction, squinting into the shadows. There. A pair of glowing feline eyes. A few feet away, I saw another set. And another. Just beyond the huts, a ring of tigers surrounded us, watching. A shiver ran down my spine.

A male scream whipped my head from the tigers to Julian, now conscious, his teeth bared as he struggled to break free from the constraints around his wrists and ankles as the gloved woman inserted several bone-colored needles into his wound. The tribesmen holding Julian leaned in with their weight on the long poles, tightening their grip, securing Julian's limbs before he accidentally grazed a bare leg. Now unable to move, he seethed, face contorted with pain as he watched the woman accept a steaming bowl of something. Leaning forward, she poured the hot clear liquid over his wound. Julian roared in agony.

"No!" I cried out, making to move forward. A spear jabbed the air dangerously close to my chest, stopping me.

My cry caught the attention of Featherman, who towered over the operation with his arms crossed over his chest. At a casual wave of his hand, four tribesmen turned and marched toward us, spears leveled. They prodded us, herding Max and me away from the scene. Farther and farther back we went, until we were forced through the narrow entrance of a tiny hut. A cloth door dropped, closing us in. Crouching, I peeked under the bottom of the door, and spotted heels. The tribesmen were on guard. I rose and turned to survey the hut, which held nothing but a wooden bowl and a reed mat in the corner, illuminated by the firelight shining through a tiny window near the ceiling.

I ran to the window. First on tiptoes, then jumping, I tried to reach the bottom sill so I could pull myself up and see outside. It was too high. "Max. Come here," I hissed. In three steps, he was beside me. "Stand right here." I pushed him up against the wall. "And stay still." Throwing my arms over his neck, I hoisted myself up onto his back.

So this is what a horse feels like, he grumbled.

"Shut up, Max!" I retorted. "You owe me, after all of your lies!" I kicked off my winter boots. With my hands pressed against the cool, hard mud wall of the hut for balance, I stood on Max's back and peered out the window.

I had a prime view of the bonfire and Julian, who lay unmoving, eyes closed, his face now pallid. They had stripped off the rest of his clothing and covered his entire body in what looked like soggy green leaves. The four women still encircled him, their hands linked, their eyes closed, their mouths moving in unison as they chanted softly.

"Is he going to be okay?" I whispered to Max.

I don't know, Evangeline. I'm sorry. By his tone, I knew the big dog was being genuine.

The woman with the gloves stood to accept another large bowl. Walking around Julian, she carefully poured a clear liquid over the leaf covering. At a snap of her fingers, someone handed her a burning stick.

My jaw clenched as I watched, my apprehension growing as the burning stick approached Julian's still body. The chanting women grew louder and more boisterous, until they were all shrieking at the top of their lungs like a bunch of lunatics.

"No . . ." I moaned, gripping the base of the window and watching wide-eyed as, with just a pass of the tiny brand, Julian's entire body went up in flames. "No!" I screamed, at the same time that Julian let out a skin-peeling shriek, his back arching severely.

I lost my balance and tumbled. Max, moving with his lighting speed, dove underneath me to cushion my fall before I could hit the hard ground. Lying on top of the massive werebeast with my heart pounding in my ears, I began to cry. I didn't stop for a long time, weeping openly into Max's side, my anger with Sofie and Leo for sending us to such a horrific place growing with each minute. This was worse than the mountains, way worse. And now they were burning Julian alive and I would be alone. "Why would they abandon us to these monsters, Max?" I asked through my sobs.

Max responded with a nuzzle to my cheek. *Leo was protecting you from Ursula, remember?*

I sat up, using the sleeve of my coat to wipe my eyes. "Well, where is Leo? Why didn't he come too?" Silence met my question. "Max?" My voice wavered with uncertainty.

My brothers took Ursula down. She's gone.

"And Leo? He's okay, right?" No answer. "Max!"

I'm sorry, Evangeline. Whatever life he had left in him, he used to send us here. He's with Maeve now.

Leo . . . dead? The news brought a fresh round of tears. I fell back to lean against the cool wall, a large, painful lump forming in my throat. Everyone was dying around me—because of me. Leo; probably Julian; next it could be Max or Sofie. When would this all end? When the necklace came off, I realized. I looked down at the thing, resting on the outside of my parka, and the sudden urge to rip it off my body overwhelmed me.

Don't you dare, Max warned as if reading my mind. It stayed my hand. For now.

ର

After staring at motionless heels for what seemed like hours, I saw the guards' feet shift. A clawed hand curled around the edge of the curtain to pull it back. Squeezing through the narrow opening, four men carried Julian in on a simple stretcher of wood and cloth. They set him down gently, then turned and walked out without a word or glance in our direction. A woman from the circle entered behind them, placing a bowl and a neatly folded stack of clothes in a corner. As she left, her eyes skimmed over Max, but she said nothing.

Now alone, I crawled over on my hands and knees. "Julian?" I whispered. He didn't answer. Discouraged, I inspected his upper body to see that it appeared unscathed by the fire that had engulfed him not long ago. The women had removed all of the green, leafy substance and covered him from the waist down with a small hemp blanket. A patch of that gray paste, now dry, covered his wound. I peered at his face. It was still ghostly pale, though slightly less pallid than before. A sheen of sweat covered his forehead and several drops rolled down his cheek. I didn't know if it was due to his body fighting infection, or the oppressive heat.

So swept up by the activities of the tribe and Julian, I hadn't had time to feel the drastic temperature change. Now that I gave it a second's thought, I realized I was drenched in sweat. No wonder—I was dressed for temperatures at least a hundred degrees colder. If I didn't get out of these layers soon, I'd likely pass out.

I began peeling off my winter gear, beginning with my hat, until I was in nothing but my gray long johns. Even those were too much. I crawled over to the pile of clothes in the corner. Julian's things, torn and bloodied, lay on top. Underneath them was a two-piece set of clothing that matched what the women in the tribe wore—whatever that was called. Glancing over at Julian to make sure he was still unconscious, I ordered Max to turn around. He obliged, and I quickly pulled off the long johns and slipped on the outfit. *Thank the heavens they aren't one of those topless tribes,* I silently celebrated, looking down at the skirt and the strip of cloth meant to be a shirt.

"Julian?" I whispered again, sliding back over to him. Nothing.

He needs to rest, Max said. *As do you.*

In answer, I balled up my coat and, placing it under my head, lay down next to Julian's still body, reaching out to hold his hand. It would be a long time before sleep finally came to me.

ॐ

I awoke to sunlight streaming in through the tiny window. Beads of sweat ran down my cheek; the hot, muggy air was uncomfortable even with the little that I wore. Max was stretched out on one side of me, unmoving, his eyes closed. I knew he wasn't sleeping, though. He didn't sleep. The previous day's nightmare flashed in my mind then. I bolted upright and spun around.

Julian's eyes were open a crack.

"Julian!" I exclaimed, throwing myself on him without thinking, earning a groan. "Sorry!" I quickly sat back up to gaze at him. "How are you feeling?"

Julian licked his lips several times. "Water . . . " he finally croaked, reaching up to paw the air with a weak hand.

There's water in the bowl in the corner, Max instructed.

I scurried over to grab it and bring it back to Julian's side. "Can you sit up?" I asked softly, sliding my hand behind his neck to help him get up to his elbows. I held the bowl up to his mouth. He gulped the entire contents down.

"Thank you."

I shifted my makeshift pillow under his head and eased him back.

"What happened? The last thing I remember was snowshoeing . . . and the wolf."

I swallowed, not sure where to begin. "We went back to the chalet after . . . " I hesitated. "After Max figured out that Valentina had been possessed by Ursula."

Julian's brow knit as he searched his memory. "Right. She was—"

"A witch. A bad one."

"Right." He paused, thinking. "What happened after that? How did we get here?"

"Leo—" I choked; saying his name pulled at the already gaping wound in my heart. "He sent us to another safe location." The giant lump in my throat was unmovable by this point.

"And my sister?" His head rolled slowly from side to side as he looked around the hut. For Valentina, no doubt.

How did I tell him that she had been torn apart by Max's brothers? "Valentina has been gone for weeks, Julian," I said instead, my voice quiet.

He frowned, trying to comprehend what I was saying. Realization finally clouded those brown eyes. Tears welled. "My sister's dead."

Max was on his feet and heading over to the door to nose aside the curtain and peer outside. This was too much for him to handle. It was too much for me, as well. "I'm so sorry, Julian," I said, a fresh batch of tears rolling down my cheeks, the pain of watching my closest friend lose his entire family agonizing.

Julian rolled onto his side, away from me, likely to hide his tears. The action shifted the hemp blanket covering him, revealing his entire bare backside. Feeling my cheeks flush, I was about to avert my eyes when something caught my eye.

A small cross-like tattoo on his hip.

I gasped. "You're—"

Despite his grave injury, Julian's body stiffened and he quickly rolled back, realizing what he had just revealed: the mark that branded him part of the People's Sentinel. But why was it not on his hand, like all the others?

Max was by my side in an instant. *What's wrong?*

"You're—" I started again but stopped to swallow, realizing that as soon as the words came out of my mouth, Julian was as good as dead. He was the enemy. Max would destroy him, regardless of whether he had saved my life.

Recognizing the situation, Julian pleaded silently with his teary eyes.

But why? How? How was the son of Viggo's beard family part of the enemy without Viggo knowing? It explained his hatred for vampires. But . . . how? A flood of questions entered my mind then and I knew I would never get answers with Max hovering. "Probably still thirsty," I told Max, grabbing the bowl and thrusting it toward him. "Can you go fetch some more water?"

Do not use the word 'fetch' with me, Max responded crisply. *And have you noticed I don't have opposable thumbs?*

"You'll figure it out, Max," I said, trying to sound casual, but failing. "Unless you want me to go out there while you stay here and comfort Julian."

With a grunt, Max plucked the bowl out of my hand with his teeth and pushed the curtain aside, practically running out of the hut.

I crawled over and peeked around the curtain to watch him as he sauntered among the huts, staggering slightly. *He must be starving by now.* The place was deserted. The remnants of the bonfire smoldered in the center of the clearing. In daylight, I could see the place clearly for what it was—a tribal village in a dense jungle. At least thirty huts formed the perimeter of the clearing. Two tigers sat outside each hut door as if on guard, their tails swirling back and forth as they watched the mammoth dog traipse through their village. Across the way, opposite our hut, sat a much larger hut than all the others. Four tigers guarded it. That had to be the Featherman's hut. I guessed he was the chief.

When I thought Max was out of earshot, I turned and dove toward Julian, my hands landing on either shoulder, pinning him roughly to the ground.

"Ouch!" he cried.

"Shut up, you liar!" I whispered sharply.

That earned a wince. "I didn't lie."

"No, you're right. You just conveniently left out an important truth. You and Max have a lot more in common than I thought!" I tempered my tone, realizing that my whisper was likely loud enough to carry in the quiet of the jungle.

"Do you blame me?" Julian whispered back. "How could I tell you? Especially after that first night, when you pretty much condemned every one of us!"

"Can you blame me? You want all of my friends to die!"

"No, I don't! I mean, I did, but not anymore. Please, let me explain!" Julian pleaded.

With my jaw set stubbornly, I sat back on my knees, crossed my arms over my chest, and demanded, "Explain, then!"

Julian struggled to sit up. He met my stare with guilty eyes. "Two years ago, these men approached my parents with an offer. They said they'd help us break free of the vampires." He pausing for a moment to regain his breath, his breathing shallow. "At first my parents weren't interested. I mean, they didn't need to do anything for the vampires except sign some papers every now and then and collect stupid amounts of money. Not exactly high-risk. But a few months later, the men came back with an offer to top whatever my parents were being paid. That, of course, sparked their interest." There was contempt in his voice. "All we had to do was get marked—" he gestured to his hip "—and report in to a phone number if we heard or noticed anything strange. My parents agreed to it."

"And you?"

Julian snorted. "My parents could be quite . . . persuasive." As if sitting up was too hard, he slowly eased himself back. He stared up at the ceiling for a long moment before continuing. "They threatened not to pay for my med school unless I complied." His head rolled to look at me now. "So of course I agreed. I mean, what did I care about a bunch of vampires? It was obvious these men wished them harm. I figured we'd all be better off if they actually succeeded in getting rid of them. I didn't know about the curse, or about this underground Sentinel group and its alliance with the witches . . . I didn't know about you." He stared at me, a strange look on his face.

I exhaled loudly, and some of my anger went with it, replaced with a mixture of pity and confusion. Pity that his own parents would drag him into such a mess, and confusion over how they actually pulled off tricking a two thousand-year-old vampire who could read moods. "But how? I mean, how could Viggo not find out that his beard family were double agents?"

Julian shrugged. "It wasn't that hard, really. We never saw them. The first time I ever stepped foot inside their place in Manhattan was the day you were there. Why would they suspect anything? The men told us that if we kept our markings hidden, we'd be fine."

I added to his explanation. "And Viggo is so arrogant, he never suspected someone could top his bribes."

Julian nodded, rolling his eyes. "It took a lot of money, but it happened."

Something still didn't sit right with me. "You parents just took the Sentinel's word at face value?"

Julian chuckled. "No . . . the Sentinel told them that Viggo and

Mortimer wouldn't be around much longer, so if they wanted to be taken care of, they'd be smart to take the deal. My parents accepted on the condition that they got several large advances up front. So I guess they figured that they couldn't lose, either way."

"Boy, were they wrong," I muttered, imagining their last few moments of life and shuddering. "Sorry," I added.

"Yeah." Julian's voice was hollow. "But luckily they didn't learn anything valuable to the Sentinel while they were there."

I felt my eyes widen as realization dawned. *No, but you have.* Julian knew everything there was to know. Everything that I knew, I had stupidly divulged to him. Enough to harm the vampires. Enough to destroy everyone I cared for.

Max pushed through the curtain then, water splashing out of the bowl as he tried to balance it upright within his jaws. He walked it over and leaned down to within Julian's reach.

"Thanks, Max," Julian murmured, taking the bowl. He lifted his head enough to drink from the edge of the bowl, his worried eyes locked on me the entire time.

If only you knew, Max, I thought, my focus shifting back and forth between the two of them.

When Julian finished, he half-placed, half-dropped the bowl on the floor and wiped the water from his chin with the back of his hand. "For what it's worth, I regret ever agreeing to it."

Regret what? Max piped in.

"Sure you do, now that you got caught," I answered bitterly.

Caught doing what? Max asked, his tone agitated.

"No . . . now that I know you. Now that I know the whole truth and what could happen if this comes to blows."

I pressed my lips together as I weighed my options. I could tell Max right now and end any threat Julian could ever become to Caden and the others. But . . . he had saved me from Ursula. He had attacked his own sister—her body—to protect me. I owed him. I didn't have to trust him. But I needed time to think things through. While we were exiled to yet another remote part of the world, he couldn't cause too much trouble. It would only take a few words from me to end him. "Nothing, Max," I finally said, adding with an air of triumph, "You're on a 'need to know' basis."

Max grumbled in displeasure but said nothing.

The worry in Julian's eyes lifted slightly. *You're not off the hook, you liar.* I turned my back on him. Hugging my chest to my knees, I lamented over everything. At least I didn't feel like a complete idiot this time. The Foreros had fooled everyone, not just the ever-gullible, naïve Evangeline.

Uncomfortable silence filled the hut as I stared at the mud wall for what felt like hours. Finally I heard the soft sound of snoring. Good. I could easily avoid talking to him for the rest of the day if he wasn't awake.

9. ILLUSIONS

It was my first time in Viggo and Mortimer's jet cabin since the trip to New York with Evangeline. With four vampires taking turns pacing around in it, three of them beside themselves with grief over the loss of Fiona only hours ago, it didn't feel quite the same.

Escaping from the Fifth Avenue palace had been easy, but not graceful. Since crashing through an army of witches to escape behind the wheel of a car was too risky, even in the Hum-V, we used the sewer system access from the garage, weaving through muck, rats, and other vileness for a mile or so to resurface in Central Park. From there it was a simple act of grand theft auto and tripling the speed limit to get us to Viggo's airfield in record time.

We likely could have run to the plane in the same amount of time, had it not been for Bishop. Mage struggled with the broken-hearted vampire every step of the way. All he wanted to do was turn around and dive back into that battleground to avenge Fiona's death, a reckless move that would mean certain death for him. I even tried a few calming spells on him, but none seemed to work, his anguish overpowering all. I found myself wishing that Mage could compel him to follow peacefully. In the end, Mage kept Bishop alive with brute force, dragging him kicking and screaming through the tunnels, her tiny arm around his broad neck in a headlock. Their difference in size almost made it look comical. I was surprised she bothered, but I felt grateful that she did. Losing one of them would be hard enough for Evangeline. Losing two . . .

Now we flew south toward the remote South American island where Evangeline waited, guarded by a group of demons created in one of my magical blunders. A part of me overflowed with joy that I would finally see my girl again. And when we did meet, it would be without the mask I had so stoically worn to hide my true feelings for her, to alienate myself from her. I would no longer need to lurk within the shadows to be near her. Life would be different now.

I sighed. No, life was not yet different. I needed to be a long way off from joy right now. I had failed to break the deadly curse hanging over her. She was still hunted and now Viggo and Mortimer knew exactly where she hid. I silently admonished myself for not moving the tribe from their original location. It had seemed like too much of a hassle at the time, the island was so isolated, so perfect for concealing that sort of creature. Evangeline was still in great danger, until I figured out how to lift that blasted curse. Then Caden could transform her, something I was sure she wanted, and she would no longer be a fragile human.

Standing at the front of the cabin, I swept my eyes over its occupants, assessing the atmosphere. It was one of complete and utter despair. We had all taken a turn in the jet's shower, washing the sewers off our bodies. Caden and Mage had pilfered fresh sets of clothes for all of us from the other private planes at the airfield. The physical evidence of the attack was long gone. But all I had to do was glance at Bishop, who sat in a seat off to himself, his forehead pressed up against the window as he stared out at the night sky with empty gray eyes, to see that the witches' attack had wounded us gravely. My heart ached for the young man. He had just watched his love of seven hundred years burn! The sickness now growing inside him was one to which I could relate. It was dangerous, for him and everyone around him. We'd have to watch him closely.

"Miss Sofie?" The pretty young flight attendant, Jasmine, poked her head into the cabin, pulling me from my dark thoughts.

I turned to smile at her. I had summoned her and the two pilots on our way to the airfield and then compelled them to fly without Viggo's consent. The three of them were on call twenty-four hours a day, seven days a week, with the expectation that they'd be ready to take off within an hour's notice. It was an unreasonable demand, but they didn't work much and they were paid handsomely for it, making them willing to cater to Viggo's eccentricities, taking residences nearby and dropping everything to run at the ring of their phones. Of course, they had no idea what their employers were, other than assuming they were involved in seriously shady business. "Yes, Jasmine?"

"You asked me to tell you when Mr. Viggo arrived at the airfield. The tower called. He just did."

How predictable. So Viggo and Mortimer had made it to the airfield to take the jet I had already commandeered. They'd be pissed, realizing I had duped them to get a head start to Evangeline. Not that they'd be surprised. I was actually shocked they'd waited in the Warehouse as long as they had. "And?"

"And they tried to take another plane, but all of the cockpits had been vandalized."

My eyes shifted briefly to Mage, who offered a tiny smile. She and Caden must have busted up the electronics while looking for clothes, to buy us a bigger head start. *Smart thinking.* Now Viggo and Mortimer would have to find a plane as well as a pilot.

"Thanks for the update, Jasmine." I smiled warmly. As she was turning away, another thought struck me. "Oh, Jaz?"

"Yes?"

"Have you heard anything over the news about an explosion or terrorist attack in Manhattan . . . anything at all like that?"

Jasmine's perfectly-sculpted brown eyebrows furrowed as she shook her head. "No, Miss Sofie."

I smiled again. "Thanks." That meant the witches were containing the attack, keeping it under wraps. For what reason, I didn't know. But every day the vampires stayed out of the news kept us away from being exposed, and the fated world war from beginning.

Jasmine pulled her head back into the cockpit, leaving behind a hint of floral-scented shampoo, and closed the door. I heard the lock click and chuckled. If we wanted in, we'd get in, but if a lock made them feel safe, have at it.

"So what does that mean? Will they still come?" Amelie asked, looking up at me with wide emerald eyes from the same seat that Evangeline had occupied on her way to New York.

"Oh, I'm sure they will. We just stalled them slightly. They'll find a way to get there; we'll just be there before them and, I hope, be gone by the time they arrive." That remote island off the southern tip of South America where the tribe lived was the absolute last place on earth Viggo wanted to go. But if that was where Veronique's pendant was, then as sure as the sun would rise in the morning, that's where he would go. I just hoped it didn't require a massacre to get there.

"And what happens when we get there?" Caden asked, his arm wrapped protectively around his sister, worry marring his beautiful face. "Who is this 'tribe'?"

"Ah, yes. My creation." I felt my lips curve up in a smile, though nothing about that tribe deserved a smile. I strolled over to take a seat—the same one I had occupied when flying with Evangeline—and asked, "Did Evangeline ever mention the spell I cast that inadvertently cursed her?"

Amelie and Caden's heads bobbed in assent. "She said something about some . . . fates?" Amelie offered.

I nodded. "Yes, the Fates. They're basically like the gods of the witches. I liken them to a group of overweight housewives sitting around a table, thinking up ways to twist hopes and dreams into some perversion of a solution," I explained sardonically. Mage chuckled softly, amused by my interpretation. I turned to give her a flat stare. "But—oh, that's right. I forgot, Mage. You know all about the Fates, don't you! That slipped my mind. Much as it slipped yours."

Mage cocked her head, then dipped it slightly as if to acknowledge my jibe with a silent "nice one."

I turned back to Caden and Amelie. "Of course, I have no idea what the Fates would look like if they took on physical form. I don't even know how I managed to call on them the first time. There's no manual for getting ahold of them. It's kind of like humans praying to their god. I just sort of stumbled upon them when I was desperate to turn for Nathan . . . "

I realized I was babbling and quickly regrouped my thoughts. "Anyway, forty years after I cast the first Causal Enchantment—the kind of spell the Fates grant—I began getting impatient. When I get impatient, I start doing . . . reckless things." Nathan had always been quick to point that out. "I began testing the Fates, casting all kinds of Causal Enchantments, attacking the problem from different angles to see what they would throw back at me. One of these spells was an attempt to erase my original one altogether, as if it never happened—to change fate back. I knew it was a long shot, but what did I have to lose? Well, sure enough, the Fates came back with an 'idea,' all right." I gave them my best sarcastic eye roll. "They turned this remote tribe in the Amazon into the anti-magic of that wielded by vampires and witches."

"Interesting," Mage murmured, her expression pensive. "That's the second of these Causal Enchantments that didn't exist in our Earth." I didn't miss the scowl on Caden's face when Mage said "our Earth."

They still hadn't come to terms with her manipulation of their memories. I couldn't blame them.

"Are you positive?"

Mage nodded adamantly. "And why does the original vampire from your Earth not look identical to me?"

"It doesn't make sense . . . " I agreed softly, speaking more to myself. Another piece to this Fates puzzle that didn't make sense. I hated broken puzzles. "If our worlds are parallel, someone like me should have been in yours, casting the same Causal Enchantments, destroying the vampire venom." Amelie and Caden nodded in silent agreement, their expressions reflecting their confusion. In my peripheral vision, I noticed that even Bishop had perked up.

"It's like you didn't exist in our world," Mage said. "Like you are unique to your Earth. Perhaps planted here to alter the course of things."

I mulled over her theory. "Planted by whom?"

"The Fates?" Mage suggested. "I mean, how many parallel worlds do they reign over? Mine, yours, how many others? Maybe they get bored with watching the same thing happen over and over again, seeing the same faces . . . maybe they decided to throw a wrench into the works."

I had never thought of that. Was I a wrench for the Fates? Was my very existence, my constant drive to test the boundaries of magic, a by-product of these gods' need to spice things up? Maybe the Fates lounged around in their sweats and rollers, watching, waiting to see what ideas their crazy jester would come up with next. The very idea twisted my stomach into knots and ran my blood icy cold. Was I their entertainment?

Mage's voice pulled me from my silent brooding. I looked up to see them all watching me. How long had I drifted off in thought? "So then, this tribe—what are they, exactly?" she asked.

Right. The tribe. I pushed a stray lock of hair off my face. "Good question. I'm not quite sure." I gave them the rundown—the toxic skin, the unsightly appearance, how their own magic counters witches' magic within a ten-mile radius, the tiger deal I made with them to protect Evangeline. "They worship the god of fire. I don't know . . . " I rolled my eyes when Mage looked at me questioningly. "But what exactly their magic can do, I'm not sure. One day, if we survive this coming war, maybe I'll experiment. That's why I kept them alive and hidden all this time. For now, I'm happy to stay as far away from those wretched creatures as I can."

"Why tigers?" Amelie asked suddenly.

I shrugged. "No reason that I can think of except companionship. They're the only creature that isn't affected by their touch. They have a slew of the animals in their village and I promised to bring them more as part of my deal to keep Evangeline safe, should she show up there. Whatever the reason, they're great for negotiating."

"That's just the kind of stupid, arbitrary stuff that the Fates come up with," Mage added, her tone flip.

"So this tribe is dangerous. We want to get in and out as quickly as possible," Caden acknowledged. "What do we need to do?" " I noticed the creased picture of Evangeline in his hands then, the one I had secretly passed him weeks ago. Many times, I had caught him off in a corner, gazing at her face. It was an endearing picture. But a picture just didn't cut it next to the real thing . . . And that reminded me of something I needed to do before I felt completely safe with him around her.

I stood and walked over to the bar fridge. Reaching in, I grabbed several bags of blood that I knew would be there—Viggo had stashed blood everywhere. "We find the tribe." I began tossing bags out to the group. The one I threw in Bishop's direction hit his knee and dropped to the floor; he made no move to grab it. "Hope they don't kill us, and get the hell out of there with Evangeline." I ended at Caden, who held his hands out in anticipation. "Not you." He frowned, as did Amelie, her curls bobbing as she turned from Caden to me. "I need to know I can trust you."

"Haven't the last twelve hours proven anything?" Caden said.

"Yes, but I'm worried your emotions will get the better of you when you see Evangeline for the first time." By emotions, I meant lust. Lust was as much a driver as fresh blood and Caden, being in his early twenties, was definitely no shy schoolboy. "I need to test you."

Caden arched an eyebrow, a worried question in his eyes.

I walked over to the cockpit door and knocked. Jasmine's head popped out almost immediately. "Would you mind coming out for a moment? Just for a sec." I reached out to take her hand.

She nodded and stepped into the cabin, scanning the others. I pushed the door closed behind her. "What lovely brown eyes you have," I cooed, steering her attention back to me with my fingertip on her chin. She smiled shyly, no clue of my real intentions—that I was zoning in on her irises, pulling her eyes in to mine until our focus was locked. In seconds, she was staring vacantly back at me, compelled. "You are going to walk over to Caden and offer him your blood," I said.

"What?" Caden barked out behind me. "Are you nuts?"

I ignored him. "Ready?"

She nodded dumbly.

Holding her hand, I turned to look at Caden. "I need to know that I can trust you."

His jade eyes shifted between Jasmine and me, full of doubt. "How is this going to prove anything, Sofie?"

In answer, I plucked a few hundred helix links. With a quick disguising chant—the same kind that Ursula used to turn herself into a sweet old bird-feeding lady for Evangeline—I let my magic loose. It swirled around Jasmine's body like a tornado, visible only to Mage and I. We all watched as Jasmine's hair lightened and grew six inches longer, as her eyes lightened to milk-chocolate brown, as her skin paled.

As she turned into Evangeline.

I heard the sharp intakes of breath from the others. It was spine-chilling to see this mirage, even for me, and I was the one who had created it. "Now, if you would please—" I gestured toward Caden.

With slow, catatonic steps, Jasmine walked over and sat down in the free chair beside him, opposite Amelie. Gathering her hair and pulling it back, she leaned away from Caden and arched her back to expose her long, slender neck. "Please. Go ahead," she offered, her voice identical to Evangeline's.

I swallowed the anxiety in my throat and watched Caden blink several times, awed by the illusion. *Please, control yourself.* If he didn't defy the urge that was now electrifying his entire body, there was no way I was bringing him with me to the tribe.

Caden's jaw tightened. "No," he growled through clenched teeth.

I allowed myself a small smile. He had passed the first step. But this wasn't the real test. Sailing over to the illusion's side with just a thought, I yanked a sharp piece of metal from the underside of her chair. Grabbing her wrist, I slashed the metal across it, opening up a wide gash.

All four vampires hissed. *That's fine. This is as hard as it will get for Caden around Evangeline.* If he began feeding on her, he wouldn't stop until she was dead; I could almost guarantee that. So he needed to fight it.

Jasmine held her wrist up to Caden's mouth. "Go on," she offered sweetly.

Caden gritted his teeth tighter. Sickness stirred in my stomach. I knew this was torture. If this were a human version of Nathan sitting in front of me, offering me his wrist, I didn't know that I could refuse. And that's why I needed to be sure.

Icy blue-green eyes turned to glare at me. He was fighting the transformation, his whites now tinged with red, his pupils dilated, tiny veins beginning to grow and throb. "This is ridiculous. Get her away before I kill her," he whispered, his voice agonized now.

My answer came fast and hard. "If you want to see Evangeline again—ever—then you will control yourself. I will sacrifice a thousand Jasmines before I let anything happen to my girl."

The warning seemed to spark a new level of control in Caden. When he turned back to look at the illusion, it wasn't with hunger in his eyes. He searched her features, all but ignoring the bleeding wrist under his nose. After a moment, he lifted his hand to run his finger along her chin, down her neck. "She looks so much like her," he murmured.

Please, control yourself. Please. A metal creak echoed through the cabin. Glancing down, I realized that my fingernails had punctured the ivory leather upholstery and warped the metal frame of the seat. Taking a deep, calming breath, I released my grip and turned back to Caden.

We remained like that for a long time—Caden and Amelie staring at a bleeding replica of Evangeline, Mage watching with interest. Bishop had turned to stare out the window again, back in his own private hell.

Finally, when the pool of blood on the floor by her seat began to worry me, I reached out to her. "Thank you, Jasmine," I called, lifting the illusion and the compulsion. The fog in Jasmine's eyes lifted, and they skittered around the cabin in confusion. "You poor thing! That's a nasty cut on your wrist." I took her by the hand and helped her up. "You should get that looked at when we land."

As if my words had permitted her to feel pain, she flinched. She held up her wrist and stared at it with wide, shocked eyes. "How . . . how'd I do that?"

"Glass." The lie rolled easily off my tongue. Lying had become second-nature to me many years ago.

"Glass?" she repeated, scanning the floor around her for the evidence.

Mage appeared beside me, holding up a broken shard of a wine glass from who knows where. "Yes, see?"

Jasmine stared blankly back at her. I felt a twinge of guilt for putting her through this.

"Here, this should help." Mage swiftly went to work winding gauze around her wrist—plucked from the never-before-used emergency kit under one of the seats. She handed the woman an ice pack from the freezer. "Press this up against it," she instructed, offering her a warm smile. "It should help stop the bleeding."

"Yes, it will be as good as new with that," I added, placing my hand over the pack and quickly weaving a few threads of magic into her wrist to close up the wound and speed up the healing. We didn't need her bleeding out in the cockpit.

"Oh, okay. Thanks," Jasmine murmured, slowly walking back toward the cockpit, glancing over her shoulder at all of us several times.

Not until I heard the door lock click did I smile. "And now we know," I said. Caden returned a grin of his own, his relief unmistakable. Relief that matched my own. I could trust Caden with Evangeline.

Satisfied, I strolled past him to take a seat in a vacant corner, grabbing a blood bag on my way. I needed time to strategize. How would I get Evangeline out of there? And where in this world could we go to hide from Viggo and Mortimer?

Unfortunately I didn't get much strategizing time, as Mage slid into the chair across from me. "Well, that must make you happy. One less threat to Evangeline?" she asked almost tentatively, as if testing the waters. Likely wanting to see how I would react to her, now that we were not busy hunting mutants or fighting off witches. Now that I knew what she was, the powers she held, the danger she presented. Frankly, I wasn't sure what to make of Mage anymore. For someone I openly claimed not to trust, there was a large part of me that felt betrayed when she revealed her secret, as if she should have told me sooner. It was stupid, really . . . and yet it was impossible to ignore. I searched her face for an inkling of what she was thinking. Nothing. Unreadable. "Yes. One less danger."

"So what are we going to do now?"

"We?" Such a small, unassuming word, and yet it weighed so heavily, coming from her. It implied we were a team.

"Yes, I thought . . . " Mage stumbled over her words, an odd thing to witness the five thousand-year-old vampire doing. And then it happened. As she looked down at her hands folded in her lap, I saw the mask drop. It was fleeting, but I saw underneath—saw grief; loss. It was a long moment before she looked up again. "There's nothing I can say to make you trust me, is there?"

I felt my jaw set. "No. I don't believe there is."

She nodded, and determination flashed in her eyes. "Fine. Read me."

"What?" I blurted.

"Read me," she repeated.

But I was already shaking my head, feeling my forehead furrow deeply. "I heard you, but . . . what?"

Mage heaved a loud sigh. "Back on Ratheus, when I first found out about you—about a witch who was also a vampire—I had to admit that I was intrigued. And impressed. Then, when I met you . . . when I got to know you, I realized how alike the two of us are."

"We are nothing alike!" I snapped.

"No?" The tiniest smile crooked her mouth. "Powerful women, witch heritage . . . Of course, I'm not a witch anymore, but I still remember those days. We both want to save this world. And neither of us enjoy killing innocent people." The smile slid of her face. "We've both suffered terrible loss. We're both lonely."

"I'm not . . . " My words drifted away, unable to form that one lie.

"Really? And where is your family? Your friends?"

I paused, the mention of friends reminding me of Leo. Pain ripped through me as I thought of my old companion for the first time since the witch attack, of the delivery of his message, of how the connection cut off so abruptly, so completely. There was only one way that could happen. Death.

"I have no one," Mage offered when I didn't speak. "Not one friend. Except you."

I opened my mouth to deny her claim to this supposed "friendship," but she was already talking again. "I should have told you. I should have trusted you." She looked down at her hands. "I'm sorry."

"Well . . . like you said. There are no words left to make me trust you."

"I did say that." That steady, confident "Mage voice" was back again. "So read me. You will know everything about me in thirty seconds." She crooked her head, smiling. "Maybe a minute. Five thousand years is a lot of memory to rifle through. You will see that my intentions are genuine. You will see that I don't have some grand scheme. I am here to help you protect Evangeline and this world."

I wanted so much to believe her, I realized as I gazed at that tiny, pale, Asian face. At my . . . friend. I never would, though. Not until I uncovered what she could not hide.

Without another moment's hesitation, before she could renege on her offer, I sank a dozen magical tendrils into her body. They sailed in as if invited through a wide-open door, snaking into Mage's memories and thoughts as they had done with Caden. Only here, there was more—so much more. The moment five thousand years ago, when she realized what that Fates had turned her into; her first human kill and her horror as she gazed down on her victim. Regret tainted her every thought. Regret for testing the Fates with such a superficial request. Regret as her own family of sorcerers shunned her with disgusted sneers and ghastly screams.

I wove in and out of years, jumping from decade to decade, one century to the next; through the common stages of denial and then acceptance, of eccentricity and then a craving for normality; through the overwhelming boredom, the recurring urges to end her eternal life. So many years, besieged with melancholy and distrust as her strength grew to undefeatable heights. Cycling through one male companion to the next, with no desire to stay; guarding her back as those around her plotted to usurp her from her invisible throne. And then suddenly . . . a face. A woman's face. Young, beautiful, vampire. Just like that, it was as if the sun rose over a horizon, and warmth blossomed within my heart. Yolanda. That was her name. A sister. A friend. Mage's best friend.

From that point on, Mage's memories took a turn toward a blissful place, the days filled with laughter and peace. Mage now had an ally, someone to watch her back, someone to trust wholeheartedly. There were no more thoughts of death. Not for six hundred years.

Until suddenly, that security was yanked out from under Mage, vanishing in a haze of darkness and fire delivered by witches and baited by the Sentinel. I watched as Mage stepped through carnage to find Yolanda's dead eyes staring up from where she had fallen. Like a twig snapping in half, something broke in Mage then. I felt her tumbling backward, back into darkness, only it was so much bleaker this time.

In the next memory flash, I was peering out over a sea of heads in a football stadium. Cameras were everywhere, aimed to capture any angle. It was a really big game. Mage's attention was on the football team in the green and white uniforms. She had previously traced two of them as Sentinel spies. In their football gear, she wasn't sure which ones they were. She decided it didn't matter. She'd just kill them all.

And that's exactly what she did. On live national television, in front of millions of spectators, a vampire slaughtered an entire football team to avenge her best friend's murder.

Filtering through the rest of Mage's memories, I watched the war unfold through her eyes, the eyes of the catalyst who brought about the end of the world. Through the moment when she realized the grave impact of her rampage, however noble the intentions may have been; through her desperate attempts to stop the devastation; through to the migration to the South American continent that she would rename New Shore; through her order to exterminate three-quarters of the vampires because there were simply too many to keep the peace. The aftermath was a long, endless stretch of regret during which guilt ate away at her dark soul. So many times, Mage held flint and stone in her hand, ready to step into a blazing inferno. Only the seer's words stayed her desire, burning into her mind as surely as if they were on fire. A parallel world. A second chance, perhaps. A chance to do right. If only she could get a second chance . . .

The last images that flashed through Mage's mind were of Evangeline's friends being dragged, bound by Merth; of Evangeline's terrified face, and Mage's urge to come forward and comfort her, knowing there was no point, that her reputation as an evil tyrant was all that had kept the masses from turning on her. And then my own face appeared in her memory, my red hair framing my face like a lion's mane, my eyes set with crazed determination as I wielded fire balls, leveling dozens of Ratheus vampires. Mage had an opening. I saw it now. She had regained her senses quickly—unlike the others—and she could have killed me. She thought about it. But there was something about me that intrigued her. An instant kinship that stayed her lethal hands. She let me live.

By the time my magical threads released Mage, I was leaning so far forward in my chair that I was surprised I didn't fall out. Dazed, I slid back, my eyes wide with shock as I stared openly at her, not because she was so horrific, not because the span of her lifetime was overwhelming, but because so many of her own memories and emotions reminded me of . . . my own. I swallowed several times before opening my mouth to speak, only nothing came out. I was utterly speechless. Drained of all suspicion in less than a minute.

Mage smiled sadly at me. "So you see, you and I are not all that different."

With a small nod, I whispered, "I guess not," and left it at that. There was nothing else to say. Just like that, seeing her for what she was, all of my apprehension vanished, all doubt of her intentions slid away. I now had a true ally in this war. I now had a real friend. It was . . . comforting.

I glanced over to see Caden, Amelie, and Bishop watching us intently, no doubt eavesdropping on the conversation. By the relieved looks on their faces, they'd figured out what had happened and they were pleased with the outcome. It meant Mage was genuinely on our side. Against Viggo, against the witches and the Sentinel, against all threats. We needed her.

Mage cleared her throat. "So after we get Evangeline, then what?"

Back to the plans. "I guess we could always go back to the cabin in the mountains, if it's still there. Whatever happened between Leo and Ursula may have burnt the thing to the ground. I won't know until I make a few phone calls."

"And who is this Ursula?"

I rolled my eyes. "Long story. Psycho jealous witch. I'll explain later."

"Speaking of jealous psychos," Amelie piped up. "What do you think happened to Rachel?"

Mage and I groaned in unison. "I hope the witches finish her off," Mage muttered.

"Yeah." Though doubtful. That would be too easy for all of us.

"Now, will we be taking this plane the entire way? You said it was an island?"

"No. We have another three or four hours, then we'll need to stop over and get a smaller plane, but one big enough to carry seven of us, plus Max," I answered.

"You mean six," Bishop growled from his corner, thinking I had accidentally and cold-heartedly counted Fiona.

"No, Bishop," I answered as gently as I could. "There will likely be seven. I don't imagine Leo sent the entire staff with Evangeline, given the tribe would not handle that well. But I'm thinking he might have sent Julian."

"Julian?" Caden asked.

"Camila's son—the woman you all killed on the first night? I sent him with Evangeline to the mountains at her request."

Caden's eyes narrowed. "And what's this son, like . . . ten? Twelve years old?"

Oh-oh. I know where this is going. I hadn't thought of this. "In his early twenties."

"No need to worry," Mage added, chuckling.

"I'm not worried," Caden quickly threw back. He stood and began pacing. "So she's been in these mountains with this twenty-something-year-old *guy* for the past month. After I tried to kill her."

"Caden . . ." Amelie said, rolling her eyes. "She's madly in love with you."

Caden scowled at his sister and marched off into the opposite corner. He was worried. And now so was I. A jealous vampire was an irrational one. Which made for a lethal one.

10. UNTANGLE

"You said Sofie is coming to get us out of here?" I asked Max, my hand holding the cloth door back as I appraised the sleeping village. The tribe was nocturnal, Max explained, and so all was quiet except for the occasional stirring of a tiger, guarding the huts. Now, though, with the sun passing below the tree line, they would rise.

Uh-huh.

"When?"

Dunno. Max had resorted to one-word answers where possible, likely to conserve his energy. He was starving and he wasn't permitted to hunt. Sofie had warned him against hunting while on the island. The tribe considered all animals food for their precious tigers. They'd kill Max if he dared deprive the tigers of food.

We stayed in the hut all day, except to get water from the basin a few times—and I wouldn't have done that, if not for the sweltering tropical heat. I dragged Max along with me each time, clinging to him like a terrified child, constantly reminding myself to breathe as the tigers' eyes lingered on me, their noses twitching as they sniffed the air, their tails writhing excitedly. Max said they wouldn't attack. I wasn't so sure.

"I hope she comes soon. This place gives me the creeps." I dropped the curtain and wrapped my arms tightly around my chest.

Max sighed heavily. *She'll come as soon as she can, but I don't know when that will be.*

"And you're sure she knows we're here?"

Oh, yes. Leo would have made sure of it.

A sharp pain, at the mention of my dear old friend.

She doesn't want you near these things any longer than necessary. It could be days, or weeks—

"Weeks!" I felt my eyes bug out at the possibility. "No, it wouldn't be weeks. Not if you aren't allowed to hunt here!"

I can last a few weeks without food.

"You've already lasted a few weeks without hunting because you were too stubborn to go in the mountains!" I reminded him.

She could be on her way right now.

"Really?" Excitement nudged aside my worry for Max momentarily, as a bubble of hope grew. Sofie, on her way? What would I say to her? What would it be like around her, now that I knew the truth? But more importantly—"Will she come alone?"

Max didn't give his answer any thought. *Likely. I can't see why she'd be traveling with any of them. Too risky. They're likely still uncontrollable.*

And just like that, Max burst my bubble. Of course Caden wouldn't be coming with her. Only a month had passed. It felt like forever but in the grand scheme of things, a month was nothing. A blink of time.

I heard rustling behind me. Julian, shifting in his sleep. Since I had discovered his dirty little secret, I refused to speak to him. It wasn't too hard, given he slept most of the day, only waking to call out for water. I had the spiteful urge to withhold it from him, to let him know how angry I was with him, but I knew that would prove fatal, in this tropical heat and in his condition. Plus Max would suspect a serious problem if I acted so cruelly. In the end, I made sure my nails dug into his neck a little as I lifted his head toward the water bowl.

Julian was terribly weak but Max thought he would survive, thanks to whatever the tribe had done to him. That was twice now that he should have died but was saved with magic. If Max found out about Julian's secret identity, I doubted magic could save him a third time.

I dearly hope she brings something for me though, when she comes, Max grumbled, interrupting my thoughts on Julian. *Something warm and bloody.*

I turned to look at the werebeast who lay sprawled on the cool floor, his hungry eyes zoned in on the sleeping man. I knew what he was thinking. "Don't you dare, Max," I warned. Guilty eyes shifted over to me. "Go hunt! Before they wake up."

I'm fine, he said half-heartedly.

"Look at you! You're definitely not fine. We're in a jungle. There's got to be tons of warm, bloody things for you to eat!" I shuddered. "I'm sure the tigers can spare a few mice, or rats, or . . . whatever rodents there are out there." I checked the darkening horizon. "Go now! You can be back before they wake up."

Do you know how many rats I'd have to catch?

I cringed. "I'd rather not."

Besides, they'll know.

"How?"

They just will. I can't. I need to stay alive to protect you.

"I don't see how good a big heap of fur lying on the ground will be to me," I muttered.

A chorus of feline roars filled the air then, earning a small yelp of alarm from me. Julian stirred again, but his eyes remained closed; a thin layer of sweat shone on his forehead. Cautiously lifting a corner of the door flap, I peeked out again to see the tigers now on their feet, stretching lazily. Then, one by one, the tribe emerged.

One hell of an alarm clock, right?

"Uh-huh." Ducking back to avoid being seen, I watched through the crack as they quietly went about their business: the women carrying baskets of various fruits, the men dragging wood toward the fire pit, all of them glancing frequently in my direction. One woman cradled a young boy of maybe two in her arms. As they passed, his glowing, jaundiced eyes grazed mine.

"Are they human?" I whispered.

They were until eighty years ago. Then the Fates transformed them into those things. They still live and die like humans, eat like humans, breed like humans. In the beginning, the tribe was half this size. They've multiplied over the years.

"So, they always looked like . . . this?"

The Fates did that to their eyes. The teeth are just bad genes. The piercings, they've done to themselves. Max snorted. *I don't imagine the inbreeding has helped much.*

Within minutes, loud snaps and crackles announced another raging fire. Across the clearing, I spotted the tribal leader walking toward the pyre, his big feathered hat making him appear two feet taller. "They sure like their fire, don't they," I murmured.

They worship the god of fire.

I glanced back at him. "Seriously?"

Max grunted in response, not bothering to lift his head.

I began to worry. Losing Leo was bad enough; I couldn't lose Max. I had no idea how long it would take a werebeast to starve to death, and I wasn't going to find out. I needed to get permission for Max to eat. "I'm going out there to find you food," I announced. "I'll be back."

That earned a chuckle. *Don't bother. Those damn cats are too precious to them.*

I ignored his skepticism, wagging a warning finger at him. "And don't you so much as lick Julian while I'm gone." Inhaling, my nerves fluttering wildly in my stomach, I pushed the curtain back and stepped out.

At least a dozen heads whipped around to look at me, but no one approached; no spears waved in my direction. The chief, who now sat on a chair carved out of a tree stump, looked over, his unsightly eyes settling on me for a short moment before shifting back to the flames.

He's the one I need to convince. Eyes locked on my target, I moved forward, my legs suddenly stiffening so I walked jerkily. He watched me approach, intrigue in those hideous orbs. When it was clear I was coming to speak to him, a quick bark in his native garble scattered everyone, granting me a wide berth.

I stopped about four feet away from him, and swallowed. "Do you speak English at all?" I asked. Those sickly eyes bored into me, but he said nothing. *Clearly not. How am I going to convince him to let Max kill on his land?* As I stood there, desperate for an idea to miraculously fall onto my head, the chief's attention drifted down to my necklace, his brow puckering slightly as if he noticed something. His mouth opened to speak, exposing his rotted teeth. But then, with a quick glance over at our hut, he clamped his mouth firmly shut.

I glanced over my shoulder to catch a snout poking out from behind the curtain of our hut. Max, watching. Always watching.

A female pulled me back, mumbling. Her hands and arms clad in a pair of long gloves, she held out a bowl of small red berries. Up close, I could see they were crafted out of some sort of reptilian skin. Snake, perhaps.

"Thank you." I smiled, accepting the bowl. Gloved fingers reached forward to pick out a berry. She gestured toward her mouth. *Eat*, she was saying. "Yes." I smiled again. "I understand." If only someone would bring a nice fresh carcass in a bowl to Max . . . That gave me an idea, one that required my mediocre skills at charades. I pointed at the hut, then at the bowl.

The woman nodded as if in understanding. She snapped her fingers and another woman ran over, carrying a second bowl of berries. For Julian. I shook my head. "I mean, yes, for Julian. But what about Max?"

She stared at me "Big dog?" I said slowly and loudly, spreading my arms as far as possible. Still no acknowledgement. I sighed. Placing the bowls of fruit down on the ground, I dropped to my hands and knees and pointed at the bowl. No response. "Woof!" I barked. A chorus of high-pitched shrieks sounded, and I felt my face redden. They were laughing at me. I decided I didn't care. Max needed to eat.

Suddenly the chief spoke. "Demon dog . . . need blood?"

He does speak English! "Yes!" I rushed to my feet. "Max needs to eat. He's starving."

The chief stared at me for a long moment and I began to doubt that he did understand. Finally he opened his mouth; one word escaped. "Crocodilus."

I frowned. *Crocodi*—"Crocodile?"

He nodded once, as if passing a ruling. "Crocodilus. Demon dog eat." He waved dismissively toward the jungle. A few tribesmen snickered but I ignored them, proud of my accomplishment. Max wouldn't starve now. "Thank you! Thank you!" I exclaimed. Not thinking, I reached forward to shake his hand. Luckily the chief had lightning-quick reflexes. In a split second, he had the blunt end of a spear jabbing into my shoulder to block me before I made contact with him.

Flustered, I picked up the bowls of fruit and rushed back to the hut. *Way to go, Evangeline. Shake the hand of a poisonous man. That would end your problems quickly.*

Max was waiting for me by the entrance. "Did you hear?" I exclaimed, grinning, as I placed the fruit down beside Julian.

Of course I heard, he muttered.

For a starving werebeast, he didn't sound too grateful. "Well . . . what are you waiting for? Go catch a crocodile!"

Did you also happen to notice the laughter that went with his permission?

I frowned. "Yeah . . . so what?"

Max sighed in exasperation. *Crocs hide in the water so they're harder to kill. Plus they taste like rubber tires and their blood, like ink.*

I grimaced, his description about as unappetizing as the thought of eating mice and rats. "Will they satisfy your craving?"

I suppose, Max answered reluctantly.

"Well then, go! And I don't want to see you back here until you're full of rubber!"

And leave you here? Are you nuts?

I rolled my eyes. "Because it'd be better for me to go into the jungle with you—full of snakes and tarantulas and God knows what—to watch you wrestle crocodiles for dinner. I'm probably safer right here in this hut than anywhere else in the world right now."

Max answered with a deep harrumph. He knew I was right. *Okay, but stay in here. Don't get into any trouble.*

"Don't touch them and I'm good, right?"

You almost blew that one with the chief a minute ago . . . nearly gave me a heart attack. Okay, I'll be back as soon as I can. With that, he ran out the door with renewed vigor, likely from the prospect of hunting. He trotted past a crowd of jeering tribesmen, letting out a few growls, but not stopping. At the edge of the clearing, he turned to glance back at me.

"Go!" I waved him on impatiently. That's all it took. He tore off into the jungle.

Intent on heading back into the hut to devour the bowl of berries—and Julian's, if he didn't wake up soon—I was a little disappointed when the chief summoned me to him with a wave. *Don't touch them and you'll be fine,* I reminded myself as I headed back to the fire. Once again, his men scattered as I approached.

"Sit," he ordered, pointing his spear behind me to a small tree stump two of the tribesmen rolled into place three feet away. Obediently, I perched myself on my makeshift chair. He followed suit, settling down in his throne.

We sat in silence, staring at the fire, watching the men feed it from the opposite side. It was now double the size as the previous night's fire, and the heat it produced made the tropical temperatures that much more uncomfortable. Sweat poured down my forehead. I briefly considered moving back, but I suspected that would insult the chief's god of fire. So I wiped my brow and sat quietly until I couldn't anymore. "Thank you for letting Max hunt," I said.

He nodded, a tiny smirk on his mouth. *He understands me . . . I wonder where he learned English?* More awkward silence followed. Finally he said two words; two I hadn't expected. "Cursed heart." He pointed at my necklace.

Reaching up to roll the pendant in my fingertips, I nodded. "Did Sofie tell you that?"

He shook his head. "I see."

Frowning, I looked down at the opaque black heart, then back at him. *He sees?*

"Two souls trapped. I see. One is you. One is green-eyed girl. Long brown hair. Curls."

That matched Veronique's description, based on the portrait in Viggo's parlor . . . but how could he see it?

He held his hands up, his fingers intertwined. "Tangled."

I bobbed my head up and down. "Yes. Kind of, I guess. They're bound together."

Leaning forward, he rested his elbows on his knees and stared levelly at me. "I . . . untangle?"

I felt my brow knit together. "What . . . do you mean?"

He entwined his fingers as he had done before, then pulled them apart. "I untangle two souls."

I swallowed, sure he meant something different. "You mean . . . so they're not bound together?"

He nodded once.

Blood rushed to my ears as excitement made my heart pound. "You can do that?" I whispered.

He nodded again, adding casually, as if offering to wash my car. "I do now?"

"Now?" I repeated like a dim-witted parrot. "Sure. Yeah, I mean— yes, please! Seriously?"

With a nod, a flick of his wrist, and a flurry of barked orders, he sent tribesmen dashing in different directions like a pack of gerbils. They returned with long wooden poles and the same platform the chief had sat on the night before. I watched in amazement as they positioned stands around the outside of the fire and erected all four posts in under a minute. *I guess he does his magic from up there.*

The magic that would release me from my curse. Was this really happening? I looked down at the pendant. This seemed too easy. Sofie had spent years looking for a way to break the curse, and this abomination with the feathered hat and hideous eyes figured he'd just untangle the souls. Of course! So simple. Too simple. Could something go wrong? "This won't hurt either of us, will it? Will I be safe? Will the other soul be safe?" I suddenly asked. The last thing I wanted to do was get Veronique killed. She didn't deserve that, and I was as good as dead if it happened.

With a disapproving frown and a dismissive wave, he promised with an air of certainty, "Both souls free."

I allowed the smallest sigh of relief. Free at last . . . Free of this curse. Free of my hunters. Free to be with Caden, forever. Free to become . . . not human. I surrendered to the tidal wave of shock as it washed over me, the very idea too wild to be real. I would do anything to be free. Anything at all.

The chief stood and marched over to the platform. He thumped on it with his spear, then looked over his shoulder at me. "Get on."

Wait a minute . . . Alarm bells sounded. I looked at the platform and at the posts, reaching at least fifteen feet into the air over the blazing fire, and then back at him, putting two and two together. He expected me up on that platform, hanging over the raging fire. "Umm . . . " I faltered, images of me tumbling into the flames suddenly coming to mind. "Are you sure I should be the one going up there?"

"To free your soul. Yes."

Was it freedom through death? "I won't . . . burn, will I?"

"No." So confident, so firm. "Get on wood now. You will be free."

Free . . . Slowly rising from my stump, I took one step, then another, and another—sure that someone else's legs were moving my body there, because I couldn't feel anything from the waist down. I finally reached the platform. It was about two feet by three feet in size—not a tightrope, but not exactly huge. Gritting my teeth and giving the hut and the woods a quick look—I knew Max and Julian would never approve of this—I stepped onto the platform.

The entire tribe closed in. Even the tigers seemed to perk up. Everyone wanted to see the god of fire free me. Or burn me alive.

My stomach knotted. "I don't know if this is a good—"

"Kneel!" the chief ordered, the blunt end of his spear pushing down hard on my shoulder.

My legs buckled and I went down. *Get out of here, Evangeline! Get off this board, now!* my subconscious screamed inside my head, and yet it was somehow drowned out by a soft, subtle cooing: *Free . . . free . . .*

The woman who had worked on Julian the night before appeared with a large jug. She lifted the spout to my shoulder and tipped it. Clear, hot liquid streaked down my body, covering my arms and torso, running over my back and thighs until it coated my entire body, pooling behind my knees. When her jug was empty, she stepped away.

The chief nodded. The drummer began pounding his instrument in a steady, slow beat. Two groups of men flocked in with another set of long posts, these ones much thinner than the ones around the fire and with two-pronged ends. I watched as they each hooked the ends into the little divots on either side of the platform. "Do not move or you will fall," the chief warned, his words instantly stiffening my body until it felt as hard as the board on which I knelt. Moving in unison, the men lifted me.

I crouched, paralyzed by terror as I rose steadily toward the top of the four posts above the fire. At one point I squeezed my eyes shut, sure I was about to pass out. I kept them closed until a jostle indicated the men were placing the platform onto its four supports. Cracking one lid and then the other, I peeked out from this new vantage. The top of this contraption was even higher than I had anticipated, I realized as I looked down upon the roofs of the little huts and the leaping flames below. The rising heat just barely warmed my body, I was that high above it.

The heads of the Death Tribe swayed back and forth as they circled the huge, blazing fire. There was no escape.

11. THE RACE

"Dear God," I whispered, looking down at the fiery carnage on the waves below. Pieces of what looked like a large cargo plane lay scattered on the ocean's surface, the water extinguishing the flames as each piece sank. We were about ten miles from the eastern shore of the island.

"What are the odds?" Caden murmured as we flew over the mess in our tiny Cessna, heading for the west side of the island where a long, sandy beach would serve as landing strip. Everywhere else was too densely forested.

"Those aren't odds," I growled. "That's Viggo. He must have hijacked a Fed Ex plane. It would have had enough fuel to get all the way here." I shoved my hair off my forehead. "Bloody idiot! Like that won't attract attention."

"Do you think he's made it to her yet?" Mage asked quietly.

The very suggestion set Caden off. "Land this plane now—into the trees, if you have to. I don't care," he ordered the pilot.

"No," I countered, though I was ready to open the door and drop out of the night sky, just to get to her. But we couldn't crash. "We'll need this plane to get Evangeline out of here. They can't be far ahead of us. They won't just walk in there, it's too risky. They'll approach with extreme caution. That should buy us a bit of time." *We're coming, Evangeline.*

12. VISIONS

The man in the tiger head pounded his drum with zeal, and my heart pounded along with him, amplifying the deafening beat. Hungry flames danced below me, taunting me, licking the posts that held the platform up but somehow not setting fire to them. At fifteen feet in the air, my wood platform was high enough that it would not catch fire, but close enough that the scorching heat rising up from the growing fire was now borderline unbearable. Sweat poured down my face and body, mingling with the clear, unidentifiable liquid to leave a sticky film on me. I wasn't too concerned about that. I was more terrified that any shift I made would rock this contraption and send me plummeting to my death.

The tribe's chanting grew louder and angrier, culminating in a chorus of hair-raising screeches. From my precarious vantage point, I watched the chief walk up to the flames carrying a basket. One of his hands was gloved with that snakeskin material. My curiosity piqued, I very slowly, very carefully, leaned over, just enough that I could see him pull out a dagger and swipe it across his palm. Blood gushed out of the gash. I squinted. *That can't be right* . . . The liquid coming out was . . . blue! He had blue blood?

He held the dagger up against his mouth. His lips moved in a chant.

Then he tossed the blade into the flames. His lips still moving, the chief leaned over and stuck his gloved hand into the basket. When it emerged, it was with a jet-black snake coiled around it. With a forceful swing, he threw the live snake into the fire. It writhed in the flames for a few seconds before growing still, succumbing to the fire.

The tribe's shrieking continued, some of the screeches so high that they rang in my ears, making me cringe. Then the cats joined in, their low roars balancing out the cacophony. I peered beyond the glare of the fire to see the beasts pacing back and forth along the perimeter of the clearing, their tails twitching angrily. But wait—their attention was directed outward, into the darkness, as if something was in the jungle beyond. They watched, waited. *Please don't be Max,* I prayed. If it was, he'd be looking for the right moment to do some sort of impossible canine leap up here to pull me down, likely burning himself alive in the effort.

While I watched the tigers and worried about Max, a blue glimmer filled the sky around me and an icy cold sensation kissed my chest. I looked down to find the heart radiating with the same brilliant blue light as it had when I plugged it into the portal. Whatever the chief was doing was working.

Beneath me, the flames rose, leaping closer and closer, tendrils reaching up to caress the edges of the platform. The scorching heat I expected didn't come, but I cowered all the same, my arms hugging my body as if to protect it. And then the flames reached me. Just as Julian had been engulfed the night before, now the flames crawled up my skin, wrapping my limbs and torso in a fiery cocoon. Surprise dampened my terrified paralysis—I felt no pain. The flames danced over my body without singeing a single hair or a single thread of my clothing.

Allo? a woman's voice suddenly called in my ear, distracting me from my fiery coat. My head darted side to side as I looked for the source.

"Hello?" I answered tentatively.

Allo? Est-is temps? the woman said. I recognized it as French and I could tell she was asking a question based on the inflection in her voice. *"Oui! Enfin!"* she cried out.

My eyesight blurred as swirls of bright lights replaced the jungle and the tribe. I blinked repeatedly, trying to focus on the world beyond. Finally the light spots disappeared and my eyes focused. Only it was as if I were underwater, my vision wavy, my hearing muffled. I found myself in the atrium—a horribly mangled version of it; the balconies now heaps of brick and stone, the gardens burned to the ground. Dozens of little fires smoldered all over the heaved cobblestones. And the air! I didn't know if it was the heavy black smoke that hung overhead, blocking the view of the glass dome, or something else, but a foul stench curled my nostrils.

A group of women stared at me. I didn't recognize any of them and by the shocked, unfriendly looks on their faces, they had no idea who I was, but they weren't particularly happy to see me. Discomfort washed over me under their gaze. Fumbling nervously at my side, my fingers grasped folds of soft material; I looked down at a gauzy white dress covering my body. Chunks of white marble lay around my feet—the crumbled remains of the statue.

"Who are you?" a commanding voice shouted. I glanced back up to see a middle-aged woman in black leather staring at me, flames dancing on each of her fingers. A witch.

Veronique, the voice said and I realized that it had come from my mouth. But it wasn't me; I wasn't Veronique, I was Evangeline. *Where is Sofie?* the voice—Veronique—asked tentatively, unsure of her English.

Cold sweat broke out over my body. My confusion grew—what had devastated the atrium, and how was this voice that wasn't my voice speaking? One of the smoldering heaps on the ground caught my attention. A hand. The heaps were bodies. *Oh God . . .* My wide eyes drifted over all the little flaming piles, too numerous to count, until one caught my attention. It hadn't fully burned, and the face was angled toward me, dead violet eyes staring in my direction. Fiona.

I screamed.

13. LYING IN WAIT

The jungle seemed more dense than I remembered from my last trip here four years earlier, to negotiate the deal with the tribe. It hadn't been a pleasant exchange—not surprising. They were deceptive, repulsive creatures, programmed by the Fates to hate my kind, both witches and vampires. Even with some level of affinity to me for creating them, it didn't take long for the chief to threaten to touch me because he didn't like my "vampire smell." I was alone then. Now I was bringing four vampires with me.

As we ran through the jungle at breakneck speed, ferns and other foliage whipping our faces, I felt the telltale signs of the tribe's proximity. The magical purple helixes floating within my body began breaking apart and fizzling out. Soon there was not one thread I could grasp. I felt naked without my magic. I hated it.

"We're close?" Mage asked, discomfort tingeing her voice. Whatever sorceress's magic she had must have vanished as well.

"Fire. That way," Caden called, nodding to the north, just as a whiff of burning deadwood hit me. I instantly veered in that direction to lead the way, but Mage grabbed my arm and pulled me back. "I'll go first. I'm faster than you." She was gone before I could respond, Caden on her heels. Bishop, Amelie, and I took off in pursuit, tearing soundlessly through the jungle.

In minutes we cleared the jungle undergrowth at the edge of the tribe's village—a collection of simple huts. They were guarded by a dozen tigers, already aware of our presence. Beyond them, the tribe circled a giant pyre, hands linked, chanting in that shrill, nails-on-chalkboard screech. The sound of it, of their mysterious black magic, sent shivers down my spine.

My eyes immediately zeroed in on the fire—on the structure above it. On the platform where a blonde girl knelt, her body engulfed in flames, surrounded by a brilliant blue light. I heard her screams.

Mage grabbed my arm a split second before I would have plowed through the line of tigers and lethal bodies to rescue Evangeline. Her vise-like grip stalled me. "Think, Sofie," she warned. "You'll certainly die if you go in there, and we don't know what they're doing yet. She's not burning."

But it was too late. I'd lost all ability to think when I spotted Evangeline up there, screaming in terror, her slender, frail body enveloped in flames. If I needed to breathe, I don't think I was capable, anxiety so tightened my chest. She wasn't burning, as Mage said. But what were they doing to her? What *would* their magic do to her? My blood ran cold with the fear of that unknown, my brain concocting all kinds of horrible scenarios. Would she turn into one of them?

"Let's not run haphazardly into this," Mage counseled. "Viggo and Mortimer don't have her yet."

I nodded slowly, peering over to see Bishop and Amelie with their hands on Caden's shoulders, restraining him. Thank God Bishop had buried his grief long enough to be of some use to us. I felt Mage's grip on my arm loosen slightly, but not completely.

Mercifully, Evangeline had stopped screaming. I looked back out at the horrific scene before us—and noticed the horde of tigers concentrating on another side of the jungle, guarding the spot as if someone lay hidden within. I'm sure someone did. Two someones. Viggo and Mortimer were here.

14. FREEDOM

I barely noticed that the flames had disappeared from my body or that the furious drumbeat and the chanting had fallen silent, I was so overwhelmed by the terrifyingly realistic image of Fiona's dead eyes. It wasn't real. It couldn't be real. The atrium was fine, Veronique was in her statue until Sofie released her, Caden and my friends were safe.

But the fear still gripped me, even as the tribesmen hooked their pronged poles to the platform and brought me down from my perch. In seconds I was at ground level beside the fire pit, still kneeling and unable to move. The tribeswomen flocked forward to surround me. One of them bent and reached toward me with her snakeskin-covered hands—toward my chest. Toward my pendant, still hanging around my neck.

I watched in a catatonic state as she cupped the pendant with both hands, then closed her fist over it. And then yanked on the chain.

I heard the snap as the clasp broke. My breath caught as I waited for the onslaught of agony that I'd felt the last time the chain broke. I was still waiting for it as the tribeswoman placed the pendant on my palm. She gave it a gentle pat and stepped away.

I looked down at the once-deadly black heart nestled in my palm, now harmless. Tears slid down my cheeks. The Death Tribe had freed me of my curse. I was finally free.

My first instinct was to thank the chief. Too wobbly-legged to stand, I crawled off the planks. Somehow I managed to push to my feet, the pendant clutched tightly in my grasp. I squinted through the dark, seeking the bright-feathered headdress. There it was, about fifteen feet away. But the chief's attention was glued elsewhere—on the jungle. His men had lined up on either side of him, spears at the ready.

There was no need to be so on edge with Max . . . So who was out there? "Sofie?" I called hopefully, my voice trembling.

Feline snarls and roars erupted, tribesmen shouted. To my left, a tiger yelped in pain. My head whipped in that direction in time for me to see a body flying out of the darkness into the tribal throng, stabbing at them with multiple spears and scattering them before landing two feet away from me.

Rachel's citrine snake eyes locked on me, glittering with hateful intentions.

15. KAMIKAZE

We watched in silence as they gently lowered the platform. I tried to see Evangeline's face, but a crowd of women immediately swarmed in to surround her, blocking my view. "What are they doing to her?" I hissed.

"I don't know, but it doesn't look like they're trying to hurt her," Mage said. "Besides, Viggo can't get to her if they're there, right?"

As usual, Mage had assessed the situation clearly. Between the circle of tribeswomen around Evangeline, the tigers, and the tribesmen armed and ready along the perimeter of the clearing, focused both on our end and the other, Viggo would consider it too risky to come through yet. He was insane, but not in the stupid, kamikaze way that was required to get to her.

"What do we do now?" Caden whispered.

I sighed. "I'm going in. They should be okay with me. Once I get to her, I can—" I stopped abruptly as my ears caught Evangeline calling my name. A second later I spotted long, raven-black hair flying through the air from the opposite end of the clearing, its owner sailing over the tribesmen and tigers, flinging spears in every direction. Several tribesmen went down, and a tiger yelped, wounded.

Rachel. Heading straight for Evangeline. And I couldn't get to her in time.

16. RACHEL'S PLAN

Rachel didn't say a word. She didn't smile. She was on a mission. Grabbing me roughly, she spun, putting her back to the fire. With her arm around my neck in a deadly headlock, I became her shield. "Stay away or I snap her neck, you parasites!" she shrieked.

"Please!" a new voice cried out.

Unable to turn my head, I strained my eyes to the right. A slender, red-haired woman stepped into the clearing and moved toward the crowd of angry tribesmen, her hands held up in surrender. Sofie! They parted enough to allow her past, closing in quickly behind her.

Sofie's mint-green eyes fell on me for the first time since the day she sent me from the atrium into my safe haven. She had apologized to me then. Now I saw that same pleading, contrite look in her ghostly pale eyes. "Stand down!" she ordered, her voice confident. She turned her attention to the chief. "Let us come out from the shadows and no one else will get hurt. Otherwise, many more will die, I can promise you that."

Let us come? My heart, pounding against my chest wall, skipped a beat. Who else was here?

The chief, kneeling over the fatally wounded tiger, paused as if weighing his options. Then he barked an order. Every tiger dropped to its belly in submission. The tribesmen followed suit, dropping to one knee.

Satisfied, Sofie sang out, "Come out, come out, wherever you are!"

Who was it?

From the jungle stepped two tall figures in custom suits. Viggo and Mortimer. Even in the depths of a tropical forest, they had found me. They approached slowly until they stood about thirty feet away from Sofie and from Rachel and me, the last point in a perfect triangle.

"Of course you'd bring that lunatic with you!" Sofie scoffed, earning a growl from Rachel that rumbled in my ear.

"And aren't I glad that we did!" Viggo exclaimed, adding, "My darling Rachel, that maneuvering was fantastic! Your battle skills are top-notch."

"I was highly motivated," she purred, her grip on me tightening until I found it difficult to breathe.

"Hello, Evangeline," Mortimer called. I hadn't heard that booming voice in a month, and would gladly miss it for a thousand more. But he didn't wait for my response, his attention quickly zoning in on my unadorned chest. "Where's the necklace?" he demanded.

Three sets of brilliant irises bored into me, Sofie's minty green ones wide with genuine surprise.

I swallowed, mustering as much courage as possible. "Here," I answered in a quavering voice, holding up my arm. I let the pendant drop so it dangled from its chain in front of me. Sofie's eyes almost bugged out of her head. "I don't want it. You can—" I didn't even finish offering it before a gust touched my cheek and the pendant disappeared from my grasp. Just like that.

"I don't believe it!" Viggo exclaimed, staring down at the pendant now in his clutches. So quickly, so smoothly, I couldn't even tell he had moved. That was that. They had what they needed from me. Was it enough to let me be?

It didn't matter because now Rachel had me, and it wasn't the pendant she cared about.

"Let her go, Rachel," Sofie warned, her surprise quickly buried, her tone cutting.

"I don't think so . . . Come near me and I'll snap her neck, you puke-eyed witch!" Rachel shrieked, grabbing a fistful of my hair, so violently that she ripped several strands out at the root. "Tell him to come out. Only him," she hissed at Sofie.

Him? Could it be . . . My pounding heart stopped altogether.

The crowd parted. A tall, lone figure stepped from the dark jungle, moving past the ring of tigers and tribesmen to glide toward me like a dream. Firelight caught the jade in his eyes.

Caden.

Suddenly it didn't matter that Rachel's claws dug into my flesh, ready to tear me to pieces. What mattered was what was going on in Caden's mind. The fears and doubts that I had buried deep to survive in my exile exploded to the surface. Had he changed his mind about me? Had time and distance dulled his feelings? Did he ever truly care? For these few seconds as he approached, my hope hung from the edge of a cliff, seconds from either falling or being pulled to safety. I held my breath.

Our eyes locked. I saw Caden's eyes. The stunning green eyes I remembered, the eyes I thought I had lost forever. In that one look, every ounce of doubt, every moment of fear, every horrific memory washed away. As if pulled by a magnet, my body yearned toward him, desperate to feel him close again.

Rachel yanked me back. "No, no, little girl. That's far enough." Her grip around my neck tightened. "Is there anything you want to say to your dear human?" she called out to Caden. "Last chance." She said it so airily, as if she were offering the last bite of a cookie before she took it for herself. But she wasn't offering a cookie. She was promising death. After all this, after all we had been through, after lifting the curse, Rachel would end me.

"We have bigger issues than petty revenge, Rachel," Sofie called out softly. "We're on the brink of a war."

War? What did Sofie mean?

Rachel's fingers dug into my neck like tiny daggers. "There's always time for revenge."

"She's suffered enough." Sofie's tone was pleading, and her eyes brimmed with distress.

A vicious cackle in my ear tensed my shoulders. "She hasn't even begun to suffer."

From the corner of my eye, I noticed Caden shift his weight and flex his hands by his sides, as if ready to make a move. Unfortunately, so did Rachel. She pulled me even closer, until her body pressed up against my back, until we were like one. "Any sudden moves and I'll snap her neck like a twig. You'll never make it here fast enough to stop me," she warned. Her arm loosened its grip and her hand slid to my chin to pull my head back until my neck was exposed. With her mouth grazing my ear, she whispered, "You thought you could outsmart me? Lie to me and get away with it? Say good-bye, little human."

I swallowed, tears now streaming down my cheeks.

"You'll never get out of here alive if you kill her," Caden warned. "You might have a chance if you don't—"

Rachel giggled softly. "Who said I was going to kill her? But make one move toward us and I certainly will."

"Rachel, you won't—" Caden began.

She cut him off. "Come on! You've got front row seats to watch!"

Oh God. Watch what? Rachel ripping my teeth out, one by one? I felt faint, my legs weakening, but Rachel gave my body a swift jerk up as she continued talking.

"Then you'll see me leave with her. If you don't follow, you might see her again. Follow, and I'll hand you her heart. Simple."

She had it all planned out. She would do whatever she wanted to me—it no doubt involved torture in front of an audience—and then she'd escape. At that moment I dearly wished I would lose consciousness. But of course, it was one of those few times that I wouldn't.

Her fingertip caressed my neck. "Why would I give her a quick death when I could drag it on for years?" she drawled. Another surge of panic tore through me. What did she mean?

Sharp pain rocketed through my body as Rachel's teeth clamped onto my neck, the ferocity of the pressure making me sure she'd rip a chunk of flesh out. I gave a strangled gasp as the pressure intensified, my eyes catching the panic on Caden's face. Sofie had dropped to her knees, her hands covering her mouth and nose, her green eyes wide with anxiety.

Rachel was drawing on my blood so fiercely that my limbs grew heavy in mere seconds, my energy draining away. Was that her plan? To bleed me dry? That didn't make sense . . .

The pressure abated suddenly and a familiar burn began coursing through my limbs. It brought disturbing memories back from that first attack on Ratheus, when the blonde vampire had pumped venom into me. Rachel's plan finally hit me. *I can drag it out for years,* she had said. She wanted to turn me so she could stalk and continuously torture me.

Suddenly, the situation didn't seem so bleak. The pendant was off, the curse gone, and if I could get away from Rachel, I'd have what I wanted—to be with Caden forever. Sure, I'd have to deal with an eternal game of cat-and-mouse, but I'd have Sofie and Caden by my side to help fight her.

Just like that, I wasn't afraid anymore. Rachel was giving me what I wanted. My mouth actually curved into a smile. Now, I welcomed the venom. I craved it. Rachel's fangs in my neck wasn't pain. It was bliss.

Don't worry, I tried to communicate as my eyes rolled lazily up to land on Caden. *Everything will be okay.*

On the brink of unconsciousness from the massive loss of blood, I was only faintly aware when Rachel retracted her fangs and released her grip on me, shoving me away from her as she let out a howl of agony. My legs immediately buckled, too weak to hold me up. I would have dropped to the ground, had it not been for strong arms swooping in to scoop me up. I felt my body sail away from the heat of the fire.

Rachel continued to scream, just as the blonde vampire had cried out before he was poisoned with his own venom, only Rachel's screech was ten times worse. What was happening? Unable to summon the strength to move my head, I let it roll to the side to see Rachel. She was on her hands and knees, her face contorted, hateful, glowing eyes fixed on me. She opened her mouth to let out a skin-peeling scream just as Mortimer appeared beside her. Grabbing her by the throat with his powerful hands, he lifted her and launched her backward into the center of the pyre. Her shrill scream abruptly stopped as the flames enveloped her body.

A hand slipped behind my head and lifted it up, ever so gently. I found myself staring up at Caden, his face a mixture of happiness and confusion. No hideousness, no blood lust. Just the Caden I knew. My Caden. And then I lost consciousness.

ႣᏒ

When I came to, I was lying on a soft surface, staring up at a white ceiling, the sound of a loud engine humming in my ears.

"It's about time," a familiar male voice whispered in my ear.

I rolled my head toward it. Caden was lying beside me, his head propped on his arm, watching me intently. "Caden!" I croaked, and immediately began coughing, my throat parched.

"She's awake!" a raspy voice called a second before a curly mop of hair appeared to hover upside down over my face.

"Here, sit up." Cool fingers slid behind my neck and helped me into a half-sitting, half-lying position. I was on a bed, I could see now. Wrapping his arm behind my back, Caden pulled me toward his muscular body.

Sofie appeared with a tall glass of cloudy, urine-colored liquid in her hand. Those pale green eyes gazed down at me with a look I hadn't seen in years—the look my mother used to give me as she tucked me in at night. Adoration. My heart suddenly warmed, the urge to wrap my arms around her neck overpowering. "Apple juice. Drink," she murmured in that gorgeous French accent I adored so, handing me the glass and smoothing my hair back off my forehead as she sat down beside me.

I took a big mouthful while my eyes roamed the room. It was tiny, containing nothing but overhead compartments and a double bed. Textured silver and white wall paper covered the walls. Wait . . . I'd seen this wallpaper before. We were on Viggo's jet. "How did we get here?" I asked between gulps.

"Not easily. You've been unconscious since last night," Sofie explained, adding with a grimace, "We had to leave the island rather quickly. Rachel's stunt burned some bridges for me." Memories of Rachel flooded back then. My hand flew to my neck to feel the bandages. "It should heal nicely with time," Sofie offered with a sad smile.

Rachel's venom . . . I frowned in confusion. "But Rachel turned me, didn't she? I shouldn't need to be healed. When will the transformation start?" I asked. I didn't feel any different, but I had no clue how this whole process worked.

Caden leaned forward, laying a soft kiss on my cheek. "Drink up," he said. "We need you strong."

I obeyed the order, my eyes unable to leave his face, my fingers reaching up to trace his slender nose and soft lips. Was this even real? He leaned forward to press his mouth against my fingers, closing his eyes and inhaling. Worry flickered through me as I remembered the last time he had caught my scent, but it quickly vanished as his eyes opened again, the beautiful jade eyes that I could lose myself in. "How did you learn to control it?" I asked, tears welling in my eyes. Tears of delight, of relief.

Caden guiltily averted his eyes. "By drinking a lot of blood. A lot."

I grabbed his chin and forced his face back to me. "Good." I smiled, trying to tell him it was okay.

He leaned in to press his forehead against mine. "Thank you for understanding," he whispered.

I leave you alone for an hour and this is what happens, Max's voice grumbled in my head.

"Max! They found you!" I exclaimed, struggling to turn around.

Tell Curly Locks to move it! Max muscled his way in, earning a grunt of protest from Amelie. Ignoring her, he affectionately nuzzled against my cheek.

"How was the rubber?" I teased, smiling.

Rubbery . . . . You broke your promise. You were supposed to keep out of trouble.

"I know. I'm sorry, Max. The chief told me he could undo the curse if I got on the platform, so I did and—"

"You agreed to go up on that pyre?" Sofie suddenly trilled. "Dear God, Evangeline! And here I thought they forced you onto it . . . Have you learned nothing about reserving a shred of doubt?" she scolded, running her hand through her hair, shifting it into a wild mane. She sounded like . . . a mother.

"He said he could get the pendant off! What else should I have done?" I answered defensively.

"You should have waited for me to figure it out!" Sofie threw back.

"Well, given Viggo and Mortimer showed up before you, I'd be dead if I'd done that. Now, at least I'm free. Viggo and Mortimer can have Veronique and I can have," I paused to gaze over at Caden, "what I want, forever."

He hesitated just a second then, ever so slowly, leaned down to kiss my forehead. "You always had me, forever . . . pendant or not."

But Sofie didn't let it go. "You shouldn't have done it, Evangeline."

I couldn't miss the grave disappointment in her voice. "What's the big deal? It worked! See?" I gestured to my chest. "It's off!"

"Oh, Evangeline," Sofie moaned, rubbing her face with her hands. "There's something you don't understand about that tribe. I should have warned you not to let them touch you with their magic, but I didn't expect this. Why didn't I expect this!" she admonished herself.

I swallowed, a sick feeling rising in my stomach. "But they got the pendant off . . . "

"Yes, they did," she conceded softly. "Because their magic counters mine. It undoes what I've done."

"You knew they could do that?"

"Yes! I guessed it, anyway. But it's not that simple. If it was, I would have taken you to them years ago!" As Sofie spoke, Caden's grasp tightened around me, as if protecting me from the news she was delivering. "I didn't know this would happen, but after I saw how Rachel reacted, it made total sense that this is how it would work." I had no idea what Sofie was trying to say. She must have seen it in my eyes, because she paused before saying, "You're full of this tribe's magic now, magic that opposes vampires and witches. It won't let you be turned."

I heard her words and yet they didn't make sense. *Not turned? Won't let me? So Rachel's venom didn't work, after all . . .* "Well, when can I be turned, then?"

She shrugged. "I don't know. Never, maybe." The room started to spin. "I can't even heal you! It's like there's some sort of antibody for anything done by vampires and witches, coursing through your veins. I had no idea you'd do something so foolish . . . if I had, I would have warned Max." She paused to reach forward and squeeze my leg with one delicate hand. "But we're lucky it played out as it did. If Caden had tried to turn you—"

I gasped, my eyes widening as I finished her sentence in my head: Caden would have died. I instinctively tightened my grip on him, needing to feel him next to me, to be sure he was alive. A fresh batch of tears welled in my eyes.

"Come on," Amelie murmured, taking Sofie by the hand and smacking Max on the rump. "It's getting crowded in here."

Sofie's eyes flitted to Caden and a silent exchange passed between them, one I couldn't read. The others quietly left, shutting the door behind them, leaving me alone with Caden. He pulled my head to his chest and wrapped his arms around me, running his fingers through my hair until my sobs lessened and my tears dried up. "Here, you should lie down. You lost a lot of blood." He lowered me down to the bed and pulled a navy blue wool blanket up to cover my body. I was still dressed in the revealing tribal garment.

"What are we going to do?" I asked, my voice hollow, as I gazed up at him. Sadness passed across his face but he said nothing, his eyes roaming my face, his fingertips grazing my cheek, running along my lips, as if he couldn't keep his hands off me. And why should he? I was finally with Caden again, I realized. As if possessed by some crazed, hormonal person, I suddenly couldn't control myself. My hands flew behind his head and yanked him down to me with surprising force. I pressed my lips up against his as tears began streaming down my cheeks again, the sound of an invisible clock ticking away in my head. I was already running out of time.

Eventually, Caden reached up to gently untangle my hands from his hair. He broke away from my kiss and lay down beside me, chuckling. "Slow down. I'm not going anywhere."

I curled up against his chest. "No, but I will . . . soon." I wasn't sure which was worse—wearing the pendant or not. Either way, I had no control of my life. "It's impossible."

Caden kissed the top of my head and wiped the tears away from my cheek. "No, Sofie will figure it out. She's smart like that." He sounded so confident. "Nothing is impossible, remember? You taught me that."

I stretched my arm out to drape it over his side, reveling in the feel of him. I had Caden. For how long, I didn't know, but he was here, with me, something I'd feared would never happen. I needed to be happy with what I had. "At least Rachel is gone," I said half-heartedly, trying to sound optimistic. "And Ursula. And Viggo has no more use for me. So life can kind of get back to normal. We're mega-rich. We can go buy a nice condo with Amelie, Bishop, and Fiona and leave all this behind. Until I get too old and wrinkly for you, anyway," I added bitterly.

"Evangeline," Caden whispered, his voice cracking. I slid away from his chest to look up at his face. Raw pain stared back. "Fiona's gone."

I flinched as if he had slapped me. "What do you mean . . . " A vision flashed in my mind—of a destroyed atrium, strange witches, and Fiona's dead violet eyes staring up at me. I sat up. "It was real?"

"What was real?"

"I . . . I saw it," I stammered. "I saw Fiona in the atrium!"

Caden was shaking his head. "Wait a minute; you're not making sense. How could you see her?"

"I saw the witches and the atrium, and burned bodies, and—"

"What?" Caden looked at me as if I'd grown a third eye on my forehead.

I barely heard him; I kept babbling on about the weird atrium nightmare I had while on the platform. "And that voice—Veronique's voice—and the statue . . . " I gasped aloud, groping forward for Caden's arm as realization dawned on me.

"What?" Caden was growing impatient; he grabbed my chin and pulled my face to look straight at his. "Tell me. You're scaring me!"

"I think Veronique's free," I whispered. It had been real. When the chief reversed Sofie's magic, he must have also reversed the tomb spell and somehow, because of my link to her soul, I saw it firsthand. *She would be free,* he'd promised. That didn't just mean her soul. It meant her physical body.

Caden's eyes widened, then darted to the closed door. He lifted his finger to his mouth to indicate that I needed to be quiet. "Why would you think that?" he whispered.

By the time I finished quietly describing the vision, Caden was squeezing the bridge of his nose. "This is bad. This is so very bad."

"Who were those witches, Caden? What happened over there?"

Caden put his arm around me and squeezed me close to him, whispering in my ear, "Don't mention anything about Veronique to anyone just yet."

"Why?"

"Because, it'll set off Viggo and Mortimer."

Viggo and Mortimer . . . weren't they long gone? How would they find out?

Caden gave me a strange look. "Come on. You may as well see for yourself." He scooped me up in his arms and pulled me off the bed, blanket and all. I reveled in the feel of his body as he carried me through the narrow hallway into the main cabin.

The joy didn't last long. My blood instantly turned to ice as my eyes landed on the two well-dressed vampires sitting across from Sofie in the main cabin. Viggo and Mortimer. A wooden box, which I presumed held Veronique's pendant, sat between them. Of course they were here. They weren't out of my life yet.

Mortimer's dark orbs zoned in on me just as the memory of him tossing Rachel into the fire hit me. "Why?" I blurted. I could have been asking anything.

But Mortimer knew immediately what I meant. "I figured I owed you that much," was all he said, that same vacant stare giving me nothing to read, yet every answer I needed. Killing Rachel was his peace offering.

"She was quite annoying, wasn't she?" Viggo piped in, rolling his eyes dramatically.

My attention shifted to Sofie, my eyes asking, *Is this an act?*

Viggo answered for her. "We all got what we wanted. You have nothing more to worry about from us. We have no more use for you." He added, as an afterthought, "Except maybe that hundred million you swindled from us."

"She earned it! Leave it be!" Mortimer boomed, turning to level a warning glare at his adversary. What had happened between these two?

"She certainly has," a new voice said. It belonged to a tiny Asian-looking woman who strolled into the cabin, smiling at me.

My jaw dropped as she handed Sofie a bag of blood and tossed another to Max before sitting down beside Sofie. Max didn't seem at all concerned; he caught the bag with his teeth and hunkered down to suck on it. Sofie thanked her with a wink, earning a wide-eyed stare from me. What were they . . . friends? What had happened over the last month?

Amelie's giggle pulled my attention to the opposite side of the cabin, where she sat cradling Julian's head in her lap, smiling slyly down at him. Julian was still visibly pale and weak from his injury, but he gazed up at her with a goofy grin, so utterly and obviously enamored with her that it was almost comical. "How long was I unconscious for?" I asked absently, frowning as I took in this development.

"Long enough for Amelie to sink her hooks into him," Caden answered.

That wouldn't take long. Of course Julian would fall head over heels with Amelie instantly. Who wouldn't? They would make a cute couple, I decided. Except for the fact that he belonged to a cult that wanted to eradicate every last vampire, and she'd probably kill him the second she found out. Small detail.

"Are you okay with them being together?" Caden asked quietly.

I turned to see a strange look in his eyes. Fear? What was it? I had never seen it before. *He must be sensing my anxiety over Julian's secret identity.* I needed to hide it better, or I'd get Julian killed and that wouldn't help matters. Soon enough, though, Amelie would find out, I was sure. All she had to do was see the tattoo. And then what would happen . . . she'd be crushed. I forced a smile, pushing the thought from my mind, and squeezed Caden tightly. "Of course!"

"Hey, little human," a hollow-sounding Bishop called out. I turned to find him sitting by himself in a dark corner of the plane, the playful smirk I treasured replaced with a cold, lost stare. There was an empty seat beside him, one that Fiona should be sitting in. Bishop without Fiona was like . . . the world without the sun.

"Can you put me down?" I asked Caden.

He did as asked. Giving his hand a squeeze, I walked over to sit down beside the heartbroken vampire. "I'm so sorry, Bishop," I whispered hesitantly, a giant knot forming in my throat.

Bishop's jaw tensed. He gave me a nod and reached out to squeeze my hand. Then he turned to look out the window, his eyes closing—shutting me and the rest of the world out. The old Bishop was gone. Probably forever.

With a sick, hollow ache blossoming in my chest, I quietly stood and walked back over to wrap my arms around Caden, tears welling in my eyes. I fought them this time. There was no time for tears right now. "How did this happen?"

Caden sighed. "Sofie? Where do you want to begin?"

Sofie gestured at two empty chairs beside her. Clinging to Caden, with a wary eye on Viggo and Mage, I walked over with him to sit down.

For the next hour, Sofie and Mage—her new "BFF," it seemed—told the entire story, from the moment Sofie shipped me off to the mountains to finding a badly-mangled Max in the swamp next to a pile of half-eaten crocodiles. I caught myself glancing over at Julian whenever the Sentinel was mentioned, and each time, I met Caden's frown. *Be careful, Evangeline. You're going to give Julian's secret away.*

By the time Sofie finished, I was sure all the color had drained from my face. I had to swallow a few times to keep the bile from rising to my mouth as the nausea kicked in. "Ratheus is Earth?" I whispered.

Caden pulled me close to him. "I'm so sorry, Eve. I didn't know. I swear it."

I reached for his hand and pulled it to my cheek, closing my eyes to revel in his touch for a long moment while I thought. Right now, right at this very moment, Sofie's sister was out of her statue and vulnerable to a horde of crazy witches and the Sentinel. She could be dead already. If Viggo or Mortimer found out—I looked up to see cold blue eyes dissecting me. *He's trying to read me!* He wouldn't be able to read anything definitive through my sheer terror right now, thank God—those two would do whatever it took to get her out, even if it meant blowing up a square block of Manhattan. To be honest, I wasn't sure if Sofie would act more rationally. And how long would it take before she figured out that the tribe's magic had reversed the tomb spell? Caden was right. I had to keep this to myself.

"So what's the plan? Are we going back to New York?" I asked vaguely.

Sofie shook her head. "Veronique is safe while she's in that statue. They've kept the attack under wraps, but if we go back there now . . . who knows what kind of spectacle they'll make."

I averted my gaze to my hands and bit my bottom lip, distressed by the knowledge that I was betraying Sofie by not telling her what I knew. I now had two volatile secrets to keep. Suddenly the fact that the Death Tribe's magic coursed through my veins, preventing me from getting what I desperately wanted, seemed trivial. A repeat of Ratheus was coming. "What are we going to do?" I whispered, unable to keep the distress from my voice.

Sofie's answer was calm and clear. "Simple. We change fate."

ABOUT THE AUTHOR

Born in small-town Ontario, Kathleen published her first book at the age of six with the help of her elementary school librarian and a box of crayons. She is a voracious reader and the farthest thing from a genre-snob, loving everything from High Fantasy to Chick Lit. Kathleen currently resides in a quaint small town outside of Toronto with her husband, two beautiful girls, and an exhausting brood of four-legged creatures.

Asylum is the second book in the Causal Enchantment Series. Look for Book 3 in early 2013.

CPSIA information can be obtained at www.ICGtesting.com
Printed in the USA
LVOW131452250512

283343LV00011B/26/P